Maiden Lane

Border City Blues

MAIDEN LANE

Michael Januska

DUNDURN
TORONTO

Project Editor: Shannon Whibbs
Editor: Allister Thompson
Interior design: Courtney Horner
Cover design: Courtney Horner
Printer: Webcom

Library and Archives Canada Cataloguing in Publication

Januska, Michael, author
    Maiden Lane / Michael Januska.
(Border city blues)

Issued in print and electronic formats.
ISBN 978-1-4597-2335-1 (pbk.).--ISBN 978-1-4597-2336-8 (pdf).--ISBN 978-1-4597-2337-5 (epub)

 I. Title

PS8619.A6784M35 2014   C813'.6   C2014-901034-6   C2014-901035-4

1   2   3   4   5   18   17   15   16   15

Conseil des Arts du Canada   Canada Council for the Arts   Canada   ONTARIO ARTS COUNCIL / CONSEIL DES ARTS DE L'ONTARIO / an Ontario government agency / un organisme du gouvernement de l'Ontario

We acknowledge the support of the **Canada Council for the Arts** and the **Ontario Arts Council** for our publishing program. We also acknowledge the financial support of the **Government of Canada** through the **Canada Book Fund** and **Livres Canada Books**, and the **Government of Ontario** through the **Ontario Book Publishing Tax Credit** and the **Ontario Media Development Corporation**.

Care has been taken to trace the ownership of copyright material used in this book. The author and the publisher welcome any information enabling them to rectify any references or credits in subsequent editions.

J. Kirk Howard, President

Printed and bound in Canada.

Visit us at
Dundurn.com | Definingcanada.ca | @dundurnpress |Facebook.com/dundurnpress

Dundurn
3 Church Street, Suite 500
Toronto, Ontario, Canada
M5E 1M2

Here's to Mercury Retrograde
and all the other celestial phenomena we use to try to explain
ourselves.

"Look at him," the gypsy said in the dark.
"Thus should men move."
"And in the day, blind in a tree with crows around him,"
Robert Jordan said.
"Rarely," said the gypsy.
"And then by hazard. Kill him," he went on.
"Do not let it become difficult."
"Now the moment is passed."
"Provoke it," the gypsy said. "Or take advantage of the quiet."

— Ernest Hemingway, *For Whom the Bell Tolls*

ONE

SUNDAY, FEBRUARY 4, 1923

Chapter 1

LURKING BELOW
THE SURFACE

Three stood back on the frozen shore, muttering obscenities at each other. Another was tinkering with the car parked on the ice. The other two were positioned further out, rolling their eyes back and forth across a stretch of scrub in the middle distance. In winter, in the colourless light and with the trees stripped bare and everything else covered in snow, it could be difficult to get one's bearings. You had to find those few familiar lines and edges and hang on to them, sometimes for dear life.

"I see something," said Thom, lifting his chin, "there, near the head." His hands were tucked under his arms and he was bobbing from foot to foot.

Lapointe saw it too — a faint, flashing light. He turned and gave Mud his own signal: a woollen-gloved thumbs-up. It was on. Standing at the driver's side, Mud reached across the steering wheel and double-checked that the coil switch was off. He then shifted the spark lever a few notches and opened the throttle. Stepping around to the front of the vehicle, he held his breath, gripped his shoulder, lowered his arm, and pulled the crank up once, twice, and then a third time, finally igniting the engine. He let the pistons warm up then returned to the controls, opened the throttle a couple more notches and listened. She was primed. His work done, he held his wrist and gently tucked his hand back into his coat pocket.

Gorski approached him. "Remember," he said, "this one favours the right."

"And that's why I'm aiming soft left," said Mud between his teeth.

"You sure you're okay?"

Mud's lungs were pumping out thick plumes of steam. "Yeah, I'm fine."

Gorski had got the T off his brother's used car lot, and Mud procured the whisky from an export dock. The documentation said the liquor was destined for warmer climes, Cuba to be exact. The way he figured, it was just bootleggers stealing from bootleggers so it wasn't really a crime. He had no idea why he felt the need to reason that one, but he did. Once an altar boy, always an altar boy, he guessed.

"This thing have enough gas?" Shorty was the nervous one, and rightly so since this was his gamble. Mud thought they should have experimented first with a few cases of Cincinnati Cream or maybe even some tap water, but for some reason Shorty felt the need to jump in with both feet.

"I told you once already," said Mud. "Now can I let her off her leash before she's empty? Hey, Lapointe, move unless you want to get run over."

Lapointe stepped aside.

The next part was going to be tricky. Mud double-checked the angle of the vehicle against its target and then gave it a slight hip-bump. With his good arm he lowered the cinder block onto the clutch and with the other he gripped the hand lever, eased it into gear, and then let drop the full weight of the block. The T sputtered forward. He trotted alongside for the first forty feet or so until he was confident the engine was dedicated to firing. He slapped her on the rear fender and said his goodbyes. Off she went. He rode his steel-toe Red Wings to a sliding stop, did a sloppy U-turn, and shuffled back across the ice to join the others on the shore.

A ten-dollar jalopy carrying cases of whisky worth over five hundred. Shorty couldn't watch. He turned away to observe instead the dawn filter through the spindly poplars along Front Road. The gang was standing on a spit that curled into the river at the mouth of Turkey Creek. They were surrounded by the remnants of Petite Côte, sandy farmland first plowed a century and a half ago by settlers from Quebec and soldiers discharged from the Detroit garrison. Shorty was letting himself become distracted by idle thoughts. There was a wood stove burning somewhere nearby, its smoke softening the crisp air. He imagined a kitchen coming to life with him sitting at the big table, warming his hands around a mug of coffee, patiently waiting on a hearty breakfast, something to do with eggs and sausage. Anything but the leftover pastrami-on-rye he had discovered wrapped in a road map on the dashboard of his car. In moments like this, and more and more often these days, he would ask himself, *What the hell am I doing?*

Thom and Lapointe were passing a flask back and forth. They were the ones who had stumbled upon this lead in a roadhouse across the way in River Rouge. It was the kind of place where business meets pleasure, and vice versa. A conversation was had over glasses of beer, and by the time their pony keg was empty the two parties were shaking hands. One of the details they agreed on was that sending the carrier vehicle the entire stretch, well over a mile, was far too risky, so Fighting Island would be used as a relay point. After the shipment safely reached the island, it would be then up to the Yanks to manage getting it to their shore. If the operation came off smoothly, this would be the drill whenever Shorty's gang had supply and the river was an ice road.

But right now it looked like they were already into some trouble. The car had shrunk in the distance so it took the boys a moment to notice their gas buggy had stopped moving. It found a combination of ruts and jagged ice where the surface had buckled in a recent thaw. The rickety T was spinning its wheels and going nowhere fast. It also looked as if it might even be shifting off course.

"Son of a bitch," said Lapointe.

Mud called back Shorty's attention and, anticipating a certain response, held up both hands, looked him straight in the eye and said, "Give her a minute."

But before anyone could utter another word or make a move, Three Fingers was sprinting across the ice on those long legs. The only sound that could be heard in the stillness was the faint noise of the engine struggling and Three Fingers' feet slapping down hard — he always preferred to run barefoot.

He slowed up as he neared the car. When he reached it he dropped onto his tailbone and, propping himself up on his elbows, set his feet against the bumper and started rocking the vehicle. He had to turn his face away from the exhaust shooting out the tailpipe and the granular slush being thrown by the spinning tires.

Just when it felt the T might free itself, there was a crack and a slosh. Its front wheels fell through the ice and the car was now resting on its front axle. Several crates of whisky shifted forward inside the gutted sedan and slammed into the footwells. One of the crates knocked the cinder block off the clutch, causing the engine to gear up. The T tilted some more and the rear wheels were lifted off the ice surface. She had nowhere to go but down.

Thom and Lapointe looked again for the signal light on the island, hoping the Rouge gang might step in and meet them halfway. They saw no light, no flash, not a flicker. There was another crack and the front axle broke through the ice, leaving the car teetering on its transmission. Three Fingers could hear the boys calling out.

"Ease up!"

"Don't move!"

"Roll away!"

This could be death, he thought. *A current of cold and careless water here to take me away, out of the sun and away from my family, from everything. I know I shouldn't be afraid.*

But he was.

There was a groaning, like from the joints of a sinking ship. Three Fingers was stretched across a mosaic of fracturing ice. His feet were growing numb as the sheets and shards supporting him sunk below water level. More cases of whisky slid across the floor and slammed into the footwells. And then in one silent, breathless gulp, the Huron went down with the automobile.

"Chain!" yelled Thom.

The boys threw off their hats and coats and ran out onto

the ice. Thom was the anchor, then Lapointe, Mud, Gorski, and Shorty.

At first there was no sign of Three Fingers, just the sound of the air gurgling out of the sinking T, which had abruptly halted, nose down, its rear wheels sticking up out of the water. Seconds passed, and then a hand gripping a hunting knife reached up through the floating chunks of ice and stabbed the lip of the hole. Three Fingers pulled himself up. He was yelling at Shorty and pointing at something down below.

"No," said Shorty, "forget the booze."

But it wasn't the crates of whisky that Three Fingers was on about. There was a sandbar, and tangled in its weeds was something else entirely.

Shorty was within a few feet now, crawling on his belly with Gorski gripping his ankles when the Huron went down again, this time intentionally. Shorty was preparing to reach for him when a figure surfaced, a ghastly, half-decayed body nearly frozen stiff. Three Fingers then sprang up, gasping for air and, bracing himself against the sunken T with one hand, reached for the knife still standing in the ice with the other. Shorty grabbed his arm while the Huron held on to the body. The boys slowly dragged them ashore.

There were a few *oh my God*'s.

"What the hell?" said Lapointe.

"You nearly got yourself killed," said Shorty.

"Not to mention the rest of us," said Mud.

"L-ook," said Three Fingers, "l-ook at his t-teeth."

Most of the flesh was gone from the corpse's face, but those long, jagged dentals were undeniable.

"Jesus," said Shorty, "it's Jigsaw."

Mud kneeled down to take a closer look, turned to Three Fingers and said, "How did you know?"

"He g-grabbed my l-leg."

The others exchanged glances.

"He didn't," said Gorski.

"But why did you drag him up?" said Shorty.

"Did you think you could save him?" said Mud.

"Forget him; he's miles past dead," said Thom. "Let's fix on saving the Indian." He and Lapointe threw one of the Huron's arms over each of their shoulders, and that was a good thing because Three Fingers was about to fold like a card table. They helped him into the fishing cabin that stood near the mouth of the creek. Once inside, they stripped him of his wet clothes, wrapped him in his coat and a couple dirty blankets, and sat him in front of the little potbelly stove. Thom got it going with some matches and loose bits of the interior. The cabin was about the size of a cell at county jail, but nowhere near as sturdy. Holes in the walls were stuffed with rags and newspaper. The stench was the only thing holding the place up. It smelled of stale cigar smoke and sour mash.

Outside, standing over Jigsaw's frigid remains, the other boys got to putting their hats and coats back on, wrapping themselves up a little tighter, taking extra care to tuck their gloves deep into their coat sleeves and fasten their buttons up to their necks.

"Why the hell did he have to drag him up?" muttered Shorty, and then he turned away, squinting in the direction of the hole in the ice. It looked like the T hadn't sunk any deeper. *Yeah*, he thought, *must be a sandbar*. And now the whisky was there for the taking — by anyone crazy enough. *Goddamn*.

Lapointe came running out of the cabin, stabbing the air behind him with his thumb. "Hey, I think the Indian's snapped or something. He's muttering all kinds of stuff that don't make any sense."

Gorski and Mud immediately went over. Shorty followed.

Three Fingers had his feet resting on top of the stove. He

was thawing out. "It w-was like he was w-waiting for me ... to c-come for him ... t-tangled in the w-weeds." He was sitting in the only chair in the place, looking up at them, still shaking and shivering but somehow managing a smile. "Always the l-last place you l-look, right?"

Shorty could feel Gorski's eyes turn on him but he refused the invitation.

"What's he on about?" said Lapointe.

Shorty ignored Lapointe. "Let's not start with that," he said to the Huron.

"I know what he's talking about," said Gorski.

"What?" said Thom.

Shorty sighed and Mud shouldered his way over to the window to stare at a pane of glass that was greasy on the inside and frosted on the other. It wasn't much of a view. He knew what was coming and wasn't interested in hearing any of it. Gorski took this as his cue and proceeded to tell the tale for the benefit of the new guys.

There was a long-standing rumour that the late crime boss Richard Davies had brought a fortune in cash and bonds down with him from Montreal, and kept it locked away somewhere in the Border Cities. It was his working capital, the stuff he was going to use to bribe, buy, and build his little empire. Thom and Lapointe had heard about Davies and how he was taken down last summer — gunned down, that is, along with Jigsaw — but they hadn't heard anything about any lost fortune. Gorski made it sound like something out of a Rider Haggard novel.

Three Fingers sat up. He was starting to feel his legs again. "He knows something," he said, pointing at the door. "He knows something."

"Who?" scoffed Shorty. "Jigsaw?"

"Think about it," said Gorski.

Mud turned away from the window. "I don't think you're gonna get him to talk."

"Maybe we should frisk him."

"You volunteering?" said Shorty.

"No," said Gorski, "I —"

"I'll do it," said Thom, the son of a pig farmer. He went back outside and the others, except for Three Fingers, followed.

There was a dusting of snow on the body now, like confectioner's sugar on death's dessert. He carefully picked up Jigsaw's remains, cradled them in his arms, and set him down on the fish-cleaning table that stood between the cabin and the creek.

"You sure he's dead?" said Mud.

Jigsaw got cut, blown apart, and sewn back together again so many times in France, he looked like a living rag doll. He had seemed indestructible.

"Yeah, he's dead," said Shorty. "It's been almost half an hour and he hasn't said a word. Remember how he liked to talk?" What Shorty was remembering was how Jigsaw used to take pleasure in mocking and berating him.

Thom found a knife in one of the drawers and started cutting into Jigsaw's stiff, tattered clothes, first his mackintosh and then his suit jacket. Thom handed the sections with pockets in them over to the boys to thaw and inspect.

"What are we looking for?" asked Lapointe.

"We'll know when we find it," said Gorski.

The process would have brought tears to the eyes of Jigsaw's tailor.

"Nothing," said Thom. "No surprise, I mean look at the rips and tears in his clothes. The fish, the reeds, the rock have been picking and scraping away at him for … how many months?"

"Keep working," said Gorski.

Thom looked at Shorty, who silently nodded his okay, and then Thom forced the blade into the pockets of Jigsaw's trousers. There were areas where the fabric was fixed to his body. He poked any gaps he could find and sliced them open wider, like he was filleting a pickerel. More of the same nothing.

The cabin door creaked open again, slapping the clapboard.

"Look at this." Lapointe was running toward them, holding one of the lapels from Jigsaw's overcoat. He and Three Fingers had been holding some of the larger pieces of the coat over the wood stove. "Feel it … there's something in there." He handed it to Shorty and Shorty massaged the fabric between his fingers.

"Gimme that knife."

Thom gave it to him and Shorty started sawing the folds open.

"What is it?" said Lapointe.

"Well, well, well." It was a key, an old fashioned-looking one, slightly longer than Shorty's palm, with a couple big teeth on one end and a few loop-dee-loops filled with coloured glass on the other. He rubbed some of the grit off it. It looked like a dull brass.

"See," said Gorski, "this proves it."

"It proves nothing," said Mud.

"But it must be important," said Shorty, "otherwise why go to the trouble of hiding it like that?" The reality of the thing suddenly opened up possibilities. The sun was rising over the trees now. Shorty turned and studied the object closely in the morning light. "It's an answer," he said. "What we're looking for now is the question."

Mud couldn't believe how easily Shorty could sometimes get sold.

"What's that supposed to mean?" said Lapointe.

"It seems obvious to me; all we need to do now is find the lock that fits the key."

"Obvious, maybe," said Gorski, "but not easy."

"So we're going on a treasure hunt?" said Mud. "Don't forget, we just lost half a grand worth of rye. I don't imagine those boys in Rouge are too happy with us right now. We made them pay us half up front, remember? They'll be looking for some sort of compensation, some gesture to put us back in good faith."

"And if we find this fortune, or whatever it is, we won't need them," said Shorty.

"Waste of time," said Mud. "We should be pulling jobs."

It was like watching your parents fighting. No one wanted to risk losing Mud. He had a level head, and when he set his mind to something, it got done. But he was always testing Shorty's leadership. Shorty knew that. He knew he would always have to prove himself. He felt they might have a real chance here. If they found the money, it would not only prove something about his instincts and leadership, it would also set everyone up real nice, maybe even for good. And they'd remember him well for that.

"Tell you what," said Shorty, looking for a compromise, "why don't we give ourselves until the end of the week? Five days. If we don't find anything, we drop it and move on, get back to regular business, reach out to the group in Rouge again."

"We should be reaching out to them right now," said Mud, "before they decide to reach out to us, if you know what I mean." Three Fingers had just joined them. He smelled of smoke and was still naked except for his boots and blanket. Mud considered the rest of the crew: Lapointe in his dungarees and heavy plaid coat, looking every bit the corn and radish farmer; Irish Thom in his threadbare hunting gear; Gorski and Shorty, the city boys in their suits and long overcoats tailored to conceal a variety of weapons and contraband substances. Mud himself was from the city too, but with one foot still in the factory. His hand, arm, and leg were throbbing. He knew it was his own fault for trying to make a repair on the assembly line while it was still moving. Hit by a car. *Stupid*.

"All right," said Mud, "until midnight Friday."

The others smiled while Shorty kept a straight face. He knew they hadn't really won Mud over or convinced him of anything. This was all against his better judgment. It was a compromise that, unless Shorty played it well, might not even last the week.

"Agreed, Friday at midnight."

"And what about the Guard?" said Gorski.

Ah, shit, thought Shorty.

The regulars stayed quiet while the boys from the county started again with the questions. It was going to be like discussing religion or politics, or a little bit of both.

Thom seemed agitated. "Are we talking about the provincial cops? Because if we are —"

"Did you have to go there?" said Shorty. He glanced over at Mud, who he could tell was trying to hold his tongue. "There was no Guard, remember?"

"The Guard is real," said Gorski. "Just ask the folks who ran into them."

"Bogeymen," said Mud.

"Drop it about the Guard," said Shorty, trying to regain control of the group. "All the same, we'll be keeping our mouths shut about our activities, right?"

"Okay," said Thom, "but who the hell is the Guard?"

Shorty looked over his shoulder. The sun was becoming lost in the cloud cover that was rolling in. He was imagining that farmhouse again, with the big table in the kitchen and all the warm food smells. He did this while he listened to Gorski and felt Mud's annoyance with the man he referred to as the Polack.

"After the boss — Davies — got killed," said Gorski, "there

were these guys who come down from Montreal looking for his money."

Mud was absent-mindedly kicking a small rut in the packed snow. Some of it loosened and hit Gorski. He ignored it.

"I'm telling you it's true," said Gorski. "People I know seen them."

"Your people are either drunks or idiots or both," said Mud.

Gorski decided to take the hit and continued. "They'd corner guys in stairwells, in alleyways; they'd appear in guy's bedrooms at night and ask them questions about Davies, Jigsaw, and Jack McCloskey. They were deadly."

"Maybe we should toss the key," said Lapointe. "We don't need trouble like that." Suddenly, for Lapointe at least, the key had the potential to unlock the bad as well as the good.

"What do you think it could be for?" asked Thom. Shorty was holding it out again in the palm of his hand, for all to see. "It doesn't look like it's for a storage box."

"Looks like a trunk key," said Gorski.

"Na," said Lapointe, "it's a door key. You can tell."

"Where would we even begin to look?" wondered Thom.

"Riverside."

"The Prince Edward."

"The pool hall."

"We might need help," said Thom.

"You feel like splitting it a few more ways?" said Shorty, incredulous.

"People are bound to find out," said Thom.

"Are you saying you got a big mouth?" said Mud.

"We're all of us going to keep our mouths shut," Shorty repeated. "Got it? If we don't, this could bring a whole heap of trouble on us. All kinds of trouble."

"Or a fortune," muttered Gorski.

As far as Mud was concerned, he had already spoken his piece. At the same time, he told himself he would have to do a little bit better than just go along for the ride. This was going to be an all-or-nothing affair. While the other boys speculated, he took Shorty aside.

"Are you going to tell him?"

They were standing close.

"Yeah," said Shorty, looking around again for that farmhouse. "I'll tell him. I'm supposed to meet with him anyway."

"What do you think he's going to say?"

"I don't know. Maybe he'll say we got lucky."

Mud leaned even closer. "Luck's got nothing to do with it," he said. "Luck's got nothing to do with anything."

Shorty backed away and squeezed the key in his palm. It felt hot.

Chapter 2

SLIDING ON COBBLESTONE

Morrison felt winter made him sharper. With everyone wrapped in layers, their hats pulled down low, their collars up high, and the elements assaulting his senses, he was forced to pay even closer attention to the finer details, where and whenever he could find them.

He had spotted Lavish Learmouth on Chatham Street while he was making his way toward the Avenue. Lavish was wearing a long, heavy overcoat that made him look as wide as he was tall, but he wasn't very tall. Of course, it was freezing cold out, but for

Lavish this garb looked a little too functional, not really his style, not his cut. Morrison decided to follow.

He was using this quiet Sunday morning to catch up on reports and other paperwork that he could no longer avoid. He hated being chained to his desk like that, getting bogged down in the minutiae of his job. He was looking forward to a walk to clear his head. But his head was already beginning to feel cluttered again, now with thoughts of what Lavish might be up to. He watched him waddle past Palmer & Clarke's Dry Goods and Ready-to-Wear, Douglas's Hardware, and then around the corner onto the Avenue in the direction of the river. He thought Lavish might drop into Stokes Brothers, the tobacconists, but he just kept on his way.

Despite the cold, churchgoers were heading to their services. Morrison had been passing clusters of them, families, heading toward All Saints' and St. Alphonsus. He was still passing them on the Avenue, though not as many now. Lavish, seemingly unable to control his momentum, almost knocked a couple of older ladies to the pavement in front of Elizabeth's Hat Shop. They stopped and turned to give Lavish what Morrison could only assume were their best dirty looks. Morrison thought that was strange behaviour for Lavish; he was usually very much the gentleman. He wasn't moving all that quickly, just steadily and rather purposefully. Morrison's curiosity was building.

Lavish stopped in front of the Royal Bank at the corner to let the traffic go by. Morrison paused, keeping his distance, but as soon as Lavish crossed Pitt Street, Morrison picked up the pace again. The churchgoers were starting to mingle with commuters walking to and from the docks, and Morrison was becoming anxious not to lose him.

Where is he going?

No establishment other than Pickard's Drug Store would

be open on this last block. Lavish walked right past, paused at Riverside Drive to let some light traffic go by, and Morrison ducked into the doorway at Bartlett's. He spied Lavish looking over his shoulders then crossing the Drive, stepping carefully through the ruts in the snow. Morrison came out of the doorway. He exchanged discreet nods with the traffic cop standing in the middle of the intersection.

Must be going into the British-American.

But Lavish passed the hotel entrance.

Nope.

It was now beginning to look like Lavish was heading to the docks to catch the ferry. Morrison could hear the church bells ringing.

Eleven.

He had better close in on Lavish, but it wasn't going to be easy. The slope down to the dock started right here. The snow had been swept away or trampled into patches of a snow-ice combination. Haphazardly seasoned with sand and salt, there were slippery parts still exposed. As he shuffled along toward the dock, Lavish braced himself, extending his arm against the side of the British-American.

There was a gap between the rear of the hotel and the next building. Morrison watched Lavish stop, slowly lower his arm, and steady himself. He walked like he was navigating a minefield. His next step found a patch of icy cobblestone at the entrance to the laneway and suddenly both feet went right out from under him and he landed flat on his back. Not only that, but because of the slope, he slid down and spun a little, pointing head-first like a compass needle north to Detroit before coming to a stop in front of the *Detroit Free Press* agency office.

Morrison had to get to him before any of the commuters did, so he hustled up to him with quick, flat-footed steps. At least he was wearing his galoshes. He found Lavish wiggling around like a turtle flipped on its back.

"Hi, Lavish," he said, looking down at him.

"Oh — Detective Morrison. Good morning."

"That was a nasty fall. Let me help you up."

"No, thanks — I can manage."

"Lavish, it's below freezing and you're breaking a sweat. Are you feeling all right?"

"I'm fine. Really, Detective, I can —"

Morrison found some dry, secure footing. "No, I insist. Let me help." He grabbed one of Lavish's flailing arms but couldn't lift him.

"Have you put on a little weight, Lavish?" Morrison once had to pick up Lavish and throw him into the back of the police wagon.

"Not that I'm aware of. You know, if you could just give me a kick and slide me down toward the dock —"

"Don't talk nonsense. I think it might be this coat of yours. Maybe if we just got you out of it first…."

Morrison unbuttoned Lavish's overcoat and, with Lavish resisting, wrestled the little man's arms out of it. People were beginning to pay closer attention now, but they were still moving along toward the dock. It was too cold for gawking. Morrison gave the overcoat a pull and Lavish rolled out of it and onto the cobblestone. The detective could barely lift it.

"You're packing more than wool here, Lavish. Get up."

"It's not mine."

Morrison draped the coat over his shoulder like it was a side of pork. "We're going up to my office here at the B-A to have a conversation."

"But Detective —"

"Or I hand you and your luggage over to Fields."

"No!"

"You lead."

Lavish shuffled back up the hill in his polished dress shoes, now covered in slush and sand. The wind was picking up again. He tightened his silk muffler around his neck and tucked his gloved hands under his arms. A staff member at the hotel saw Morrison coming and held open the door.

"Morning, Detective."

"Lazarus," said Morrison, "shouldn't you be home in bed?"

"Tolley phoned in sick. He beat me to it. Something's going round. Now I'm workin' his shift and mine."

"Sorry to hear that. Is my room available?"

"Yes, sir. It's been slow lately. Lots of cancellations. You want me to help you with that?" Lazarus was pointing at the coat.

"No, I got it. Give me about ten minutes; Mr. Learmouth here will need a taxi when we come back down."

Lazarus kept glancing over at Lavish, who was still shivering in his suit.

"Yes, sir."

With his free hand, Morrison waved Lavish up the stairs. "After you."

Lavish had been to Morrison's office at the British-American before. It was a dingy room on the third floor that Morrison liked to use for interrogations and dealings of his own. He paused at the first landing to let the detective catch up. Morrison weighed in at almost three bills, but despite that, as well as the booze and cigars, his engine was still in good form. Everyone figured he would just drop one day with no warning and with a smile on his face.

Room 3b was around the corner from the landing. Lavish stepped aside and Morrison paused and tilted himself forward slightly to better balance the weight of the coat while he searched his pockets. He pulled out a ring of keys with a bottle opener as a fob and jingled them around until the right one fell between his fat fingers. When he opened the door he gestured for Lavish to enter.

It was just this side of shabby. There was a time the British-American was fancy, but that was back when hotels offered a toilet on every floor. Now they offered one in every room. They were falling behind the times. Morrison let the overcoat slide off his shoulder and onto the bed.

"We had an agreement," he said to button-lipped Lavish Learmouth.

"I told you it's not mine," Lavish repeated.

"Don't insult me with talk like that." Morrison pulled his automatic knife, a Presto, out of his hip pocket and got to work on the lining of the overcoat. "I could have hauled you into headquarters, but I didn't want you to suffer the embarrassment."

Lavish turned away. He couldn't bear to watch.

"There must be five or six dozen flasks in here, Lavish."

"Sixty-six." He thought he should let Morrison know right then and there that he was going to be keeping a strict inventory.

"Who's your tailor? That Jew whose brother has the speak on Erie Street?"

Morrison removed one of the flasks from its sleeve, opened it, and took a long drag on it. Lavish protested.

"Detective!"

Morrison wiped his mouth with the back of his hand. "We have a deal, Lavish: You keep the information coming and I turn a blind eye to your bootlegging activities. Our deal includes a standing appointment Friday afternoons, and you stood me up last week. And the information in previous weeks has been a little, shall we say, on the light side. And then you go and pull something like this?" Morrison was pointing at the coat.

"I'm sorry, Detective."

"Sorry nothing. I'm confiscating this whisky. It's good stuff too, by the way."

"All of it?"

"All of it. Now, where did you get it? Are you doing a job for someone?"

Looking down, Lavish counted the stains on the carpet and suddenly noticed the bed had been moved. Only by about a foot. He wondered what it might be covering up. Something fresh.

"Yeah, it belongs to Jacobs — his brother, that is."

"I heard he was moving some inventory."

"He paid me fifty bucks and said I could keep the coat. I'm supposed to be meeting a guy in Detroit right about now."

"A friend of yours? Is he a professional?"

"No, on both counts."

"Forget about him then. And forget about Jacobs. Listen, I'll give you a chance to earn it back."

"How?"

Morrison stole another sip from the flask and took a step closer to Lavish. "I've been feeling a little in the dark lately, and it's not just because of the time of year. I'll give you two days to come across with something good for me."

"Like what?" said Lavish, blinking.

"Start with Shorty Morand. Ask around; I want to know what he's been up to. I've been hearing things. I'll keep your shipment safely locked up here. Depending on the quality of the information you have for me, and how quickly you get it to me, determines how much of it you get back."

"What is it about Morand?"

"I don't know. And I can't go poking around for no reason. He knows my habits, he knows my routine."

Morrison pocketed a fresh flask and the two headed back

downstairs. Morrison could see Lazarus helping guests with their bags, taking them out to awaiting taxis. When he returned, Morrison approached him.

"Here's money to cover a ride home for Mr. Learmouth." Morrison handed Lazarus a five. "Also, no one goes in that room."

"Yes, sir."

"I'll be back tonight." Lazarus went out to hail another taxi and Morrison turned to Lavish. "Remember: two days. If you come up with anything right away, I'll be at my desk, shuffling paper, otherwise, leave me a message here at the hotel. I'll be checking in regularly."

"Got it."

Morrison headed back through the doors and out into the cold, patting the bulge in his breast pocket. It would definitely improve the coffee at headquarters.

Chapter 3

TUMBLERS

"And then Gorski brought up the Guard."

"Jesus, Shorty." McCloskey was standing with his back to the middle of three floor-to-ceiling, half moon–shaped windows that were squinting at Riverside Drive, one hand pressed against his forehead and the other resting on his hip. The room, which actually took up the entire third floor of the building, was empty. He was wrapping up an inspection of the refinished floor when Shorty arrived. Shorty appeared a little more anxious than usual so he had asked him to go first. So far, he wasn't liking what he was hearing.

"You told me," said Shorty, "to show some initiative."

"Yeah, but more along the lines of your deal with those boys in Rouge. This is a little different. Not only does it sound like a waste of time but it's also going to fill the boys' heads with a bunch of nonsense."

Shorty appealed. "Jack, you know I don't buy into any of this bunk about the Guard, but why not let us run with this lost fortune thing for just a few days if for any other reason than to clear the air of it, and then we'll get back to regular business and never touch it again."

McCloskey reached in his breast pocket for his cigar case. He gave it a squeeze and it popped open. His last three White Owls. He pulled one, snipped the end with the cutter he kept tucked in his vest, then started patting his other pockets, looking for his matches. Shorty came forward with his.

"What was it you told Mud?"

McCloskey was getting the cigar going.

"I told him until Friday at midnight — and, Jack, that's not to say we'll turn away any business that falls in our laps in the meanwhile."

"You're damn right," said McCloskey. "Show me this key again."

Shorty handed it to McCloskey, who turned to the window and examined it closely in the northern light.

"Shorty, there isn't a single scratch on this key."

"So?"

"So how do you know it's ever poked a lock?"

"Maybe the lock hasn't been poked yet," said Shorty. "C'mon, let me run with this, Jack."

McCloskey returned it to Shorty. "All right, you run with it, but I want to be kept informed. And if I come across any leads I want you and the boys to follow up on, I don't care what day or hour it is, you're going to drop whatever it is you're doing and get back to work."

"Got it."

"You can tell the gang we talked," said McCloskey, "but this is your game. I've got enough on my plate right now."

Shorty saw this as an opportunity to change the subject. He looked around. "So this is our new place?"

"Like it?" McCloskey walked out into the middle of the floor. "It still needs some work. I've got some guys coming back tomorrow to check the wiring before we finish the walls."

Shorty was inspecting some of the details. "Nice," he said.

"The previous tenants, they went under. I guess even insurance firms lose the occasional bet."

"One too many in this case. I have a question," said Shorty.

"Shoot."

"How are we going to get the pool tables in here? In the last place, Green had them hoisted from the alleyway up and through a freight door, you know, like a piano. I don't see any way we can squeeze these tables in." He looked around. "Unless we're having them assembled in here."

"I changed my mind. We're not going back into the billiards business."

This caught Shorty a little off guard. "What sort of business are we going into then?" And by business, he meant their front operation.

McCloskey pulled a small silver case out of his other breast pocket, one not nearly big enough to house a row of cigars. He pried it open, lifted out a vellum business card, and presented it to Shorty.

BORDER CITIES WRECKING AND SALVAGE

Surplus and Used Auto Parts

Domestic and International Sales

112-16 Mercer St. PHONE SENECA 1008

Shorty blinked. "Wrecking and salvage, Jack?"

"We're going to buy for pocket change any old clunkers we can get our hands on, chop them up and sell the parts — on both sides of the border. It's a growing business and very profitable. Pay next to nothing for the car and its parts for, I don't know, 500 percent? Anyway, that's the legit part."

"I'm with you so far," said Shorty.

"These parts we're moving around, we pack them with straw, newspaper, and a few bottles of rye. That's how it's going to work and that's how it's going to get done, and in a few months we'll be moving more whisky than headlights."

"All right ... but do you know much about this stuff, Jack?"

"Not much, but I know people who do. We just need to put our heads together."

"The address ..." Shorty was examining the card again, turning it over and over, looking for some sort of clue. It all sounded good but he had a feeling he was missing something.

"I just signed the papers. Used to belong to this fellow named Sklash. He's retiring. We can talk more about that later." Jack was excited now and started pacing about the room. "The finer points of the deal need to be work out." He checked his watch. "Oh — I'm late for another meeting. Tell Gorski and Mud I'll be touching base with them about all this — sometime next week."

"We're still using the British-American?" said Shorty.

"Yeah, for now. And keep me up to speed on your quest or whatever this is, okay?"

"Sure, boss." Shorty touched the brim of his hat and tucked the business card away. He started slowly down the narrow stairwell but then picked up his pace to the point where he almost collided with a passerby on the sidewalk. He stopped, noticed his hand was hurting, and realized he was squeezing the key again. Jack had taken the news better than he thought he would. Shorty guessed it helped that Jack had other things on his mind. He looked up and down the Drive. *Wrecking and salvage*, he said to himself. He crossed the street to the Crawford Hotel, where the guys were waiting for him in the bar.

"So what did he say?" said Mud.

Shorty looked around the bar. Reformed, all of them. The place had been busted one too many times in the past couple weeks and was now bone dry. The Crawford had lost its protection and its game, and now most of the rooms upstairs were empty. The rummies had moved on, but they'd be back.

"He said we can run with it — but only to the end of the week like we all agreed."

"What's the matter?" asked Gorski, sensing something else was in the air.

"Nothing. Jack's just got a lot on his mind right now, you know, what with getting back in business and all."

"Anything we should know about?" said Lapointe.

"No, not now," said Shorty. "Let's stay focused on our game. I have to make a call." He got up from his chair, went up to the bar, and asked for the phone. The boys looked at each other but didn't say anything.

Before the end of the hour, Shorty was sitting across from Olive McTavish in a booth at Lanspeary's Drugstore. She was one of the elevator operators across the street at the Prince Edward Hotel. The rest of the gang was sitting tight in Shorty's Studebaker parked around the corner on Pelissier, mumbling into their coat collars.

Olive was about to start her shift; Shorty bought her a milkshake for lunch. He asked the soda jerk to put an extra egg in it for her.

"Good?"

"Tasty."

"Great." Shorty got right to the point. "Now, me and the boys want upstairs."

She was gently working the 'shake with the long spoon. "Where upstairs?"

"You know where upstairs. Is it occupied?"

"It's off-season."

"Yeah, I heard all the beaches were closed. You're going to let us in the back door so the house dick doesn't see us, and then you're going to take us up the service elevator."

She held the spoon halfway between the tall cup and her thin, painted lips. "You wanna short-sheet the beds?"

"You're awful cute today, aren't you, Olive?"

Shorty and Olive had a bit of a history. They'd gone to school together at Cameron Street Public. They were sweethearts for a while, but when Olive got a job and started taking long walks with a bellboy named Gerry, Shorty's nose got out of joint. The fact of the matter was Olive didn't want the complications that went along with being the girlfriend of an entry-level gangster. She wanted a simpler life. Shorty insisted he could give her that. Olive told him to take a good, long look in the mirror and be careful not to burn himself on that torch he was carrying. She was silent as she shovelled the last dregs of the thick 'shake into her mouth.

Where does she put it? wondered Shorty. She came up to his chin and looked she weighed about as much as a bag of grapes.

"All right. What's it worth to you?"

"Five," she said.

"A fin? For that I can get the concierge to give me a guided tour of the hotel and a hot meal at the end. All I want is a peek inside the suite."

"I could lose my job if I get caught, Shorty."

He looked at the pyramid of soda glasses behind the counter

and wondered if he could knock them all down with one saltshaker. He sighed and reached for his wallet.

"I feel like I'm displaying a horrible precedent."

She smiled.

"And what's this going to buy you if you get caught?"

"It'll let me drink my sorrows away."

Shorty was glad the others weren't here to witness this. He told her he would bring the boys through the alley behind the hotel, just off Park Street, in ten minutes.

"There's a door to the left of the loading dock. I'll be there," she looked at her watch, "in fifteen."

Right on time, she let the boys in, and when they started with the stomping of the boots inside the door she told them to shush. "Be quiet and wait here." It was the loudest whisper they had ever heard.

Mud put out his cigarette and Lapointe pulled out his flask. Olive reappeared presently and waved them down a short, ugly, cinder-block hallway to the service elevator. She locked the car so that it travelled non-stop to the eleventh floor. When it halted she opened the scissor-gate slowly. It was dead quiet; the only thing running was the red carpet to the window at the end of the hall. The gang followed the tiny elevator operator to the door of the deluxe suite that back in the day had served as Richard Davies's second home.

It suddenly occurred to Shorty how crazy it was to think there might be anything belonging to Davies left in the suite, or even the smallest clue to the whereabouts of his fortune. After law enforcement from all levels of government and of varying degrees of corruption had turned the place inside out, there'd surely be nothing to work on. Not only that, but by the time the hotel finished putting the place back together again there was a long list of reservations from tourists and honeymooners wanting to stay in the rooms formerly occupied by the infamous Richard Davies. In other words, the suite had seen a variety of traffic. But Shorty had to start somewhere.

They examined every lock in the place, in desks, closet doors, armoires, even the gramophone case. They looked for strong boxes, trunks, grips, wall safes, and loose floorboards. Whenever there was a break in the action, they discussed the Guard and whether or not they could trust Olive. Paranoia became the hardest currency. They found nothing and came to no conclusions.

"Don't you think someone would have found it by now?" said Mud.

"Maybe they just didn't look in the right place," said Thom.

"Or maybe whoever found it absconded to South America," said Mud. "What now?" He continued kicking the ball back into Shorty's end.

"Yeah, what now?" said Lapointe.

Shorty stiffened. What was it Three Fingers said after he found Jigsaw's body? *Always the last place you look.* He turned away from the window on the Avenue to find Three Fingers staring at him. The Indian was always doing that and it always threw him off. What Shorty didn't know was that the Huron believed answers were found in people's faces, regardless of whether they knew it, and not in hotel rooms or in spoken words that might as well have been written in blowing sand or melting snow. He saw something in Shorty's face. The others came back from taking one last look around the place and gathered around their leader.

"Maybe we should take the key to a locksmith and hear what he has to say," said Thom.

"No, not yet," said Shorty. "Let's try the house."

Shorty led them back down the service elevator and this time straight through the front lobby. Sure, they were turning a few heads but Shorty didn't care. The five bucks he gave Olive burned him. So did the boys' attitude up in the suite. He paused at the cigar shop and asked the tobacconist for a box of White Owls. The tobacconist pulled the box out of the humidor and set it down on the counter. Shorty opened his jacket to his waistcoat, exposing the butt of the revolver he had in his holster, and then picked up the box and pushed his way out and through the revolving doors onto the Avenue. He didn't even smoke. He just wanted to walk away with something. The gang followed without saying a word.

It was treacherous along Riverside Drive. Frozen ruts kept stealing the wheel away from Shorty while parts of the road exposed to sun were smooth as glass. Just yesterday, one of the city's leading barristers and his wife were driving along this very same stretch when, in an effort to avoid an oncoming vehicle that had veered into their lane, the barrister hastily applied the brakes, causing the car to skid and topple down a thirty-five-foot embankment, landing on its side on the frozen Detroit River. The barrister had to kick a hole through the ragtop so that he could drag himself and his fainting wife to safety. *Now that's someone I'd like to have in my corner*, thought Shorty.

When they reached the house, he pulled up Esdras, the nearest side street, and parked a few doors up from the Drive. The boys climbed out of the Studebaker and traipsed through the snow toward the entrance. It was set back, nearer the water's edge. The first thing they noticed was the fresh tire tracks in the driveway.

"Cops?" said Shorty.

"No," said Three Fingers.

"What interest would they have in this place any more?" said Mud.

Shorty pulled his coat lapels tighter around his neck. "C'mon."

The snow had drifted against the hedge along the driveway. Three Fingers leaned into Shorty and said, "Look — footprints where the tire tracks stop."

Gorski noticed too. "That's a big pair of boots."

"I don't like this," said Lapointe.

As they made their way carefully up the tiled stairs, Gorski picked up where he had left off and told Irish Thom and Lapointe how Davies had been running a smuggling operation from this house, and not just liquor either but guns and munitions too. Davies, he said, was arming strikebreakers on the other side of the border, trying to stop the spread of socialism in every blue-collar town between Detroit and Chicago. What Gorski didn't know, what didn't make it into the papers, was that Davies was also fanning the flames of racial unrest. He sold the whole thing as a package deal. He had been a man on a mission.

The front door was open a crack with icy snow wedged in the gap. Davies had been renting the property from a businessman in Detroit. This businessman never stood up to claim the property after the incident. Clearly he wanted to distance himself from the whole affair. He probably wrote it off. As with the hotel suite, the police and the Mounties had taken turns scouring the residence. No one on the street had heard whether or not they had turned up anything of interest. There was a fallen section of ceiling behind the door. Thom carefully forced it open.

The place was a disaster area: bloodstained walls, broken windows, crumbling plaster, and cold and snow blowing in from every crevice. Shorty started having flashbacks to that fateful night. Memories he thought were lost and forgotten were resurfacing, just like Jigsaw.

"You okay?" asked Mud.

"Yeah, sure." Shorty started to think more about the police. If the police had found anything pointing to Davies's working capital, someone in the department would have spilled. How long could someone keep money like that a secret? On the other hand, a dirty cop might have kept it to himself. But if he did, why would he have stuck around? While Jack was recovering from his wound, Shorty and the boys kept had close tabs on all the Border City Blues. No one had voluntarily left the force in the last several months, and no one had been discharged. The Mounties were a different story, however: an unknown variable.

Being the only ones who had ever set foot in the place before, Shorty and Mud split the group.

"There's two or three rooms down the hall as well as the way to the cellar. The kitchen and the dining room overlook the river."

They started poking around. More fresh footprints, damp with snow; handprints on dusty, overturned furniture; and recently exposed wall frame where sections of plaster had been pried off. It was bad enough that no one knew exactly what they were looking for, but to be sifting through a mess like this made the venture that much more challenging. Three Fingers examined the fresh hand and footprints.

"The Guard was here," he said.

A few heads popped around corners.

"Recently?" asked Shorty.

"Not sure," said the Huron, "but they have been here."

"Someone was here, but what tells you it was the Guard?" asked Mud.

"They probably know about the key," said Gorski.

"How's that possible?" said Shorty.

"They were always one step ahead of everyone else," said Gorski. "They have this sixth sense. They anticipate, they see, they know."

He sure could tell a story.

"Weren't they also supposed to have gone through this place last summer?" said Shorty, sounding more and more like a believer.

"But when they failed to turn up the money," said Gorski, "they probably figured all they had to do was wait until a certain snake lifted his head out of the grass."

"Who's the snake?" asked Thom.

"Charlie Baxter," said Shorty. He needed to sit down. He righted one of the chairs.

"And who would that be?" asked Lapointe.

"The guy who shot Jack," said Shorty. "Davies's bodyguard and the only one from his inner circle still unaccounted for."

"Some bodyguard he turned out to be," said Lapointe.

"Baxter was on a riverboat cruise with his sweetie — Davies's girlfriend — when Davies got killed." Shorty pointed at the big brown stain on the wall. "Right over there." It was his turn to tell the story. "There's plenty of speculation about what happened to Charlie Baxter after he shot Jack. Did he mean for his boss to get shot so that he could steal his fortune and run off with his girl? And did he try to kill Jack in order to prevent him from getting to the fortune before he did? No one ever believed Baxter tried to gun down Jack just to avenge his boss's death. There obviously wasn't that kind of loyalty there. There had to be more to Charlie Baxter."

"And where's the girl?" asked Lapointe.

"Ever heard of Pearl Shipley?" said Shorty.

"Hasn't she been in some pictures?" said Thom.

"Small ones," said Mud.

Lapointe's eyes got big and Thom started breathing heavy.

"You're steaming up the windows," said Lapointe.

Lapointe slapped Thom's shoulder and Shorty leaned back, folded his arms together, and continued. "Anyway, accounts are sketchy. Piecing it together, it sounds like Baxter had been following Jack all morning, and at the Michigan Central train station pulled a gun on Jack while Jack was sitting in his car. With his boxer's reflexes, Jack shouldered open the unlatched door, throwing off Charlie's aim. Jack took the bullet between his chest and his shoulder. The strange thing is, it was the exact place his brother took a bullet in a street fight."

"Where's Baxter now?" asked Thom.

"No one knows," said Shorty. "It sounds like he used the chaos at the train station to disappear. And the cops were so distracted by the events from the previous night, they kind of forgot about him. Maybe it would have been different had it been a homicide."

The boys who hadn't heard the story before were listening intently, not minding the wind blowing through the crumbling house. Mud lit a cigarette and quietly poked through the rubble. Three Fingers was busy watching the river from the sunroom at the back of the house.

"Jack was well-liked and respected by all, even his enemies. Whether they knew it or not, he was the glue holding the city together — or at least the city that we live in. Depending who you ask, you'll hear that either the Guard got Charlie, that he went over to the States, or that he went back up north to the lumber camp that Davies recruited him from."

There was a pause, and then Thom asked the question that was on everyone's mind. "Do you think the Guard knows we have the key?"

"Again," said Mud, "how would they know?"

"If they did, they'd be all over us by now," said Gorski.

"Maybe they're waiting for us to make our next move," said Lapointe. "Maybe they're just waiting for us to lead them to Davies's fortune."

"They're watching us right now," said Three Fingers as he re-entered the room. He didn't talk much, but when he did he had everyone's undivided attention. The gang held their maybes and stood very quiet and very still for a moment, looking around the place and listening. Nothing but the wind off the river, whistling through the holes and cracks in the house.

"Whatever you might believe," said Shorty, "I don't think this is a good place for us to be right now."

"But we came here to have a look around," said Thom.

"Look at this place," said Shorty, turning slowly around the room with his arms outstretched. "But don't look too hard because you're liable to knock it down."

"It's been picked clean," said Mud

"By the vultures," said Three Fingers.

They were quiet again, feeling the cold, the emptiness, and the dark, bottomless pit of this sorry address on Riverside Drive.

"This house drinks from us," said Three Fingers.

Shorty had heard enough. "We should split up," he said.

"But we gotta watch each other's backs," said Gorski.

Shorty pocketed the key. "Okay," he said, "you can start with mine." He knew the Guard had been here. He had felt their presence before. Hell, he had even seen them. But he wasn't going to get into that with the boys. He had never told anyone what he saw, not even McCloskey. Part of him didn't believe it. The other part just hoped he would never have to experience them again.

Chapter 4

BULLETS, RYE, AND REMEDIAL GYMNASTICS

Afternoon

"Maybe you should just sit down."

McCloskey was pacing about the room. He was in one of his moods again. "Not right now," he said and then he sat down. He was in Clara Fields's apartment, in her reading chair.

"Do you want to —?"

"I don't want to talk about it," he said.

"All right."

And then he started talking. "I still don't remember."

"Remember what?"

"You know."

"Sorry," she said. She sat back on the chesterfield with her ashtray in her lap and a lit the cigarette she cradled between her fingers. She gave him time to put his thoughts together. This was becoming a ritual of theirs, quite different from their past rituals.

"There's the war, but it's not like I'm trying to remember that … it surfaces occasionally … this is different … last summer —"

"You know what happened last summer," she said.

"I know what people told me, people who were there. But there's still that gap, those lost hours. I just feel like something important is missing, some place, or someone."

McCloskey's memory had been returning gradually, progressing backwards, from when he was convalescing, to arriving at the hospital, to being at the train station, seeing Charlie Baxter's face and the gun in his hand, to the gunshot, and then the memories stopped and his mind was blank, and then his memories picked up again at the night before, in the storm and the gunfight at the house on Riverside Drive.

"Does it matter?"

"It bothers me. It's like an open wound … that needs to be sewn up."

"What do you remember?"

"I've told you everything I remember," he said.

"Let's walk through it again. Start from the last thing you remember, before the blank hours."

"You … at the cemetery … after Billy's funeral."

"You really remember that?"

"What you mean?"

"Like you said, do you remember details because you were told them, or because they are your actual memories?"

"It's a memory, I know it now. I can see all of it, from my

point of view. We separated, you and me, and after that it goes blank." McCloskey rubbed his face with his hands and sank back further into the chair.

"And what is the very first thing you remember after that?"

He reached over, picked up Clara's cigarette case from the end table, and got one going. He exhaled at the ceiling. "Sitting in a wheelchair on the grounds of the hospital. It's sunny. There are other patients. Everyone's in white. There's music playing on a gramophone."

"All right, let's back it up again. You don't remember leaving the cemetery?"

McCloskey stood up and started pacing the room again. "I know I got in my car." He sat down, this time in a little wooden chair that was part of the dinette outside the kitchen. He turned the chair around so that he was facing Clara. He gripped the arms, then relaxed, took a deep breath, and closed his eyes. He was quiet for a moment.

"I'm driving ..." he said.

"Where?"

"Downtown."

"Keep driving," she said softly. She was being careful not to prompt him, not to fill his head with any images that were not his own. She wanted all of it to come from him, naturally.

"The river," he said. "But I see people ... and the skyline of Detroit ... I must be near the ferry docks."

"Are you sure?"

"I think so."

"That's good. Have any ideas what you might have been doing down there?" Clara let him concentrate. Maybe a minute passed.

He shook his head. "No, no I don't." He opened his eyes and straightened up. "I need a drink."

"I think I have some rye."

"Ginger ale."

That stopped Clara in her tracks. "Did you take the pledge?"

"No, I'm just not feeling like it."

Clara disappeared into the kitchen. McCloskey heard the icebox door open and the pop of the bottle top. "Do you want a glass?"

"No, thanks."

She reappeared and handed him the Vernor's.

"Let's go for a walk," he said.

"Don't you want your drink?"

"I'll take it with me."

They bundled up. McCloskey wrapped Clara in her raccoon coat. "Do you have to feed this thing?" Clara tied McCloskey's muffler snug around his neck. He donned his wool fedora and she slipped her feet into her late husband's, Jack's brother's, galoshes. McCloskey grabbed his bottle of Vernor's.

They headed down the stairs and out, pausing at the street corner. "Well," said Clara, "where to?"

"Let's just go around the block — this way." McCloskey gestured down Erie Street toward Victoria Avenue.

There was a footpath worn through the snowdrifts. Some residents had apparently already given up on shovelling. The two were silent for a while, McCloskey stealing the occasional swig of ginger ale from his bottle. Walking the short block along Erie, they then turned north down Victoria.

Clara was waiting for McCloskey to speak first.

"Maybe I should just forget about it."

"It doesn't sound like you can," said Clara. "Did you ever go back? To the train station, I mean."

"No."

She let that go for a while before she asked if he'd like to try that, see if it triggered anything.

"Will you come with me?"

"Sure," she said.

"Can we do it now?"

She looked at her watch. "I think so."

"Let's go."

They were already at Anne Street, so they just looped down Pelissier and walked straight to his car, which was parked near Clara's. They piled into the Light Six and McCloskey wiggled it back out of the ruts. It actually handled well in the snow, better than Studebaker's Big Eight or any of the other heavier cars.

"Do you remember the route you took to the train station that day?"

"Sort of."

"Okay, try not to think too hard about it. Just drive."

McCloskey pulled over before he got to Giles Boulevard and parked the car. He closed his eyes and rested his head back.

"Are you all right?" asked Clara.

"Yeah. I'm just trying to clear my mind first."

They sat in the car, silent. It was freezing cold. Wind whistled through the bare branches of the trees. Clara looked around and saw a rug folded behind her. She grabbed it, unwrapped it, draped it over her legs, and waited for McCloskey to collect himself. When he finally did, he put the car back in gear, turned right onto Giles and then left at Victoria, following it all the way up to Tecumseh Road. He turned right, merging into the traffic.

Driving to the train station with a girl sitting next to him. This felt familiar, he thought, but he didn't say anything.

Turning right at McKay, he found the road surface slightly better, probably from being so heavily travelled by commuters. He could tell Clara was waiting for him to say something. He could feel her eyes on him.

He was letting his instincts, or whatever it was, take him

over, to the point where it no longer felt like he was in control of the car. The Light Six seemed to be ignoring the available ruts and was plowing through the half foot of snow to get to where it thought it needed to be. McCloskey parked between the entrance and the south end of the building, where the track was still visible.

He cut the engine and then just stared ahead, his hands gripping the wheel. Clara remained quiet. She could hear a passenger train to their left coming out the tunnel that ran under the river. It approached the station sluggishly, trying to make its way up the slight grade. Cold steel against cold steel. Probably ice and snow on the tracks too. McCloskey turned to look, but from where they were parked there was no view of the train.

"Looks pretty quiet in there," he said, referring to the station.

"Yeah."

"I wonder where it's headed."

"Did you want to go inside and warm up for a bit?" she asked.

"No, let's just sit here until the train pulls out. I want to see that."

She hesitated and then asked if that meant something to him.

"I don't know."

"Mind if I smoke?" she said.

"No, go ahead."

She pulled a small package of cigarettes and a box of matches out of the inside pocket of her coat. A car pulled quickly into the lot, too quickly for these driving conditions. It pulled right up to the entrance of the station. Doors opened and slammed shut.

"Just in time," she said.

He stared at the car for a while. Something else was echoing in his head.

"Are you sure you don't want to go inside?"

"Yeah, I mean, no. I never went inside. Listen — I think it's getting ready to pull out already."

And it was. He could hear the shouts and whistles on the platform, followed by the sound of the wheels grinding the frozen track. Smoke and steam above and around the station, and then finally the locomotive. He watched it pull away and slowly disappear into a gust of blowing snow that seemed to twist around the cars, creating another tunnel.

"Did you see their faces?" he said.

"Yeah," she said. "I saw their faces."

"Okay, let's go."

"You sure?"

"Yeah."

"Where to?"

"Back to your place," he said. "I could use that rye now."

McCloskey started the engine, checked his mirrors, and did a U-turn in reverse, aiming the vehicle hard at the road. "Do you think you could work my shoulder again?"

"If it'll help."

"Great. I've been thinking I'm ready to hit the gym."

She looked at him. "Are you sure that's such a good idea?"

"I need to do something."

They were heading back down McKay.

"Okay, but do me a favour and start slow."

"I'll try," he said.

"While I'm working your shoulder, maybe you can tell me about what you experienced at the train station just now."

"That's exactly what I was thinking. I think I need to loosen up a little."

Chapter 5

RUNAWAY TRAIN

Dusk

The young fireman had no sooner closed the door to the fuel car than there came a pounding from the inside. *Impossible*, he thought, *I must be imagining things*. He turned his back on the door, leaned on his shovel, and continued watching the two engineers work the controls. He still had a lot to learn.

Bam bam bam.

This time it was loud enough for the engineer and his assistant to hear over the engine. They had their hands full so they instructed the fireman to go investigate. The boy unlatched one of the swinging doors, and out came a big man wrapped in an overcoat and brandishing a sawed-off shotgun. He looked like he'd just climbed through a coal mine.

"There's a cow on the tracks," he said.

This was his opener. He said it loud enough that he wouldn't have to repeat it, probably thinking it was too good a line to waste. The engineer and his assistant pulled their eyes off the grimy wall of dials and gauges and faced him.

"Who the hell are you?" demanded the engineer.

"I gotta make a transfer; you're going to stop this thing."

The engineer hesitated, considered his assistant and the fireman who, with his thin, coal-smeared face was staring blankly at the gangster, bootlegger, or whatever he was.

"But we only just stopped at Maidstone — we're up to speed now."

"Do it," barked the big man, and he raised the shotgun so that it was eye level with the engine cab trio.

The engineer wised up quick. "Like you said, mister." He and his assistant started pulling this and turning that — all the things they needed to do to make a sudden, unscheduled stop. The fireman stood aside and waited for further orders.

It was quickly becoming dark. The bootlegger kept his shotgun fixed on the railmen while he looked outside for his markers: Three oil-drum fires in a farmer's field.

"Is that Sexton Sideroad coming up?" he asked the engineer.

"Yep."

"Okay, you'll be stopping somewhere before you cross Middle Road, so get ready. Is that cord the train whistle?"

"Yes, but —"

The bootlegger gave it a couple pulls and continued to check for his markers.

● ● ●

Four men in black sitting two-by-two and facing each other in the back corner of one of the passenger cars felt the train slowing and checked their wristwatches. One of them immediately got up and started making his way through the car in the direction of the engine. Another followed very shortly. The third remained seated while the fourth took up a position at the back door of the car. They moved in silence, with ease and precision.

The car was dimly lit, making it even more difficult to see their faces beneath their wide-brim hats, to judge the cut of their clothes, or to understand their intent. They were like shadows; rather than reflect light, they actually seemed to absorb it. After some murmuring among the passengers, the car fell silent again and no one interfered or so much as mentioned them. To many of the passengers they were invisible, and to others they seemed to represent something otherworldly. Those passengers looked away.

The train was slowing to a stop. The side of the first baggage car opened to a blast of swirling snow. A man in a big coat leaned out and started swinging a lantern. A much larger man came to the door dragging a couple of heavy suitcases. He staggered like a drunk but it was just the rhythm of the train that was throwing him off.

"There they are. See?"

"But can you see the haystack?" said the one with the suitcases. "We don't want to be waiting around here any longer than we have to."

"It's right there in front of you."

"Hey, I'm not the one with the lantern, am I? And stop swinging it around like that."

"Like what?"

"You almost hit me."

"Would you relax?" said the lantern-bearer. "I swear you're worse than my old lady."

"Drop dead, Mouse."

Barney, the one doing the heavy lifting, grabbed one of the suitcases by the handle and, with both hands, swung it back and forth to give it some momentum and then heaved it toward the haystack just beyond the narrow ditch.

The farmer got out of his Model T pickup and retrieved the suitcase. He opened it in the headlight beams. Inside the case were about a dozen bottles of rye packed in newspaper. The farmer gave his "okay." Barney started tossing the rest of the order onto the haystack. Two younger men hopped out of the back of the pickup to help retrieve it.

"Why has this train stopped?"

The first man in black had reached the engine cab just as the train had come to a halt. He didn't come by way of the fuel car but rather off the shoulder of the track, surprising the bootlegger.

"His orders," said the engineer, pointing at the bootlegger.

The bootlegger couldn't get a good look at the shadowy figure, couldn't make him out. "You a cop?"

"No."

A light flickered in the bootlegger's head. "Hey, wait a minute — this is my caper. If you want in, you're a bit late."

"This train is scheduled to arrive at Michigan Central station in Windsor at 9:15 p.m."

The bootlegger cocked his head at the shadow. "You're not after the booze?"

"No."

"Then why don't you just go back to your seat and finish your crossword before you get hurt, okay?"

It got crowded in the engine all of a sudden: the engineer and his assistant backed up against the hissing wall of dials and gauges as soon as they saw that one of the bootlegger's partners had appeared out of nowhere and was positioning himself behind the man in black. His partner was just as big, and in all likelihood just as stupid.

"Need any help finding your seat, fella?" he said.

Without hesitation and with very little effort, the man in black grabbed the fireman's coal shovel out of his hands, spun, and bashed the second bootlegger across the face with it. An explosion of teeth, blood, and snot followed. The bootlegger staggered back and down onto the gravel shoulder, rolling into the frozen ditch that ran between the track and the farmer's field.

The first bootlegger, stunned, pivoted his shotgun toward the man in black, but in one swift motion the dark figure grabbed the barrel with one hand and the bootlegger's neck with the other. The bootlegger let go of the shotgun in order to better defend himself but the figure was already pressing the bootlegger's face against the fire door. It made a sizzling sound and the bootlegger started wailing. The figure then picked him up effortlessly by his lapels and tossed him out the cab, landing him somewhere near his partner. The figure then calmly shifted his attention to the engineers and the fireman.

"You have some time to make up," he told them and handed the fireman back his coal shovel. "Get stoking."

The team didn't ask any questions and got right to work. They noticed there was a second man in black in the cab now. They looked identical, but still indescribable. They were all shadow and seemed to blend together, moving like a two-headed beast.

"Don't stop until we get to the station," one of them said. Or was it both of them?

"But Pelton —" started the engineer, pointing his thumb up the track.

"Don't stop until we get to the station," the voice repeated.

Just as Barney was preparing to heave another of the booze-laden suitcases toward the haystack, the train lurched forward and he staggered back, almost falling over with it.

Mouse obviously couldn't see it, but the farmer's face fell. He shouted something toward the baggage car that the bootleggers couldn't hear and then ran back to his pickup. He told his boys plain and simple that the deal had gone south, but not to worry, he had an idea. He suspected that his suppliers either got cold feet or just needed a little help with the personnel on the train. He told his eldest boy to hide what landed in the haystack, and his youngest boy to accompany him. The farmer threw his truck into gear, mashed the pedal, and beat a path over to 9th Concession, where he dropped down and hung a right onto Middle Road. "It'll take us out of the way a bit, but then we'll shoot back up 8th and head them off."

Barney and Mouse looked at each other. What happened? Were there Mounties on board? Mouse stayed put and kept watch on what was left of the shipment while Barney went to investigate. The big man reached outside around the still-open baggage car door for the ladder to the roof. He wasn't fast but he was surprisingly agile; as a kid he was always the one elected to climb the tree to retrieve a kite. What he hadn't bargained for was tonight's near-blizzard conditions.

Everyone in the car heard the noise on the roof. The third man in black rose from his seat and walked to the front of the car. The fourth man followed, exchanging his position at the back door for one at the front. The third then made his way outside and onto the roof. The train wasn't moving so fast yet, but the snow was blowing like mad and it was bitter cold. Also, ice was building up on the rungs that ran along the top of the car. The bootlegger didn't see the man in black until he was practically face to face with him. At first he thought his eyes were playing tricks on him. Who the hell else would be crawling on all fours on the roof of a moving train in a snowstorm?

Even this close, the figure had to shout in order to be heard. "Where are you going?"

"I need to use the john."

"Where are you going?" the figure repeated.

"You wanna punch my ticket?" said the bootlegger, cracking wise again.

"Yes." The man in black pulled a Webley out of a holster inside his coat and used it to blow a hole clean through Barney's head. The bootlegger tumbled off the roof of the car and landed in a snowdrift, limbs outstretched and looking like a big, ugly snow angel. The man in black replaced his Webley, turned back the way he came, and re-entered the passenger car, walking past the fourth, who was still guarding the front door. There was a new face in the crowd: a conductor was across in the aisle seat. The old man was sweating bullets, fiddling with the hem of his jacket but staring straight ahead, not making eye contact with the shadowy man as he entered and sat down. The train was picking up speed again, travelling faster now than it had been before its unscheduled stop. The fourth man proceeded up the aisle and left the car at the rear.

When he reached the still-open baggage car, he found Mouse positioned near the door, sitting on one of the remaining suitcases of rye and frantically waving his lantern at the farmer's speeding pickup truck. Mouse caught the figure out of the corner of his eye.

"Shit — you a cop?"

"No."

"You with the railway?"

"No."

"Then who are you?"

Back in the engine cab, the first man in black checked his watch while the second noticed a vehicle tearing up the service road, heading in the same direction and gaining speed.

The farmer made a sharp left down the next concession and stopped right on the level crossing. He put his brake on and flashed his headlamps. His boy, unconvinced that the train would stop in time, bailed out of the truck and started running home. The farmer cursed him and his mother and then sat back and lit his pipe. He was determined to get the rest of that rye. There were folks in roadhouses all along St. Clair's shores counting on him. His reputation was at stake. And then of course there was the money; he would make a tidy sum that would at least partly make up for that lousy corn crop last year. He puffed away on his pipe and thought for all his trouble that he should hold back some of his payment.

"I'll teach those fuckers."

The train was racing now and, what with no news about what was going on, the passengers were becoming a little uneasy, and not just in the car hosting the dark figures. A few looked to the conductor, but he was busy twisting his hat in his hands.

Minutes later they were shaken by a sudden impact, but the train kept barrelling down the track. Debris flew past the windows in the first passenger car. It looked like automobile parts flying past. The locomotive had thoroughly demolished the pickup. The farmer managed to jump out in time.

The train breezed through Pelton Junction, normally the last stop before the city limits. Toward the end of the long stretch broken by only one county road, they passed the Kenilworth and Devonshire racetracks and the roundhouse. Soon there were lights in the distance and a glow in the night sky, indicating downtown Windsor and Detroit. The train was charging right into the city now. The lit surroundings were giving passengers a more accurate sense of just how fast they were travelling, and tension mounted. People were gripping their armrests, purses, and bags tighter. A few of the older women muttered prayers while the men remained quiet. They were bracing themselves for the worst.

Back in the baggage car, the fourth man in black had become bored with Mouse and hurled him through a wooden fence they were passing. A few suitcases of liquor followed. The figure then made its way back to the passenger car and took a seat next to the third. The first and second figures reappeared, made their way up the aisle and took seats across from their partners, completing the dark quartet. The rest of the car remained silent. All that could be heard was the rhythm of the rails.

The train finally began to slow and the four checked their watches: 9:12 p.m. The engineer started fiddling with the gauges and his assistant began applying the brakes, something he normally didn't have to do this soon and so aggressively.

They were entering the rail yard. A signalman in the first tower rang his contact at the station and told him to get everyone off the platform. Something was clearly wrong.

Both the engineers had their hands on the brake now. The assistant had his foot against the wall of the furnace for leverage. Their ears were filled with the head-splitting, stomach-churning sound of steel on steel. The engine cab was vibrating, almost shaking. The engineer noticed his assistant's eyes were closed; sweat streamed down and mixed with the soot on his face, black tears running down his cheek and off his chin. His teeth were clenched, the engineer could tell.

The train finally stopped, the first car about thirty yards beyond the platform. It was 9:14 p.m.

Passengers, shaken and stirred and white as snow, disembarked slowly. Many took a deep breath of the cold, crisp air as soon as they got outside. It cut the motion sickness. Red caps helped the women passengers climb down off the train and through the snow toward the platform.

"Watch that last step, miss."

"Thanks a bunch," said Vera Maude, a little wobbly. She was adjusting her hat and coat when she stopped and shuddered.

"Something wrong, miss?"

"No," she said, "just got a sudden chill."

"It's this cold snap we're having. People getting chilled right to the bone."

"Yeah? Say, can you call me a cab?"

The four dark shadows stepped off on the other side of the train, boarded a freight elevator that dropped them below track level, resurfaced at the end of a tunnel on the Wellington side, and disappeared into the night.

— Chapter 6 —

THE MAN ON THE STREET

Campbell closed the Cadillac Café and started winding his way home through winter. *Not enough ginger*, he thought. *Not enough ginger.*

He frequented Ping Lee's establishment on Riverside Drive because Ping kept late hours and let him order off-menu. Campbell had asked him what was fresh, and knowing what he liked, Ping skillfully assembled a succulent chicken and vegetable chow mein. The fried noodles were filling and the chicken juicy and tender, done just right, but there wasn't enough ginger, and that's what Campbell was most looking forward to: something to gently keep his insides warm while he measured the streets of downtown. Ping had frowned at Campbell's ginger request at first. He didn't believe it should be included in this recipe that he took great pride in preparing. But he liked Campbell; he always told him he was "okay."

Campbell occasionally went to Ping just for information, but knew better than to call it that. Informants in the Border Cities, particularly those who worked or resided along the river, had a tendency to disappear. He told Ping that he sought his opinion, his sage advice.

The wisdom of the Orient.

Ping smiled the first time he heard Campbell use that phrase.

What's so funny?

Campbell eventually stopped using it.

He was looking for Ping's thoughts on Judge Gundy's decision this morning. He had a copy of the *Border Cities Star* opened in front of him on the counter. "Two Chinese Get Big Fines." It was an opium trafficking case. The fines followed a messy RCMP bust at a grocer's on the other side of the Avenue. Ping was his usual philosophical self.

Dou yan.

What?

One of his daughters happened to be standing nearby, stacking hot, clean plates. She bridged the divide for them.

He say, you cross-eyed.

Really? What else does he say?

Not much. Not tonight.

Campbell stopped telling anyone at the department about his surveys of the city streets in his off hours. He had thought they would have appreciated it, respected his desire to know the territory as well as any constable walking a beat. Chief Thompson told him he was wasting his time and the other cops said, in not so many words, that he was cutting their grass. They also thought he was checking up on them, maybe being used by Thompson to keep tabs on them. *Things didn't used to be this tangled up*, thought Campbell. Regardless, he quietly kept to his routine.

Every intersection was an open invitation to the bitter wind. Campbell pulled his overcoat collar up against the elements. It did little good. He hated doing it, but he decided to shorten tonight's planned circuit by taking Pelissier Street up to Wyandotte, and then loop back north toward his apartment once he crossed the Avenue.

The wind whistled around the slack in the telephone wires and howled through the gaps between buildings. Any warmth Campbell might have been carrying with him was quickly dissipating; he could barely feel his nose, and his cheeks smarted like they'd had a good slapping.

A strange amber flash in the big windows along the side of Meretsky & Gitlin's furniture store caught his eye. It was a reflection. He glanced up at a dying streetlight and that was when he noticed the snow swirling overhead. Pulling his collar up further, his bowler down lower, and plunging his gloved hands even deeper into his pockets, he continued on his chosen path.

No traffic on London Street. No streetcar wheels grinding to a stop on frozen tracks. No sputtering motors. No surprises. He shifted his eyes over toward the darkened Capitol Theatre as he crossed. It would have recently emptied. It was the last night for *Heroes of the Street*; he had meant to catch that one.

Probably just as well.

He continued his brisk pace. At Park Street, the businesses gave way to simple clapboard houses. They didn't hug the sidewalk and didn't throw much light. The snow was landing now and he was picking up the smell of wood and coal burning.

He had resisted long enough; he paused at the top of Maiden Lane to light a cigar. He dug deep through his layers to find it, procured under the counter from Ping, and his Ronson. The spark, a flash, and the aroma. He was feeling better already. But only for a moment.

The crash cleaved through the night. Campbell instinctively ducked, but his curiosity made him turn just in time to see a shadow hit the pavement along with broken glass and what appeared to be windowpane. He looked up and saw a curtain billowing out of a yawning gable in the third storey of the sole dwelling on Maiden Lane. He ran over. The body was splayed out in the dusting of freshly fallen snow. Blood was pooling around the head and glass fragments glittered in the streetlight. Campbell unhitched the flashlight from his belt, picked the victim's pockets, and found a wallet. He opened it, found some identification and then his mind kicked into gear.

Kaufman: Male, foreigner; year of birth 1867. Right cheekbone crushed from impact; cuts on his face attributable to glass; broken right arm raised over his head; cuts on his hand also from glass; left forearm tucked under his midsection; body twisted slightly — both feet pointing to the right.

A constable came running from the Avenue, not thirty yards away. He was surprised to see Campbell already on the scene. "I rang the box, sir." Maybe his way of saying he would have been there sooner.

Campbell noticed a neon sign hanging in the ground floor window of the house. No other light came from the window. The sign looked like an eye. Below it, painted on the glass were the words *Madame Zahra's Astral Attic*. A small parade of concerned citizens dressed in bathrobes, overcoats, galoshes, and other people's hats came staggering, bleary-eyed, out of their homes along Pelissier and the Avenue, converging on the house on

Maiden Lane. Campbell pulled the cigar out of his mouth. "Send up whoever from the department gets here first," he said, before pointing his cigar at the gawkers, "and keep these people back."

There were no fresh footprints on the front steps. The entrance was unlocked. Campbell entered. On the other side of the tiny vestibule was a longish, narrow hall. First to the right was a locked door, and just ahead on the left was a staircase, with light coming from above. He leaned against the handrail and looked up. A fixture was dangling above the second-floor landing. Campbell took to the stairs, two at a time, until they delivered him through the floor into a tiny attic apartment.

He felt as though he just passed into another world, and in some ways he had. It resembled a gypsy tearoom from a Hollywood movie. Stepping up, he first noticed the stars painted on the ceiling; then the richly patterned wallpaper; iconography and idols; fringes, tassels, incense, and candles. He was so distracted by the décor it took him a moment to notice the three people sitting around the table to his left and a fourth chair tipped onto the floor. A woman whose costume and demeanour suggested she was none other than Madame Zahra appeared calm. The other two, older, about the victim's age, appeared agitated. The trio made eye contact with him but did not move or speak. They appeared frozen in the moment. He left them in that state while he quickly examined the window, a gaping hole that went almost from floor to ceiling. In addition to the winter gusts, it was also opened to a view of the neighbourhood rooflines and the bright, distant beacons of downtown Detroit.

Campbell considered the trajectory of the body. To have gone through the window and landed that far away, Kaufman either would have had to have a running start or have been thrown with a great deal of force — and the trio at the table looked to him like a card of featherweights. He looked down again and happened to catch the station's REO as it turned from the Avenue onto the lane, coming to an abrupt stop about ten feet from the body. Campbell held his gaze until he saw a constable step out of the vehicle. He whistled and then went to the top of the stairs to greet him.

"Bickerstaff," he shouted.

"Detective Campbell?"

The constable scrambled up the stairs and into the apartment. "What happened, sir?"

"I think the sidewalk killed him," said Campbell.

"And what of these ones?"

"They haven't spoken, haven't moved. See if you can't pull that tapestry down and hang it from the curtain rod. It's Siberian enough in here already."

"Sir?"

"Nothing. Has someone contacted Laforet?"

"I phoned him from the station. He was none too happy."

"That's because he hates the telephone. But I have a feeling he'll like this." Campbell pulled out his notebook and approached the table. "I'm Detective Campbell, and," pointing behind him with his pencil said, "that's Constable Bickerstaff. Would you be Madame Zahra?"

"Yes."

"Is that your first or last name?"

In a tone that made her sound like she was used to random searches and interrogations, she answered, "I am Zahra Ostrovskaya."

Campbell's pencil hovered over his notebook. "I'll stick with Zahra for now. A man identified as Kaufman is lying dead on the pavement outside. Was he pushed out of that window?"

Zahra said she did not see him go out the window. In what Campbell figured to be an Eastern European, possibly Russian accent, Zahra went on to explain how she did not see anything because she was in a trance.

"A what? Don't — we'll come back to that." He shifted his attention to the couple. "What is your name, sir?"

"Yarmolovich. Pavel Yarmolovich. And this is my wife, Sonja. She does not speak good English."

Campbell nudged up his bowler with the heel of his thumb. "I'll decide whether or not she speaks English well, sir. Are you carrying any identification?"

Yarmolovich reached inside his coat, pulled out a yellowed paper, and handed it to Campbell. It unfolded into something resembling the Treaty of Versailles. Campbell scanned it. Thinking it official-looking enough, he refolded it and handed it back to Yarmolovich. He then manoeuvred toward a beaded curtain that he presumed sectioned off some sort of cooking area. He sliced through the hanging beads with his hand and parted it several inches. It was indeed a kitchen, about the size of a closet and about to collapse upon itself. He turned back to his host.

"Madame Zahra, would you wait for me in here?"

The detective widened the gap in the beaded curtain for Madame Zahra, who then slowly made her way up from the table. Campbell then sat in the chair she formerly occupied and turned his attention toward Pavel Yarmolovich.

"Did you throw Kaufman out of that window?"

Yarmolovich seemed shocked at the accusation. Or at least that's what his performance suggested. He denied it, first in his native tongue and then in broken English, both served hot. Campbell then turned to the woman, but before he spoke a word to her, he held up his hand to Yarmolovich, just stopping himself from putting it over his mouth. The question was going to sound ridiculous, but he had to ask it. "Sonja, did you push Kaufman out of that window?"

She glanced at her husband with an expression that could only be described as incredulous and replied, "No."

"There," said Campbell, "now that we have gotten that out of the way, am I to conclude that Mr. Kaufman jumped out of that window?"

"Yes," said Yarmolovich. Without checking with her husband first, the wife nodded.

"Please stay seated."

Campbell rose from the chair and slowly walked back toward the window, along the way examining the bits of furniture, wall hangings, and the carpets on the floor. There were no signs of a struggle, nothing looked disturbed. From the window, he paced the distance back to the table. If Kaufman had jumped, it would have to have been after a running start. He sat down.

"Now, what would make Kaufman do a thing like that?"

Yarmolovich sighed and, rubbing the stubble on his chin with the back of his hand, said, "He was talking to his wife."

"She was here?" said Campbell.

"Yes, they were arguing. Kaufman was angry, and then frightened. He got up, and then *fsht*," said Yarmolovich, smacking his hands together and sliding his right palm forward, "out the window. That was when Madame Zahra came from her trance."

"And Mrs. Kaufman, where did she go?"

"Back to the other side."

"Other side of what?"

Yarmolovich looked at Campbell like the detective was someone who had never heard of canned peaches before. "To the spirit world."

Campbell looked over the edge of his notebook and tipped his bowler back a little farther. "I'm sorry, but when you said Mrs. Kaufman was here, you actually meant …" With his pencil he pointed at the stars on the ceiling.

Without looking at each other, the Yarmoloviches nodded. Campbell closed his notebook and told them to sit tight; he was going to speak with Madame Zahra. But first he approached the constable, who had finished hanging the tapestry and was now positioned between the window and the entrance to the apartment.

"Bickerstaff."

"Sir?"

"Keep an eye on things for me here," he said, nodding back toward the Yarmoloviches. "I'm going to have a few words with Madame Zahra in the kitchen."

"Yes, sir."

Campbell entered the cooking area and found Zahra using a Bunsen burner to light what he thought to be one of those Turkish cigarettes. She was tilting her head toward it while holding back her waves of jet-black hair. She straightened up when she got it going. "The Yarmoloviches, they were helpful?"

"No, the Yarmoloviches were not helpful. Let's forget them for a moment. You started telling me something about being in a trance."

"Yes." She went on to explain how she had been conducting a séance with the couple and Kaufman, and was in a trance when the incident occurred. She claimed she saw nothing. Campbell knew the Yarmoloviches were listening; they started whispering to each other as soon as they heard their name.

"I step outside of myself," Zahra explained to the layman, "and become door through which spirits may pass into this world."

"Ghosts?"

She smiled. "I know what you are thinking — glowing apparitions, floating in air at end of your bed at night, making *voo-ooo* sounds. Tales told by ignorant peasants."

"Yeah," he said, "I guess that's what I was thinking."

Madame Zahra closed her eyes. "One cannot see them, but one can feel their presence. Sometimes they are confused and frightened, like lost children. Other times, like this evening, they want to be heard and they will speak through me."

Campbell removed his cigar. "Who was speaking through you this evening?"

She opened her eyes. "Rose Kaufman."

Bickerstaff knocked on the doorframe. "Sir, the wagon's arrived."

"Laforet too?"

"It looks that way."

"I'll be right back," said Campbell, "don't move," and he stepped out of the kitchen. "Bickerstaff, stay here and keep watch on these three; make sure they remain separated." Campbell galloped back down the stairs to meet Laforet.

A small crowd had gathered, unfazed by the still-blowing snow and frigid temperatures, fascinated at the sight of a dead body. The doctor, dressed in his Donegal tweed overcoat, cashmere muffler, and a lambswool wedge, was leaning over the victim.

"All right, everyone clear out," said Campbell. "Go back to your nice warm beds."

"Detective," said the doctor.

"Is this how you normally dress for a suicide? Did you stop at Wickham's on the way over?"

"I always try to look a little livelier than the corpse," said Laforet, giving Campbell the once-over. He stood up. "So is that what this is? A suicide?"

"I saw him hit the pavement."

"And he didn't have any help?"

"What makes you think he might have?"

"I don't know," said Laforet, looking down and pointing. "The twist to his body is rather curious. As if he turned, or tried to turn, mid-flight."

"Too late to change his mind."

"Did you see him go through the window?"

"No, I didn't."

"And yet you're certain he wasn't pushed?"

"No one up there could have pushed him, and so far there's no evidence of anyone else having been in the room at the time. I'm sorry; go on."

"Well, the twist in the body and the position of the arms suggests to me that he went out the window backwards, and then turned, perhaps instinctively bracing himself for the fall."

"Possibly. Or, like I said, maybe he changed his mind. It would have all happened in a matter of seconds." Campbell took one last good look up and down and around the scene and then said, "All right, let's go upstairs and I'll introduce you to the cast. Top floor. I can fill you in along the way."

Laforet turned his gaze up to the third-floor gable.

"You might even have time to read me the city directory."

In the apartment they found Bickerstaff straddling what had been Kaufman's chair, now positioned in the middle of the floor, and eyeing the Yarmoloviches, who were still seated at the table. Campbell called in the direction of the beaded curtain. "Madame Zahra, would you come out here please?"

She made her entrance.

"Madame Zahra, Mr. and Mrs. Yarmolovich, this is Dr. Laforet, our city's coroner and a colleague of mine."

The doctor removed his hat, walked over to Zahra, took her hand, which she had already extended, and gently grasped her fingers. He then nodded at the Yarmoloviches as he placed his hat on the table and unbuttoned his coat.

Campbell turned to the constable. "Bickerstaff — go down and make sure they don't need help with the body and then station yourself inside the vestibule. Give me a shout if there's a problem."

Bickerstaff touched his hat and made his way back down through the opening in the floor.

Campbell faced the trio but was speaking to Laforet. "Where we left off is with a domestic argument between the late Kaufman and his even later wife, Rose. But," he said, glancing at the doctor, "there is evidence that Kaufman may have been pushed."

Madame Zahra remained stoic but the Yarmoloviches vehemently shook their heads. Campbell continued. "Was there anyone else — physically, that is — in this room this evening?" More head shakes. "Madame Zahra, who else lives in this building?"

"Second floor is vacant; main floor is landlord."

"His name?"

"Old Gravy."

"Come again?"

"That's what it sounds like. Old Gravy."

"O'Grady?" Campbell had no idea where he pulled that one from.

Zahra's eyes widened and she aimed a finger at Campbell. "Yes, O'Grady. That is his name."

"He must be a heavy sleeper."

"He is away. Visiting to Chicago, I think it was."

"All right," said Campbell. He sighed and pocketed his pad and pencil. "Speaking of sleep, I think we all could use some." They all seemed to be losing focus, even the medium.

Laforet donned his wedge and began fastening the long row of buttons on his overcoat.

"Madame Zahra," said Campbell, "I'll be back tomorrow

morning. Mr. and Mrs. Yarmolovich, I'll have Constable Bickerstaff escort you home. You can expect to hear from me tomorrow as well. Good night."

It was an abrupt ending to an abrupt start. Campbell and Laforet left Zahra's first. Once back on the street, Campbell took a moment to re-examine the scene of Kaufman's death. Snow was accumulating and the blood that had pooled was now covered in white.

"Any further thoughts?" Campbell asked the doctor.

Laforet was wrapping his muffler around his neck. "I agree that none of them could have propelled him, willingly or not, out of that window. It has to have been a suicide."

"I need to know more about this man," said Campbell, looking up at the window. "Do sane people normally do things like this?"

"In my experience, it's always been sane people who do things like this."

"And what about this stuff about the spirit world?"

"My spirits come from bottles, Campbell, not Ouija boards. Are you all right?"

"I'm all right. I just need to finish my walk."

TWO

MONDAY, FEBRUARY 5

Chapter 7

PERSONA NON GRATA

Morning

'PURITY' MAN IS ARRESTED

Church Worker Charged With Rum-Running

Constable John Smith, of River Rouge, church worker and a leading spirit in the movement to make River Rouge 'pure,' was arrested last night in his alleged house of ill-fame and booze joint, at 274 Kleinlow Street, by a squad of police raiders. Two girl inmates and six men habitués were said to have been engaged in a scene of gay revelry when raiders descended upon the place.

Two cases of Canadian beer and a quantity of whisky were seized, it was reported.

Smith was brought to the River Rouge police station and released on bond. He will come up this morning for hearing on the charge of violating the disorderly ordinance. The case will be heard before Justice Samuel Barron of River Rouge. Both offenses of keeping a bawdy house and selling liquor come under the disorderly ordinance, hence a double charge was not preferred against the peace officer, police explained.

While the new police headquarters could accommodate a drill hall, a fully equipped gym, a police museum, and an identification branch, it could only afford Detective Henry Fields a broom closet of a room with a single window, one with bars on it no less, overlooking the parking lot in the rear. Apparently the room had been meant for some other purpose, but no one could remember what. Now it was all his.

He was pinning an article he had just clipped from this morning's *Border Cities Star* to a corkboard that he had to stand sideways on the floor because it was too big to fit on the wall. When the office manager had shown him the room, Fields looked around and asked the fellow if it had been built around the desk or if the desk was assembled in the room. He was only half-joking.

"The top comes off and the legs are detachable. My advice is, don't lean on it too hard."

The corkboard was covered with newspaper clippings. This newest addition was of particular interest to Fields because he had learned from one of the girls at the switchboard — one of his best sources — about how yesterday morning a gang of bootleggers tried to send a jalopy, likely filled with booze, across the frozen river near LaSalle. Their mission was unsuccessful. A farmer who had spotted the group while he was out doing a bit of hunting reported the incident. Fields's gut told him there was a connection between these suspected rumrunners and the event in River Rouge.

All of the articles on the board had to do with law enforcement on both sides of the river coming down on bootleggers, moonshiners, and other such cross-border violators of the Prohibition Act. It was his way of keeping tabs, of seeing the whole picture. It was also inspiring. To him, these law enforcement people were the real crusaders, the real heroes fighting the war. Not people like him. It was no secret that his promotion last summer to detective was politically motivated. But where did it leave him? Having to rely on a junior police officer and switchboard operator for his information gathering. He had recently walked in on a conversation in the kitchen area where he thought he heard the words "lame duck detective" come from one of the constables sitting around a table, but put it off to his bad ear and poured himself another coffee. They started talking again as soon as he walked out of the room, though he couldn't make anything out.

Fields stepped back to consider this mosaic of crime and felt a hand on his shoulder. He turned abruptly.

"Sorry, sir. I didn't mean to startle you." It was Corbishdale. "I knocked ... but you must have been deep in thought."

"Yes ... just thinking about these arrests in Rouge. You wanted to see me about something?"

"You asked me to keep you posted in the event we were able to glean anything else out in LaSalle." Corbishdale took a small pad of paper out of the hip pocket of his uniform jacket.

"Right." Fields returned to the chair behind his desk.

"The farmer confirmed seeing two vehicles and six men. He didn't recognize any of them, but he was also too far away to get a good look at any of their faces. He said three of them were dressed like they could have been locals — from the county — as opposed to the others who were in suits and overcoats. But he figured they were rumrunners, all of them, and held back because he didn't want any trouble. The vehicles appeared to be a newer-model Studebaker and an old Model T."

"And the T was the transporter. Was there any sign of it?"

"No, sir. It was definitely lost, along with its contents."

"They'll be looking for it after the first thaw. Anything else?"

"We're still trying to figure something out."

"Like what?"

"The farmer said that when he saw the car stall on the ice, one of the rumrunners ran out to try and either retrieve it or get it going again. When it broke through the ice, the rumrunner went down with it," Corbishdale was eyeballing his pad, "and the others managed to save him … and …"

The young officer was still trying to imagine all of this.

"Yes, and?"

"Well, the farmer said that the man they saved surfaced from the water holding on to what looked like a body."

Fields pivoted his good ear toward Corbishdale, who had a habit of letting his voice fade.

"Come again?" said the detective.

"He said the man surfaced with what looked to be a body, and that as the others dragged the man ashore, he dragged the body. That was when the farmer ran back home, got in his car, drove to the general store in LaSalle, and made the phone call. By the time he got back to Turkey Creek — where the rumrunners had been launching from — everyone was gone. Staff at the general store corroborated the farmer's statement and confirmed the time. Also, his wife verified the time he left and the time he finally arrived back at their house."

"And this body, where is it? Surely they wouldn't have taken it back to the city with them," said Fields.

"We don't know; that's what everyone is trying to figure out. The ground is too hard for them to be able to have buried it."

"Could they have hidden it somewhere nearby?"

"The provincial officer I spoke to said that other than the tracks they left in the snow to and from their vehicles and the nearby cabin, no other tracks lead out of the perimeter."

"Cabin?"

"Oh — that's something else. It appears the rumrunners were making use of a small fishing cabin near the shore, closer to the creek. The officer found a stove inside, still warm, containing pieces of a man's overcoat and suit, some burned, some just wet, as if it they had been thawing it out after pulling the body from the river. Strange."

"Destroying evidence, perhaps. But evidence of what?" Fields glanced over at his corkboard. "This is bizarre, Corbishdale. Why did they feel the need to drag the body out of the river? They couldn't have even known it was down there."

"You're right, it doesn't make any sense, sir."

"Maybe they did take it with them," speculated Fields, "and they disposed of it somewhere between LaSalle and Windsor."

Fields looked at his watch and then flipped back through a notepad on his desk until he got to blank pages.

"Are you thinking of going out there, sir?"

"Maybe. I have a lot on the go right now. Continue to keep me posted."

"Yes, sir."

Fields waited until Corbishdale was down the hall before he

got up to close his door. Back at his desk, he reached in a bottom drawer for the bottle of pills meant to keeping his head from feeling like it was going to split open. He shook two into the palm of his hand and washed them down with what was left of his coffee, now cold. Sometimes the pills worked, sometimes they didn't. He then pressed the palm of his hand gently against his left ear. The ringing went louder, like he was holding the ringing inside his head, letting it reverberate. He pulled his hand away. There was no doubt about it; it was getting worse.

It's been months now. Maybe there's more to it.

He got up from his desk and opened the door again. The hum of the police station dulled the ringing, or at least distracted him a little from it. Maybe he would drive out to the county and have a look around. There was nothing else for him to do here.

Chapter 8

COPELAND'S BOOK STORE

Very Maude was seated, or rather wedged between passengers, on a bench on a streetcar slowly rolling toward the downtown. *A big difference from last night's train ride*, she thought. Time was patient now, like the big flakes casually falling right now on London Street. It was a refreshing pace. The last several months had been a whirlwind for her. She hadn't come home for Christmas like she said she would; she had become caught up in her new life in New York. It had started with looking for steady work and a place to stay, and then, once settled, she tried to focus at least some of her energies on finding her writing voice. But then she found herself in a relationship, which she always seemed to be trying to salvage before it ever seemed to really get started. Strangely, she felt free again. She wondered how long that feeling would last. Probably only as long as that feeling you get when you're really escaping something. It fades shortly after you arrive.

There was a low drone of conversation throughout the streetcar. She felt out of touch. What were they talking about? The horrible weather? The price of butter? Most of the women seemed to be going to do their shopping, carrying empty bags and baskets. The men, presumably all off to work, whether to a factory or a desk, carried the smell of stale tobacco smoke. And the smell of wood fires seemed to hang from everyone's clothes. It was the common denominator. Feeling snug inside her coat, Vera Maude lowered her chin inside her muffler and closed her eyes.

Her uncle had contacted her after New Year's to tell her that her father had been ill for some time and, yes, he was sorry he had been keeping that a secret from her but he had been sworn to secrecy. He was writing her to tell her that her father had taken a sudden turn for the worse. Apparently not seeing his dear Maudie at Christmas had affected him badly. Her father had asked his other children to keep their mouths shut about it too, but he needn't have worried. None of them had kept in touch with Vera Maude after she left Windsor.

She felt terrible. She knew that her father was always torn between having her close to him and wanting her to be free to live out her dreams. As soon as she was able to scrape together the money to pay the balance on her share of the rent in the Village apartment she was sharing with two other girls, she bought a train ticket home. Her employer told her quite plainly that he couldn't guarantee her position would be waiting for her when she got back.

But this didn't quite feel like home anymore. Had the city changed, or had she? They'd never really gotten along, her and Windsor, and were barely on speaking terms when she left. Was New York really her home, her real future? The position at the bookstore might not be there when she got back, but the Village and the rest of New York certainly would be.

Time will tell. But then it might be too late.

"Too late for what?"

She was mumbling in her half-sleep. Still tired, now drowsy from the warmth of the streetcar, she tried to rouse herself. The doors flipped open and the blast of cold air was refreshing. Church Street. Several passengers waddled off, some off to pay their spiritual bills at St. Andrews's, some to place want ads at the *Star*, and some just to beat the crush at the Avenue.

Vera Maude had written Copeland's bookstore a couple weeks ago, explaining her situation and her desire for a position. She'd outlined her experience at a Greenwich Village bookshop but neglected to mention her tenure at the Carnegie Library here in Windsor, an experience she was certain the chief librarian was just as anxious to forget as Vera Maude was.

Pelissier Street. The Capitol Theatre. What was playing? The Griffith picture, *One Exciting Night*. She thought she had read something about it. She had great memories of watching shorts and newsreels, or catching the occasional vaudeville there. She had been a regular at most of the cinemas in town and kept a weekly schedule from the *Star* in her purse at all times.

The Avenue. Everyone spilled out onto the street as quickly as people bundled in layers of wool could over ice and snow.

Vera Maude walked behind the streetcar and crossed London. It was freezing cold, but she was enjoying the fresh air. Too often for her, that close, warm air, combined with the motion of the streetcar, was a recipe for nausea. And vomiting at a job interview always left a bad impression, or so she had heard. The sidewalk around the Imperial Bank was cleared, and one of the Andros brothers was out in his shirtsleeves trying to clear the space in front of their confectionery. Icing on the sidewalk. Downtown hadn't changed all that much. There was still plenty of hustle and bustle. She continued north toward Chatham Street and the Victoria Building.

She was early for her interview, so she thought she should take time to acquaint herself with Copeland's selection. She surveyed the front window first. There was a display of what appeared to be recently published books and what she assumed were bestsellers, a few of which she was familiar with.

People read differently on different sides of the border.

Chesterton's *The Man Who Knew Too Much*; Galsworthy's *Forsyte Saga,* collected; Aldous Huxley's *Mortal Coils*; Walpole's *The Cathedral*; Wells's *A Short History of the World*; Rebecca West's *The Judge*; Woolf's *Jacob's Room*; Yeats's *The Trembling of the Veil,* as well as *The Player Queen*; and old favourites to get one through the long, dark winter — mostly Dickens. Sprinkled among the books were paper hearts and St. Valentine's Day cards.

A curious display.

Vera Maude stomped the snow and slush off her boots and stepped inside. Almost everyone in the store turned around to look at her. She smiled, unbuttoned her coat, and then wiped the fog from her cheaters with her muffler. She removed her tam and stuffed it in her bag. The shop was just how she remembered it: tables near the door held stacks of recently published or newly-acquired second-hand books; rows of chest-high bookcases in the centre containing popular fiction titles; a perimeter of books in non-fiction categories that went almost from floor to ceiling; and tables at the back set up for special orders, appraisals, gift-wrapping, and mail order. Speaking of Dickens, the shop still had all the energy and chaos of a Phiz illustration. She took the opportunity to duck behind one of the freestanding bookcases to give her hair a quick tease. She was never a hat person.

Coming back around, she spied Mr. Copeland, bespectacled and stroking his short, pointed white beard, perusing the contents of a large box of books belonging to a man who appeared convinced he had just raided King Tut's tomb.

"I'll give you three dollars for the lot," Vera Maude overheard Copeland say. "And that's being generous."

"But —"

"I'm sorry, but that's all they're worth. And as you can see, I'm overstocked at the moment."

The man took it. He looked like he might be in a bad way. *What could he have thought they were worth?* wondered Vera Maude.

"May I help you, miss?"

"Oh — yes, my name's Maguire, Vera Maude Maguire … I sent you a letter about a position … you wrote me back." She presented the letter.

Copeland took the letter, examined it, his hand resting on his chest, nodded. "Ah, yes. Please step this way, Miss Maguire."

He led her between the tables to his desk in one of the inner recesses of the store, a desk covered with yet more books and even more paper. He condensed a few of the piles and cleared a space.

"If I remember correctly, your letter said you had some experience."

"Yes, I worked several months at Mr. Shay's shop in Greenwich Village."

"I'm not familiar with this Mr. Shay."

"Oh, he is a very popular bookseller. He —"

"What are you reading right now, Miss Maguire?"

"Right now?"

She couldn't possibly tell him she was reading *Black Mask*

magazine. It was the December issue, the one containing, "The Road Home," the story by Peter Collinson. What was the right answer? Her eyes fell on a title shelved behind Copeland.

"*On a Chinese Screen.*"

Copeland's face lit up. "Ah," he said, "the Maugham stories. How are you enjoying them?"

"I think they're delightful."

The old man started stroking his beard again, appraising Vera Maude. He resumed with the tough questions.

"Ours is a little shop. You've been to the big city, as they say. Why wouldn't you rather seek a position in Detroit? I mean, you might find things here a little dull, after all."

Vera Maude was feeling that Copeland had already made his decision before she set foot through the door. She went for broke, feeling badly about dragging her family into this.

"Truth is, Mr. Copeland, my father passed away recently, and I've come home to be close to my siblings and my uncle, assist them with certain matters, you know."

"Oh, I see." Copeland cleared his throat and shuffled some of his stray papers. He looked at his shoes and scratched his ear. "And what were you looking for in terms of hours? I'm afraid I don't have all that much to offer right now."

"I'll take anything you have available, Mr. Copeland."

"You say it would only be temporary. Do you know how long you plan on remaining in Windsor?"

A fair enough question. "I'm really not sure. At least until the summer."

Copeland was thinking he really couldn't afford Vera Maude and she seemed like she might be overqualified. And then there was her garb and mannerisms. He had concerns about that as well, and everything that went along with it: a certain attitude, and the politics.

Vera Maude pressed on. "I'm not looking for entertainment, Mr. Copeland. I'm looking for work, as a bookseller, and —"

"You'll be selling cards and stationery too," he said.

"I'm perfectly all right with that," she said without hesitation.

She was determined to wear Copeland down. He was actually coming around to the idea of her experience in New York being an asset.

"I can start you this afternoon. Gladys is down with a terrible cold. It's this weather, you know. Winter can have its busy periods. People stuck indoors without much to do." He was thinking out loud now.

Vera Maude nodded. There was a brief pause. Both held their breath.

"All right, I'll give you Saturdays and three days a week," he said.

"That's great." She grabbed the old man's hand this time and almost pulled his arm out of its socket. "Thanks, Mr. Copeland."

Once Copeland got his hand back he made some brief comments about the position. Soon Vera Maude was bundling herself back up again and making her way through the labyrinth of tables — meant to encourage browsing — and heading toward the door. Along the way she noticed the "Book Reviews" page from the *Border Cities Star* pinned to a board on one of the store's pillars. She had some homework to do.

She walked back up to London Street and crossed the Avenue to the other corner, where she caught the westbound streetcar and rode it all the way to McEwan. It wasn't nearly as crowded this time. It was almost an enjoyable ride. She was certainly in better spirits.

When she arrived back at her uncle's place, she found him sawing away, the newspaper tented over his face. She gently closed the door.

"What's the news, Uncle Fred?"

He sat up and the newspaper slid onto the floor. "Well, hello there. I didn't expect you back so soon. So, how did it go?"

Vera Maude smiled her crooked, dimpled smile. "I got myself a position at Copeland's — part-time."

"Good for you, girl!"

"It took some fast talking."

"You're the fastest talker I know. When do you start?"

"This afternoon, after lunch, just for a bit of training before my real shifts start. Is that all right with you?"

"'Course it is," he said with a nod.

"You'll be okay?"

"Mrs. Cattanach will be in shortly to take care of the laundry and make my supper. She's a good woman, you know."

"That's the third time you've said that. I'm betting she's not hard on the eyes either."

Her uncle winked at her. Vera Maude went into the kitchen to fix her and her uncle some tea. When she returned with the clinking tray, Fred started reading aloud a piece from the *Star*.

"'*Tomb Yields $15,000,000 in Stones, Gold — Treasure of Pharaoh Tutankhamun Proves Real Marvel*.' Ain't that something?"

"I guess so. I don't know; sometimes I think maybe they shouldn't be poking around the burial sites like that."

"Why not? It's history. And these are beautiful objects."

"It's not just going to end up in some guy's house?"

"I don't believe so. Well, I certainly hope not. Sounds like an adventure, though, doesn't it?"

"That it does," said Vera Maude. "Any other news?"

"Oh — that runaway train of yours made the front page," he said, pointing at the headline.

"I told you I wasn't kidding," said Vera Maude. "Did they say what it was all about? Was it a malfunction?"

"Bootleggers."

"You're kidding," said Vera Maude, looking over her uncle's shoulder now.

"You said the train made a stop?"

"Yeah."

"Was it" — Fred was reading aloud again — "'somewhere this side of Maidstone'?" He looked up from his paper. "And you say you didn't see anything?"

"No. But it felt like we did hit something, and I thought I saw some debris fly past my window, as if we struck an automobile or something. Like I told you, the snow was blowing all around us pretty hard. Does it say anything else?"

"No other details as of yet. Some kind of investigation is apparently underway. But no one's saying anything right now. If you did hit a vehicle stuck on the tracks, it probably was just some kind of malfunction."

Fred folded the paper and set it on the coffee table, and Vera Maude picked it up. Her eyes immediately fell on an article about a mysterious death on Maiden Lane.

"And what about this?"

"Now that's crazy. Some foreigner threw himself out a third-storey window."

"Crazy? That's terrible." Vera Maude had forgotten what a colourful place the Border Cities could be. Her mind went back to the bootlegger she had met the day she left town. McCloskey was his name, Jack McCloskey. She wondered what he was up to right now.

Chapter 9

IN THE COLD LIGHT
OF DAY

After a good night's sleep, coffee, and a Danish at White City Lunch, Campbell was ready to return to Maiden Lane, but this time without Laforet, any constabulary, or either of the Yarmoloviches. He telephoned Madame Zahra from the diner to let her know that he was on his way, to make sure she that was up and around. He had got the impression that she did most of her business in the off-hours.

Campbell folded one lapel under the other, pulled his collar up around his neck, and stepped out onto Pitt Street. With few exceptions, he always preferred walking to taking his car. To him, the automobile was beginning to seem like some elaborate scheme, something he was being forced to grow to love, told he could not do without. He would have to keep his opinions to himself, though, in case Messrs. Ford or Dodge happened to overhear him.

Wanting to absorb any bit of sun that might actually manage to poke through the clouds, he crossed the Avenue and started up the west side. Campbell put his galoshes to work. They were one size too big. Smith's had been out of his size and he couldn't be bothered to shop around, so in really deep snow he had to clench his toes to avoid stepping out of them. He had done that once, in a particularly slushy period in early winter, and he wouldn't make the same mistake twice. He really detested winter. As far as he was concerned, anyone who professed to loving winter was either out of their mind or was an athlete of some sort, pretending to be training for Chamonix.

Campbell noticed how the latest blast of snow was clinging to the rough-hewn masonry on the north side of the post office like icing. The east side was spared. Approaching Chatham Street, he had to navigate around the piles of snow spilling down and passing through the bars of the cast-iron fence that edged the little park behind the customs house. He stepped around the miniature avalanches and examined the scene. It appeared the park was being used as a local snow dump.

I guess they have to put it somewhere.

The cannon that was the centrepiece of the park, a relic of the Crimean War, was almost buried.

Or is it sinking?

Snow creates that illusion sometimes. Campbell looked down and noticed small footprints running up one of the larger slopes and how they went all the way over the fence and led straight to

the cannon. Here was an opportunity to sit astride it. No doubt
there was a snowball fight, an imaginary re-enactment of some
glorious battle. Campbell remembered a friend, they couldn't
have been more than twelve at the time, who had developed a
technique for making the perfect snowballs. When the perfect
snow fell, he would make several and line them up along a cleared
section of his porch rail. He would then go in the house and
come back with a pot of cold water and a slotted serving spoon
from the kitchen. This friend — Campbell watched him do this
— would dip each snowball into the water, raise it, and then dip
it again, raise it, and then dip it again, and finally set it back onto
the porch rail. He would repeat this exercise for the rest of his
munitions. In freezing-cold temperatures, the water would glaze
the snowball, making it a near-deadly weapon. He once, with a
throw worthy of Herman Pillette, knocked the hat, glasses, and
nearly an eye from the head of boy who just happened to be in
range. Campbell had turned to his friend in horror and saw him
smiling with glee.

War is hell.

Campbell's feet were getting cold from standing around,
so he got moving again and hustled across Chatham Street. The
snow that was patted down alongside the Victoria Building was
brittle and crunched under his feet, making it sound as if he were
walking over a carpet of saltines. He was tempted to stop at the
windows at Copeland's bookstore but kept up his pace as safely
as he could in an effort to warm his feet. It was working. He was
still waiting for that little bit of sun to come poking through
the heavy cloud cover. He knew it was getting higher in the sky,
though one could hardly tell.

He slowed up now, the cold air feeling sharp in his lungs.
Walking past Woolworth's, Campbell could hear metal scraping
on cement. He smiled. Someone had finally struck pavement.

Indeed, there was an unfortunate soul out with a coal shovel tending to the sidewalk that wrapped around the Imperial Bank.

Avoiding any potential liabilities.

Crossing London Street, Campbell was reminded of his walk last night. *No,* he thought, *not what I had been expecting, not at all.* He almost laughed at himself.

None of that comes expected.

When he had finally arrived back at his apartment last night, he kicked off his galoshes and staggered to the bathroom, where he peeled off his outerwear — he could have stood up his overcoat on the floor since it was by then frozen solid — and hung everything from the shower curtain rod to thaw and dry (it never dried). He then sat in the chair that faced the window, which faced the river, put his feet up on the radiator and lit a cigar, thereby warming both ends of his body and hoping the warmth might travel like a fuse to his core. As a Windsor police detective, he had already seen a lot, but he was recalling now how sitting there last night he had one of those *Did that really just happen?* moments.

Maybe my mind was numb too.

Campbell kept walking. No, there was no place else to put the snow. It was already piled in the gutters, the margins of the Avenue, the street corners, and anywhere else that did not translate into some major inconvenience. Minor inconveniences were allowed. He heard a motor struggling up ahead, near the Labelle Building. And not just a motor struggling, but wheels spinning as well. A horrible sound. He approached and found what appeared to be a Gray-Dort that the driver had attempted to park in the snow pushed onto the street. Unusual for this model, thought Campbell. He held up his hands as he walked around to the driver's side. The driver saw him and shouted over the engine, "I'm stuck."

No kidding.

He had no patience for people like this, people with vehicles who once they stepped inside felt they were invincible and impervious to any kind of disaster.

"Stop accelerating," shouted Campbell.

There was a margin of moraine on either side of the car; Campbell could see where the driver had backed in, but evidently he had no exit strategy.

What was he thinking?

It occurred to Campbell that he spent a great deal of time wondering what it was people could have been thinking, as in, *What were you thinking when you jumped out that window?* He would return to that later.

"All right, slow gear. I'll push from behind. Let's try a rocking motion and see if that gets you over. Do not, I say do not throw it into reverse. Understand?"

The driver, thankful for any assistance, nodded. "Yes."

Campbell stepped back to the rear of the vehicle and positioned himself behind the right fender. The driver began with the slow acceleration and Campbell, with his heels dug into the mound of snow, sand, dirt, and sludge behind him, pushed and paused, pushed and paused, until he had a pulse. Weak at first, and then he could feel the wheels were taking over. He gave it one long, hard push and the car took to the gritty moraine and sped off. Not a wave from the driver.

You're welcome.

After Park Street, it was all private dwellings, some with businesses incorporated into them — mainly professionals: optometrists, chiropractors, lawyers. The professionals tended to clear their walks, not so much the residents. The last two addresses before Maiden Lane were a real estate agent and a dentist. Campbell paused at the corner before turning onto the little lane. He wanted to contemplate the scene in the daylight. It was his first impulse, to look up at the attic window. It had already been boarded up from the inside. After trying to re-imagine the trajectory, the physics behind it, which still seemed impossible, he started walking slowly toward the building and halted once he was facing it.

He pulled out his notebook. *1 Maiden Ln. Only house on block. Occup: Mort Boyd, Prud Ins agnt; Marg Bethune, slsldy; Jn Lawley, clrk; Cath McGregor, bkpr; Mme Zahra Ostrovskaya.* None of this spoke to him.

Stranger in a strange land, thought Campbell.

Before entering, he thought he would go to the corner at the end of the block, to where he almost saw Kaufman fly out the window. He made fresh prints in the snowdrifts along the north side. The block was interrupted about halfway by an alley that looked as if it hadn't been trodden upon in a day or two.

Standing at the very spot where he saw Kaufman hit the pavement, he partially recreated the moment by lighting up. He looked up at the window again, then down the block toward the Avenue and further down, where Maiden Lane continued after a bit of a jog, and he saw wagons that were coming out of Cadwell's stables. Old and new worlds.

Which is Madame Zahra's world? Campbell wondered.

The smoke from his cigar did a tight spiral straight up into the chill air. He retraced his steps diagonally across Maiden Lane to where Kaufman's body hit the pavement. Campbell kneeled down and brushed the fresh snow off the cobblestone. There was still some glass and fragments of windowpane. He turned and looked once more up at the top floor. He had a thought, but it made little sense so he filed it away for now. He dabbed the end of his cigar gently in some fresh snow then tucked it into his hip pocket. He made his way up the steps and into the vestibule.

He checked the door to the right and found it still locked.

Before going up the stairs he walked down the hallway to the back door this time. He turned the deadbolt. When he opened the door, a drift of snow six inches higher than the bottom of the doorframe retained its shape. It had settled in. He looked down. The only indication that there were actually steps leading down into what he presumed was some sort of garden was the little wooden handrail that poked up through the snowdrift and then angled toward the house. The snow in the garden had none of those dimples that one sees when a fresh layer of snow covers older footprints, and the snow around the gate looked undisturbed. He closed the door, made his way back down the hall, and up the stairs. He knocked at the door at the second-floor landing. Still no answer. He removed his boots and proceeded up into the attic apartment. Madame Zahra was standing in the middle of the room, looking every bit the gypsy queen. She must have heard him coming.

"Welcome, Detective Campbell."

It was warm, a warmth that came maybe from the inside out. Was that possible? It was like being in chapel — physically speaking. He said nothing but instead did a lap around the room. It looked the same but different, the way rooms do in natural light, the little that there was, mainly coming from the small window in the kitchen filtering through the beaded curtain. Amber-coloured bloodshot beads. There was another small window in the gable in the middle of the long wall. A few fat candles provided the rest of the light in the room.

"Who's your carpenter?" said Campbell, facing the repair job.

"Yarmolovich has friends who build houses," said Zahra. "He says they can make window in two days. Sit."

Just to the right of the gable, in the same long wall, were two chairs, between which was a contraption that was a combination reading lamp and ashtray, with bizarre-looking serpents and other creatures climbing up the wooden pedestal.

"Do you mind if I smoke?" asked Campbell.

"If it pleases you."

Campbell pulled his cigar back out of his hip pocket and re-introduced it to his Ronson. While he was busy with that, Zahra brought over a small table with a round marble top, just large enough to hold a tea service. She then returned to the samovar in the kitchen and came back with two steaming cups.

"A special blend," she said.

Campbell blew a smoke ring at the pointed ceiling and noticed an egg-shaped crystal hanging from the apex. Another prop? He rested his cigar on the beastly ashtray.

"Thanks," he said. "I hope you don't mind my stopping by, but I woke up with more questions than I left with last night."

"Of course."

Campbell lifted his cup from its saucer. "Do I drink this black?"

"I do. But I know you English like your cream and sugar. Sorry — I only have milk. It comes from horse."

Campbell blinked. "What?"

"A horse pulls a man with milk. Is that wrong?"

"Not exactly. No matter, I usually take my coffee black, so I'll give it a try. And by the way, my father was Scottish."

"There is difference?"

Campbell let that one go but used it as his lead in. "May I ask where you are from, Madame Zahra Ostro …?"

"Ostrovskaya. I'm from small village outside of Minsk."

"So, Russia. When did you leave?"

"After the war there was another war, and then another. And then those of us who were lucky, we got out. That was few years ago. We scattered when we landed, going deeper into America and Canada. I stopped here."

"Don't take this the wrong way, Madame, but the costume,

the séances, the …" Campbell was waving his hand around the room, "… stuff. Was this you back in Minsk, or is this new?"

She smiled. "I know what you are asking, Detective Campbell. I am not trickster, and I am not gypsy like you see at the circus or at the movie show. I believe in what I do, it is real as anything in this world, or your world of facts and science and evidences."

"So last night Kaufman really was speaking with his wife?"

"Yes, I called upon her, opened door for her; no, I became door for her to re-enter this world. She was here; I felt her presence."

Campbell thought he would roll with that for now and see where it took him. "What could they have been discussing that would make Kaufman want to throw himself out the window?"

"I do not know. Like I told you, while they were communicating —"

"I know, you were in a trance. Would you care to speculate, guess what it was they might have been talking about?"

"No."

"Why not?"

She smiled. "That isn't facts."

"Right." Campbell continued. "Mr. Kaufman had no family here and he lived alone, over in Ford City. I checked. His identification says that he was also born in Russia. His papers said Minsk. Did you know him in Minsk? Was he one of the party that escaped the city the same time you did?"

She hesitated. "Yes."

"Do I need to ask the Yarmoloviches if they were also from that part of Russia?"

"No, you do not have to ask. We all escaped Minsk together. We knew each other there."

"And Rose Kaufman?"

"She did not survive."

Campbell looked up from his notepad. "It must have been terrible for you."

"Is this what you wanted to ask me about, detective? How we had to leave our homeland while foreigners fought over it?"

"It helps me to understand."

"Kaufman and his wife were separated, in the street, while there was fighting. She and few others we travelled with were trapped in a building. We waited for them in a farmhouse outside of city, near where my people camped. I was working at a café, but I went back sometimes. We waited until we could wait no longer. A boy caught up with us as we were going to Lithuanian border. He told us what had happened. He was the only one from that building who survived. He watched Rose Kaufman die. Kaufman's heart was broken. Ever since then he has wanted to speak to her, to say his farewell."

"Thank you for your time, and for the tea, Madame Zahra."

"I hope it was of help."

"If I have any other questions, I'll contact you."

Campbell descended through the floor and pulled on his galoshes on the landing below. He knew one thing: he needed to brush up on his knowledge of the occult. He also needed to talk to the Yarmoloviches. And find an atlas.

Chapter 10

BE CAREFUL WHO YOU TALK TO

Shorty decided they should take a new approach and broaden their search. But in order to do that, they might have to tip their hand, talk to some people. It was a difficult decision and not all of the gang members were in agreement. Where they were in agreement was that they had to be careful. Say the wrong thing to the wrong person and it could be followed by any variety of trouble. They might get beaten to the prize, get brought down by the law — or even worse, this mythical Guard might find them out. The Guard were still the unknown variable, and the more talk there was about them, the tenser the situation became.

According to the new plan, their first stop was going to be the pool hall formerly owned by the late Lieutenant Green, McCloskey's old boss. The boys had an in: one of the partners in the revamped establishment happened to be Lapointe's brother-in-law, Sephore "Seph" Reaume. The Reaume family had lived on the south shore of the Detroit River for almost two centuries. Their history was the Border Cities' history. Farmers when they settled, they'd been contractors for the last couple of generations, helping turn some of those tired fields into factories and warehouses. Seph was the entrepreneur — local parlance for "bootlegger." He also dabbled in a bit of smuggling, mostly out-going.

Lapointe met Seph at the café in the Herendeen Hotel on the corner of Pitt and Goyeau, just a few doors from the pool hall. Seph was sitting in a stool at the counter, but when Lapointe arrived he suggested they take a booth, away from the rest of the patrons.

"How's this?" asked Seph, pointing to an unoccupied piece of real estate.

"No, not in the window."

"All right."

They found a booth in a dark corner. As soon as the waitress touched down, Seph ordered them both the fryer's latest triumph, a pork chop–stuffed French toast sandwich. He might only be working at a café, but the man had aspirations. He had discovered the dish on a recent trip to Chicago and thought it would suit the tastes of Border Citizens. It was becoming a minor rage. While they waited, Lapointe started trying to explain to Seph what it was he and his gang were up to, but he danced around a bit too much and his brother-in-law was swiftly growing impatient. Lapointe was at least able to pick up on that and arbitrarily threw in a few details.

"Ah," said Seph, connecting the dots, "I know what you're talking about."

"You do?"

Their plates arrived and they resumed talking once the waitress was a safe distance away.

"Yeah, of course. That money and whatever else it was that belonged to that Richard Davies."

"Wha — how long have you known about it?"

"I don't know," shrugged Seph, "since last summer, I guess," and then he cut into his sandwich. He closed his eyes and took it in as if it was a fine French wine.

Lapointe was a little taken aback. "Why didn't you tell me?"

"We thought it got found, and whoever found it just kept quiet about it." Seph gestured toward the door with his coffee mug. "Your boys think it's still out there somewhere?"

"We think we never heard anything because it never got found." Lapointe shook his head and cut into his sandwich. "I still can't believe you didn't mention anything to me about it."

"It's been months," said Seph. "The trail's cold." He took another sip of his coffee. "Forget about it."

Lapointe looked over his shoulder and then leaned across the table until his chin was almost touching his brother-in-law's plate. "We found something." He was about to go off-script, and he knew it.

Seph paused, mid-chew. "What?"

"A key," whispered Lapointe. "We found it on this guy — Jigsaw."

Seph swallowed what was in his mouth and almost choked. "He's alive?"

"No, no — dead, really dead. It's a long story, but we pulled him out of the river."

Seph lowered his knife and fork. "You pulled him out of the river? Where?" He wiped his mouth with his napkin. "What the hell did you do that for?"

Lapointe put his finger to his lips and made a "shh" sound.

"Like I said, it's a long story. I'll save it for later."

Seph squinted at the chicken farmer. "You sure he's dead?"

Lapointe sat up. "Why do people keep saying that?" Now he had the sudden urge to drive back to where they dumped the body — or what was left of it — though he knew he could never find the place. It was somewhere near the intersection of Turkey Creek and Malden Road. "Of course he's dead … I mean, you should have seen him." Lapointe was shuddering at just the thought of Jigsaw's gruesome remains.

"All right," said Seph, "a key. For what?"

"That's the thing — no one knows. All we know is that his fortune might still be out there, and this key is probably tied to it."

Seph was trying to make the leap. "How do you figure?"

"It was hidden on Jigsaw — sewn right into his coat. It has to be something important, you know? So it has to be connected to Davies's lost fortune. It could unlock a vault, or a chest, or —"

"So who has it? McCloskey?"

"No, one of the boys. I had to swear not to tell. We're passing it between us."

"All right. So what is it you want from me?"

"Maybe it's for a lock somewhere in the pool hall."

"My pool hall?"

"We're going over every space, room, locale that Jigsaw had contact with."

Seph shook his head. "We renovated when we bought it last September. I saw it when it was stripped down to the studs. Trust me, there's nothing in that place that will take any key you've got."

"And the tables?" Lapointe surprised even himself with that one.

"They were stripped down, refitted, and refinished."

Lapointe sank in his seat and let his face get real long.

It was Seph's turn to ask the questions. "Where else have you looked?"

"Well," said Lapointe, slumped in his booth, playing with the crusts of his French toast, "Davies's suite at the Prince Edward and his house in Riverside."

"So people know you're poking around."

Lapointe perked up. "No, no, only you, Seph."

"Trust me, people know you're poking around. You're leaving tracks everywhere, and I'm not just talking about in the snow." Seph pushed his empty plate aside. "Did the other boys ever tell you about the Guard?"

Lapointe swallowed hard, and it didn't go unnoticed.

"So they did," said Seph. "You can bet they're already on to you and your boys."

"You mean they're real?"

"Would you want to wait until you were dead to find out if the Devil was real?" It was Seph's turn to lean across the table. "I knew a guy who saw them right after Davies got killed. This guy was in a roadhouse, Chappell I think it was, enjoying a cold beer when these four guys came in, all in black, dark as shadows in the middle of a bright summer day. The room fell quiet and they just moved about, silently, like they were looking for someone. They found him all right, sitting alone in a corner, trying real hard not to get noticed. One of the Guard picked him up and then they all surrounded him and dragged him out. My buddy tried to stop them. One of the Guard turned to my buddy. All he saw was a glimmer in this Guard's eye. It sent a chill through him and he froze. The Guard regrouped and hauled off their captive. But it was like they swallowed him up. My buddy and the other patrons gathered their courage and went to follow the Guard out the door, but they had to pause to let someone else come in. The man asked what was the matter and they told him, and do you know what he said?"

"No, what?"

"That there must be something funny in the beer, because he didn't pass anyone on his way in."

Lapointe was about to make the sign of the cross but then put his hand back down under the table.

"I'm not one to believe in ghosts and devils," continued Seph, "and I haven't been to church since I was an altar boy, but I'm telling you what I heard, and it was from someone who was there. The Guard swallowed him up and disappeared into thin air."

"That's not possible." Lapointe paused. "What did they want from him?"

"No one knows for sure. They figured he either got too close or took something that didn't belong to him, and they wanted it back."

Lapointe met up with the boys at the British-American and told them about his conversation with his brother-in-law. He conveniently left out the anecdote about the Guard.

"We're getting nowhere fast," said Mud.

"Now what?"

"Can't you see? We can't stop now," said Gorski. "We have to keep moving until we find it, whatever it is."

"We're committed now."

"I think we should let Jack get involved."

"Yeah, we need Jack."

Let Jack get involved. No one *let* Jack do anything. Shorty had always felt that something was pulling him and the other boys along. He didn't know what it was. He started feeling it as soon as they found the key on Jigsaw. If the key was a means to an end, maybe it was theirs.

It was a brief but intense conversation and they all needed
to cool off. They had finished and were standing now outside
the hotel, on the corner where the Avenue met Riverside Drive.
Shorty looked up and down, turned to the gang and said, "All
right, I'll talk to Jack again. The rest of you fan out. Davies
had his hands in a lot of pies; let's see if any of them were half-
baked. Thom and Three Fingers, take Ojibway and Sandwich.
Gorski and I will take Windsor and Walkerville. Mud — you
and Lapointe take Ford and Riverside. The key might come in
handy, depending on what you find and the circumstances, so
we'll share it." Handing it to Thom, Shorty said, "I want you and
Three Fingers to take it first. Again, be careful who you talk to, be
careful what you say."

Shorty pulled the end of the cigarette out of his mouth
and flicked it into the wind. It vanished in the blowing snow.
"If anyone finds anything, leave me a message at the desk. We'll
reconvene at the bar at nine tonight. Good luck."

Chapter 11

DREAMT OF IN YOUR PHILOSOPHY

Campbell got himself over to the library but was told, without the librarian even checking, that they did not have anything on the occult. *Not the kind of thing we carry*, she said, *not what the public is looking for.* Except for him. He was confused. What public was she referring to? The librarian sent Campbell to Copeland's. She — Daphne was her name — said that Mr. Copeland catered to *broader tastes* and could even handle special orders. She offered directions. He told Daphne that he was familiar with the establishment, though honestly he wasn't entirely, and thanked her. He stepped around a caretaker mopping up grey-brown puddles of grit and melted slush off the marble floor near the entrance. The man gave the detective a quick glance. Campbell knew that the caretaker had overheard his exchange with Daphne. Campbell paused as he bundled himself back up again.

"Is she always like that?" he said.

The caretaker made a few more swirls on the floor with his mop and, without looking up, said, "Yeah."

At the top of the stoop, Campbell checked the skies and then adjusted his hat and carefully negotiated the steps back down to the sidewalk that took him back to the Avenue.

It was nearing the end of lunch hour now and the streets were quieter. Or maybe people were eating at their desks. And the ladies didn't seem to be heading out to the shops as usual. This weather was obviously bad for business. *Maybe that's why they had to invent Valentine's Day*, thought Campbell. *More red to keep them out of the red.*

He kept his head down, which wasn't like him. He wondered what he might be missing.

Frostbite.

And then he wondered if he could tell by the character, by the marks on the exposed sidewalk, where exactly along the Avenue he was walking. He stopped, and found himself standing in front of Copeland's.

Very good.

He examined the window display and checked the titles, though they were difficult to read through the frost on the inside of the glass. Nothing he could make out seemed to suggest this was a place where he might find books on channelling spirits or on astral planes, but he'd give them a try. Two couples were exiting. He shouldered between them and passed through the door.

After peeling off his gloves yet again and while blowing into his cupped hands he surveyed the bookcases that were almost as high as the ceiling, the tables stacked with books, a cart overflowing with books to be shelved, and the stationery — boxes of paper, pens, ink bottles, notebooks and pads, writing paper and diaries. The place was an arsonist's dream. He wandered a bit, trying to take it all in. Though inhabited, it was dead silent. Compared to this, the library was a henhouse.

"May I help you?" whispered a small feminine voice behind him.

He turned. "Actually, I'm —" Campbell was tongue-tied for a moment "— looking for your occult section. Would you have such a thing?"

The bookseller put one hand on her hip, cupped her chin with the other, spun on her heel, and then returned back to Campbell. "Not exactly. But we do carry books that touch on the subject. They're scattered a bit, in philosophy, religion, science … was there a particular title or author you were looking for?"

He was studying her face, cataloguing every detail, as he always did when meeting someone for the first time. He hoped he wasn't being too obvious. Wide copper-green eyes behind the Harold Lloyd-type specs; just enough colour in her cheeks to predict a warm skin tone in the summer; and dimples when she was barely smiling. Her s's whistled just ever so slightly. And then there were the wild chestnut-brown curls piled on top of her head, held together with a contingent of hairpins. He had better hold off for now.

"Anything on theosophy?"

"Oh," she said and turned to one of the walls of books. "I thought I saw something earlier." She started moving toward a section and, holding his hat now, Campbell followed.

"You've heard of it?" he said. "Theosophy, I mean."

She glanced back to him while she wove around the tables. "Oh, sure. I worked in a bookstore in the Village — in New York — and people were always coming in and asking for —"

"You're American?" Campbell was anxious to solve this mystery girl. He didn't detect any kind of American accent.

"No," she said. "I'm from here. Anyway, like I was saying, people used to come in the store all the time looking for those kinds of books. People into holding séances or parties with a palm or a tarot card reader, Madame Blavatsky-type stuff, you know?"

She moved quickly, and Campbell couldn't help but notice her hips swinging around the table corners. He tried to stay focused. "Really? So you know a little bit about the subject?"

"Only what I picked up from the clientele," she said over her shoulder. And then she stopped moving and pointed to a few shelves in the categories that she mentioned. They were all adjacent to each other. "Have a look and let me know if you need any more help. I'll be around."

She wiggled away. He wondered if she had heard or read anything about the incident on Maiden Lane. Then again, why didn't he know anything about this latest occult craze? It was like a new foxtrot.

"I'll have a browse. What's your name in case I need to come looking for you?"

"Vera Maude."

"Thanks, Vera Maude."

She smiled and turned away to help a customer trying to flag her down, some woman waving a newspaper clipping. This Vera Maude girl took something besides herself with her when she walked away. Campbell couldn't quite put his finger on what it was. He regrouped and shifted his attention back to the task at hand: a crash course in the occult.

After a half hour or so he found a few books that he thought might be useful, some specific, others tangential to the subject. He had thumbed, skimmed, grazed through all of them. Once or twice while doing this he glanced over at Vera Maude. One time he had to move out of her way as she led a customer to the children's books section. Business seemed to be picking up. The winter could only keep people indoors for so long, even a winter like this one. Campbell settled on a couple of titles and brought them over to the register to have Vera Maude ring them through.

"A little light reading, I see."

"Not your taste?"

"Not really." She squinted through her cheaters and poked the keys on the National. One of the keys seemed to want to stick. "I like detective stories," she said.

Hm.

She handed Campbell his change.

"Thanks," he said.

"But I guess," she was saying as she bagged his purchase, "these can kind of read like detective stories, you know?"

"How do you figure?"

"People looking for answers."

Campbell folded the end of the bag over and tucked the bag under his arm. "You might have something there."

"Thanks," she said. The way she said it to all her customers. Campbell was already making his way toward the door, back out into the cold. He opened it and the little brass bell above the doorframe rang. "Come again."

Chapter 12

IT'S IN THE EXECUTION

Morrison came galumphing down the hall at police headquarters, and noticing Fields's desk light was still burning bright, he invited himself into this otherwise dark space.

Along with his low-wattage desk light, Fields was also using any ambient light from the hall in order to see what he was doing, making Morrison's presence about as inconspicuous as a solar eclipse. The big man was standing in his doorway. Fields' first thought was that his colleague was here to congratulate him on the raid that he and Corbishdale had executed this morning.

"Fields."

Fields gestured toward the chair in front of his desk. "Morrison — have a seat."

"No, thanks. I gotta be somewhere." Actually, Morrison looked like he just came from somewhere. For a man that size, he certainly enjoyed being on the move. "You probably heard about the cleaning up that the provincial police and a few of our boys had to do."

"Clean up? What do you mean?" He was drumming the end of his pencil on the report he was working on. It was hard to tell, but it looked like Morrison was wearing a slight grin. Maybe it was just the booze; a cloud of rye had just wafted toward Fields's desk. Or maybe it was something else.

"I'm talking about those coloureds on Tuscarora. Your bust this morning, yours and Corbishdale's."

In their morning raid, Fields and Corbishdale arrested a Mr. Don Henderson and Miss Oda Gray after discovering a partially consumed bottle of "white mule" on the premises. Corbishdale had got the tip from one of Henderson's neighbours who had a less than friendly attitude toward "those damned monkeys." When questioned, Gray said she and her boyfriend bought some of the liquor from Henderson first last night and then again this morning. Twenty-five cents a glass. Henderson was charged with unlawfully keeping liquor for sale and Gray was held on a vagrancy charge.

Morrison explained to Fields that a squad of provincial police and Windsor officers went back to the address a short while ago and arrested Henderson's brother-in-law, a guy by the name of Lockman, and two other fellows.

"All from Detroit," said Morrison, "and all coloureds. While Henderson was in the clink, Lockman brought his pals to Henderson's to retrieve the last of the booze — stowed away behind the wall of the root cellar in the basement."

Fields resisted the temptation to raise the palm of his hand to his forehead. He hadn't properly frisked the place.

Morrison was rocking on his heels now. It seemed to go along with the grin. He continued. "This neighbour of theirs said that there'd always been a lot of coming and going at the house. He phoned the desk early afternoon and said there were some familiar faces circling the house like vultures. That's when our group went out and nabbed them, right in the house. Our boys said one of Lockman's pals, Anderson, I think it was, was caught pouring some of the hooch on the floor while the other fellow, Blythe or something like that, ran out the back door, through a maze of chicken coops in the yard, and threw the bottle over the fence. It landed right in a neighbour's back yard."

Morrison was enjoying this, Fields could tell. Fields was making an effort not to look too disappointed in himself and kept his back straight.

"And get this," continued Morrison with a chuckle, "apparently Blythe was at one time employed as a detective for the Anti-Saloon League and the Women's Christian Temperance Union. He also said that for the past six years he's been in charge of coloured help at Windsor's racetracks. Ha!"

"Thanks for the information," was all Fields said and resumed dragging his pencil across the paper in front of him, a signal to Morrison that the conversation was over and he could get the hell out of his office now.

"Just thought you ought to know," said Morrison, and he turned and left, brightening Fields's door.

Once the big man's footsteps faded down the hall, Fields broke his pencil in half and tossed the report in his desk drawer. He then went looking to see if Corbishdale happened to be around but couldn't find him. Fields looked at his watch. It was late. Corbishdale would be home in bed right now, or at least he ought to be. What a day it had been. Fields stood in the lobby and lifted his gaze to the high ceiling, examining the corners and the plasterwork.

He had returned from LaSalle this morning with nothing: no clues to the intentions of the Canadian rumrunners, or any connection to the earlier River Rouge activities. He checked the cabin and saw the pieces of the suit on the stove and on the floor, and thought nothing of them. He looked out on the river and could make out where the hole in the ice likely was, but it was being covered with fresh snow. He spoke to the farmer, but he had nothing new to offer. And on Fields's way there and back, he had looked closely at the shoulders of the main road and the entrances to the side roads and could not make out where any vehicle would have recently pulled over or turned off.

Fields turned his gaze toward the pictures of the retired officers on the wall. He wondered what kind of example he was setting for Corbishdale. The boy's previous mentor, Montroy, knew what he was doing. He was a street-wise veteran cop who had much to teach a junior constable. When he was retired out of the force last summer, Fields decided to take Corbishdale under his wing and finish the job that Montroy had started.

When Fields had returned from LaSalle and got back to his office, he was again feeling discouraged and disheartened. Corbishdale came looking for him. He had a fresh lead, a good one. It had to do with the house on Tuscarora. Barely prepared, hardly thinking, but looking for some sort of success, some sort of valediction, he told Corbishdale to grab his coat because they were going to make a raid.

Fields's head was pounding again. And now his ear was ringing badly. When he turned, he saw that the desk sergeant was facing him and his lips were moving.

"Come again?" said Fields, turning his good ear toward him.

"I said, you all right, Detective?"

"Yeah, fine. Thanks. Just tired. Time to call it a night, I guess."

The detective returned to his office for his pills, hat, and coat.

Chapter 13

YOU WON'T FIND HIM HERE

Vera Maude pulled on her gloves and shouldered her way through the door at Copeland's. Mr. Copeland was right behind her, turning the *Open* sign around to *Come Again*. It had been a good first day. Vera Maude was able to find what people were looking for mostly, as well as point them in some new directions, all without the least bit of sarcasm or snobbery.

It's the new Vera Maude, she thought.

Winter seemed to be tightening its grip on the Border Cities. There had been another light snowfall in the afternoon. A fluffy white layer added to the heavy brown and grey ice and slush already on the sidewalks. Too heavy for a broom, merchants had been trying their best with coal shovels to push the mess into the gutter. Pedestrians, Vera Maude included, stomped their boots and galoshes on the cleared parts, sending the merchants back to work.

She was thinking about what her uncle had said last night about taking the opportunity to look up old friends. The truth of the matter was she really wanted nothing more to do with them, but wasn't about to tell him that. Many of these so-called friends were the reason she had left Windsor in the first place. Shortly before she left town, if she saw someone she knew heading toward her down the sidewalk, she'd cross the street to avoid them. She was already cutting ties.

But she felt conflicted; she wanted to connect with people, yet always wanted to be left alone. She enjoyed a good conversation, yet felt awkward in social situations. She felt harassed, yet I was often overcome by loneliness.

She walked over to the corner newsstand at Chatham Street, bought a copy of the final edition of the *Star,* and took it into Pond's Drugstore. It was warm and humid inside, what with the kitchen behind the sit-down counter operating at full steam ahead and the people milling about in their heavy coats. She found a stool halfway down the line. An overly made-up waitress pounced on her and asked if she wanted to see a menu. Vera Maude didn't need one; she could read it off the waitress's apron: chicken soup, meatloaf, and …

"A slice of apple pie, please."

"Anything to drink?"

"Tea, thanks." Vera Maude looked around. It reminded her of some of the diners in New York. It also reminded her how comfortable she felt there. She didn't mind the noise and the traffic or the streets teeming with people. Everyone was so busy, so preoccupied with their own lives. Interesting lives. They were all in it together. She never felt alone. Well, maybe sometimes.

The waitress reappeared with a little stainless steel teapot and big white mug. She then advanced to where a cluster of domed cake pedestals looked to Vera Maude like a crop of giant mushrooms sprouting from the countertop. She leaned into the apple pie with her long knife and brought the slice over to Vera Maude on a heavy plate.

"Cheese?" she asked.

"No, thanks."

"Give a shout if you need anything else."

Vera Maude tasted the pie and almost made a *mmm* sound but stopped herself. It was that good. And still warm. She continued to reflect on how things in New York seemed to be working for her, except for her relationship with Toby, the boy she had met while working at the bookstore. He told her she made his head spin. At first she took it as a compliment. Then he said it again but in a different tone. Now she thought she knew what he was talking about.

Am I really such a bitch? she wondered. She poured herself some tea and gave it a spot of milk.

Distance is a funny thing. She couldn't really see her life in the Border Cities until she was in New York, and she couldn't really see her life in New York until she was back here in the Border Cities. Now she was making her own head spin. One thing was certain: it just wasn't going to work with Toby.

She topped herself up and then ruminated further over her mug of Red Rose. When she was done ruminating, she opened up her copy of the *Star* to the movie listings. John Barrymore's *Sherlock Holmes* was playing at the Walkerville cinema, and she had plenty of time to make the evening show. She counted out some silver and left it on the counter. She jumped into one of the phone booths inside the door to call her uncle Fred and make sure he was all right and let him know she was going to be a little late. She dropped a nickel into she slot, got on her tiptoes, and asked the operator to put her through.

"Sounds good, dear. You enjoy yourself now."

"Thanks, Uncle Fred."

She smiled as she held the earpiece for a moment midway before hanging it on the side of telephone. Sometimes he reminded her of her father.

Now it was back out into the cold and the dark. She pulled her gloves on first, purchased from a used clothing store in the Village. They went up to her elbows. Then she wrapped herself in her coat and fitted her tam back on her head.

"Hey, this isn't a changing room at Smith's."

"Gimme a minute, buster!" she yelled through the window of the phone both. She'd bet he wasn't expecting that. He wanted her out and out of the way but wouldn't stand aside to let her open the door. It was like the people desperate to get on the subway car who won't let you get out of the car first.

Bundled and ready, she made it to the revolving doors and leaned into them. They suddenly took off and she looked over to see a man smiling down at her, doing all the work. He gave her a wink and she stuck out her tongue.

He probably liked that.

She considered taking an Avenue streetcar up to Wyandotte Street, where she would then transfer to an eastbound car, but changed her mind and decided to hoof it to Wyandotte instead. Walking would keep her warm, warmer than if she had to stand around waiting for the next Avenue car.

It was more than just cold now; it was bitter. And the walk was longer than she remembered it would be. She tugged her muffler up over her nose and mouth.

Vera Maude glanced down Maiden Lane, looking for any signs of the incident that was reported in the *Star* but didn't see anything obvious. A streetcar was slowing to a stop up ahead at the corner, but she knew she would never make it in time, not on this ice. There would be another one by the time she got there. And there was. It was crowded with people heading home from work. At least it was warm.

She had to stand and wasn't able to see the street very easily. On top of that, the windows were either frosted or fogging over. It was a good thing the driver was shouting out the names of the cross streets, otherwise she wouldn't have a clue where she was.

No one got off until they were well out of the downtown. She hoped they weren't all going to the same movie, otherwise she'd never see the screen either.

"Gla-a-a-dstone."

"Oo — that's me."

Vera Maude squeezed her way out the side door and stepped down carefully onto the icy sidewalk. It took her a moment to get her bearings in the snowfall. Then she saw the marquee and the people standing outside the cinema. She scurried over to the booth, bought her ticket, and headed inside.

It was wonderfully warm but not stuffy. She congratulated herself on another brilliant idea.

When are the movies ever a bad idea?

Not interested in anything from the concession stand, she settled into her seat and peeled off her layer of outer clothing. She then wound it all up and wedged it into the seat next to her.

A buffer in case it gets crowded.

They started appropriately with a recent "Our Gang" short, *Young Sherlocks,* before moving on to the more serious stuff.

When the feature was done, Vera Maude and a few others lingered in the cinema. The projectionist loaded a Pathé newsreel about bootleggers operating along the Canadian border between Chicago and Buffalo. Vera Maude was reminded once again of Jack McCloskey and her last few hours in Windsor spent eating and drinking in a downtown speakeasy in the heat of summer, back along Wyandotte Street. McCloskey had listened patiently while Vera Maude opened up to him. No, she had never heard from him after that, even after sending him a postcard, mailed to the British-American where he had said she could reach him. That was all she really knew about him, that and what she had read in the papers. She had done all of the talking that day. They had seemed to be two lonely people looking for answers. She wondered what kind of trouble he was up to these days.

Once outside, she walked for a while before another streetcar came along — probably the last of the evening. She had her choice of seats this time and picked one on the north side so that she could look in the shop windows — the ones that were still lit. She got out a few blocks before the Avenue. She was feeling adventurous.

She walked back and forth across the front of the speakeasy a couple of times. When she got up her nerve she stepped lightly down the stairs to the heavy wooden door. Three knocks got a tiny window to slide open. She had to stand on her tiptoes. Smoky heat oozed out.

"Trombone," she said.

"Dat once espired."

Vera Maude didn't recognize the voice or the accent, but she caught its meaning.

"Sorry … uh, Jack McCloskey sent me."

The doorman's eyes widened then looked her over. He must have liked what he saw because he unlocked the door and eased it open.

She stopped inside the door and searched for the table where she and McCloskey had sat. It was strange seeing another couple there. They were smiling. Had she and Jack smiled like that? A waiter walked by with a tray holding a teapot and four cups.

"Excuse me, I'm looking for Jack McCloskey. Would he happen to be here this evening?"

"You got business wid him?"

Vera Maude stiffened. *Confidence, confidence.*

"Sort of. We go back. I'm passing through on my way to Chicago and I thought I'd check in with him."

"He's not here."

"Would he be at the British-American?"

"No. Are you alone? I mean, you're not with anyone?"

Vera Maude eased back. "Hey, mister, I'm not looking —" It was the New Yorker coming through.

The waiter eased back too. "Of course not. Look, honey, Jack's not here and I don't know where you'd find him. Okay? Now if you want some tea, take a seat over there and I'll get you some."

He turned and disappeared behind a swinging door near the back of the room. Vera Maude left the speak and decided to walk all the way to the Avenue. It was snowing again, big flakes. Under the streetlights, it was like walking through the Milky Way. When she reached the Avenue, she spotted a cab heading north and hailed it. The cabbie must have seen her at the last moment because he hit the brakes, slid, and almost spun the vehicle. He straightened out and backed up to where Vera Maude was standing.

"Where to, honey?"

"McEwan, just off London — and don't get us killed in the bargain."

"Yes, ma'am."

From honey *to* ma'am.

She noticed the cabbie always glancing up at his mirror. Headlights from behind them shone into the mirror and lit the cabbie's face.

"Something the matter?"

"Nothing."

The car behind them was following awful close to be just a coincidence. Vera Maude realized it was the vehicle behind and not her that the cabbie was most interested in. She turned around and made a mental note of the make and model. The cabbie slowed to make the left onto London Street. When he completed his turn he checked his mirror and Vera Maude turned around again. The other vehicle was still following but not so close now. They didn't need to; traffic was much lighter along London Street at this time of night.

"Right or left?"

"Right," said Vera Maude. She started poking at the inside of her purse with a gloved finger.

He pulled over and Vera Maude handed him some coin.

"Is this enough?"

"Sure, thanks, honey."

Honey status restored. She climbed out and noticed the other vehicle stopped a few doors back. She turned and started making her way up the walk to the front door. When she reached the steps, the other vehicle continued in pursuit of the cabbie.

Strange.

The snow continued to fall, but prettily now, not like the blast of icy precipitation that worked one's face like sandpaper or reduced roads or masonry to rubble. She'd have time in the morning before her shift to help her uncle and Miss Cattanach clear the snow away. Once inside, Vera Maude locked the front door and turned off the porch light. Her uncle sat up in the chesterfield, blinking.

"Maudie, I was just about to put the kettle on. Would you like some tea?"

"Thank you, Uncle Fred."

"You can tell me all about the picture you saw. What was it again?"

"Barrymore's *Sherlock Holmes*."

"Ah. And did the butler do it?"

She smiled. "No, it was Moriarty. You know — bad blood."

Vera Maude kept her uncle entertained for a little while longer, until he started dozing again. He enjoyed hearing her stories much the same way her father did. Maybe someday she would get to tell him about Jack McCloskey. She had no idea how tired she was until she stood up. She followed her uncle up the stairs, kissed him good night in the hallway, shuffled into her room, and collapsed on the bed, fully clothed. It took that last bit of energy she had to strip down and slide under the covers.

She lay there, thinking about that afternoon with Jack McCloskey, trying to remember details about him and what they had said, but most of what she was left with was a feeling.

The weight of sleep settled upon her and she finally drifted off, the sound of the motor running outside only half registering. It was the car that had been following the cabbie, parked in front of the house.

Dead, past, gone.

Vera Maude was thinking about her father again now. She thought these were the most honest descriptions of death. She hated *resting* or, worse, *asleep*. Her father was dead, past, gone. Are there any signs of a life lived after death, or do all traces of it eventually vanish? Depends on who you are. A rich man might leave a skyscraper in Detroit with a portrait of himself in the lobby. A great artist might have his works collected in a museum; a writer might leave a life's work to be read by countless generations. A doctor gets a disease or body part named after him, an astronomer might name a star. But what about the rest of us?

There's all the stuff one leaves behind: a raincoat, a gramophone player, a geranium. Another category of leave-behinds is quantifiable yet somehow immaterial: debt, a magazine subscription, an unanswered letter. And lastly, there is the utterly immaterial and unquantifiable leave-behinds: hurt, regret, shock, and disappointment, or depending on your standing in society or failing health, joy or relief. Behold the laundry list of life.

What did Robert Maguire leave behind? What did his life ultimately add up to? Had he vanished all together or were there remnants of his life still out there? Would they remain vivid, or were they already fading?

All of this got Vera Maude thinking. It was the search for the meaning of a life. Where does one start? She would start with his obituary.

Chapter 14

CASTING SHADOWS

McCloskey was already warming a stool in the British-American when Shorty and Gorski arrived. He noticed them in the mirror behind the bar.

Picking up his mug of fake beer, he greeted them in the middle of the floor after they finished brushing the snow off their arms and shoulders. "Let's sit down somewhere," he said and led them to a round table, not too big, in the corner furthest away from the door. It was a bit dark, but that was all right. At least it was warm.

"I'm sure the rest are on their way," said Shorty as he unbundled himself. He knew how impatient McCloskey could be these days. This was the new Jack McCloskey, and Shorty was getting the feeling that one of his new roles was going to be shop foreman.

"Okay," said McCloskey, "let's not start until everyone gets here."

"How you doing, Jack?" asked Gorski.

Making friendly with the boss.

"I'm good. Thanks."

McCloskey still didn't quite know what to make of Gorski. All McCloskey kept hearing from Shorty was that Gorski was a hard worker and never hesitated to jump into the fray. He supposed that was good enough. In this business you couldn't let personalities get in the way.

Mud and Lapointe were next to arrive. Having the best view of the door, Shorty spotted them first and flagged them over. Mud looked surprised seeing McCloskey at the table. Lapointe had never met him, but it wasn't hard to guess who it was.

"Mr. McCloskey," said Lapointe as he offered his hand.

McCloskey accepted. "Lapointe, right?"

"Yeah."

"Call me Jack."

There was a little awkwardness and then McCloskey said, "Boys, grab some chairs and sit down," and then he held up a hand, caught the waitress's eye, said "Gracie," and made a circle with it, "a round here."

Gracie got the signal and disappeared with her tray of dirty glasses to behind the bar, where she left them for the dishwasher and started pulling pints.

"Sorry for the quality of the beverage here, boys, but I'm sure you understand, rules is rules." McCloskey checked his watch.

There was a long silence and the others started looking nervous. Just in time to perhaps save the day, or the night as it were, Thom appeared. He spotted them before they spotted him. He was covered in snow.

"You're late," said Shorty. "What, did you stop to pick up some milk?"

"No, I —"

"Forget it," said Shorty. "Jack, this is another one of our newest recruits, he goes by Irish Thom, but we just call him Thom. Thom, this is Jack McCloskey."

Thom extended a cold hand. "Nice to meet you, sir."

When McCloskey finished warming Thom's hand, he turned to Shorty and said, "They're getting awful formal out in the county these days, aren't they? Sit down, Thom."

"Where's Three Fingers?" asked Shorty.

"I dunno," replied Thom. "I told him I'd meet him back at his place in time to give him a lift here, but when I got there, the place was dark and all locked up."

"Maybe he's following a lead?" said Shorty.

"Or maybe he's passed out somewhere," said Gorski.

"None of that shit," said McCloskey.

Gorski slumped back.

"Okay," said McCloskey, "let's get started anyways. I want to hear everything you've got so far. Shorty, you can chair this meeting."

Shorty looked around the table. "Thom, we might as well start with you. What's the news from your quarter?"

Thom shook his head.

"And what's that supposed to mean?" asked Shorty.

"We hit Ojibway first, planning to work our way back into town, and got nowhere," said Thom. "Davies either never got that far, or maybe he didn't see anything in it for him."

"Not even with all the land speculating? The waterfront properties? The steelworks?" said Shorty.

"We hit the post office and then we asked around," said Thom. "We got nothing but blank faces."

"You dropped his name?"

"Yep," said Thom.

"Maybe they just didn't recognize it," said Shorty.

"The land speculating was what we asked about first, and all we heard was there's been no activity on that front for months."

"Huh. All right," said Shorty. "And in Sandwich?"

"Well, that's where we separated. Three Fingers said he knew people who used to talk about these hiding places in that town, you know, old hiding places in houses and churches used since the slavery days but now get used for liquor and other contraband. We agreed that was a good place to start."

"But you have no idea how far he got."

"None."

"Meanwhile, what were you up to?"

"I paid a visit to the salt mines," said Thom. "There was a sign at the gate, said they were looking for help. I went in, found the office, and made like I was looking for work. Anyways, while we were talking, I was also sort of trying to measure the guy out."

"What do you mean?" demanded Shorty.

"I started suggesting that I was actually looking to do some business of my own here, that I might know somebody who was dealing in something called 'libations.' He caught on, gave me a wink and a nod, and sent me to the shipping and receiving office, but before he did that I dropped Davies's name, gave this guy the time frame, and asked him about any unusual activity."

"And what did he say?"

"He hadn't heard or seen anything that might have looked

suspicious or rang any bells," said Thom. "Again, he said his pal in shipping and receiving might know something."

"Do you think he was looking to get greased?"

"No, I don't think it was anything like that," said Thom.

"Okay, so what did shipping have to say?"

"Same story, he hadn't heard of anything unusual in the last several months, at least nothing that raised any flags or eyebrows. I didn't cover all the ground there, though — it's a big place … I could go back."

"No, save it for later," said McCloskey.

"What about the roadhouses and hotels out that way?" asked Shorty.

"That was going to be our next stop," said Thom.

"Okay," said Shorty, "hit those spots tomorrow. We still have good contacts in all of them, right? People we can trust?"

"The ones worth doing business with, yeah," said Thom.

"All right," said Shorty. "And I'm assuming you still got the key?"

"Oh, yeah," said Thom. He reached deep down inside his breast pocket for it and handed it to Shorty.

"Thanks," Shorty said and then pocketed it and shifted his attention over to Mud. "Mud?"

"Well — Jack, I covered Ford. You know I'm familiar with many if not most of the factories out there, but it's still a lot of doors to knock on. With all the knocking I did, I didn't get anywhere. The people I talked to of course knew the name, but the impression I had was that it was all after-the-fact kind of stuff. You know, what they might have read in the papers, rumours, talk. I got the feeling that if Davies had any business in Ford City, it was on a higher level, with people the fellows I was talking to never came into any kind of contact with. If we go back to Ford, or any of the factories in that town, it should be closer to the level that Davies would have been operating at. I don't think he had too many soldiers, Jack, I think it was all Davies."

"Thanks, Mud. We'll come up with a new approach to Ford," said Shorty. "Lapointe?"

McCloskey interrupted. "I'm guessing nothing, right?"

Lapointe nodded.

McCloskey had been chomping at the bit the whole time, not really surprised at what the others had come up with so far. "If I can just jump in here — excuse me, Shorty — this afternoon I caught up with a few of Charlie Baxter's old poker buddies."

The boys' jaws collectively hit the table.

"Yeah, I know, it's a strained relationship. They were a little surprised to see me too. I found them above a Chinese restaurant just over here on the Drive, across from the train station. I knew that was their latest hangout. They have several in rotation."

McCloskey glanced around the table. He knew that some people had written him off. He was enjoying this. It had been a long time.

"Yeah, I let them run their little rackets because I knew they never were, or ever would be, a threat to our business. But every time they scored, I figure they owed me something. I've been keeping tabs, and I went to collect."

The boys were wondering who or what else McCloskey had been keeping tabs on these last several months.

"I told them they can settle up now by paying me in information. How good the information is will determine whether or not I let them continue."

"Can we trust them not to talk, Jack?"

"Yeah," said Gorski, "what if it just makes things more complicated for us?"

McCloskey cut right to it. "Are you talking about the Guard? Stop with the folk tales for once."

"But, Jack —" started Lapointe. He had his brother-in-law's story. Shorty glared at him. He knew Lapointe was just itching to tell it.

"What?" said McCloskey.

"It's nothing, Jack. Now, what did Baxter's buddies have to say?"

"No," said McCloskey, "I don't think you know these guys. Anyway, they told me that Baxter, when he had had a few too many, would start talking about Davies's 'reserves,' though they were never quite sure what that meant. Also, before he caught up with me at the train station, he tracked them each down to ask about Jigsaw's whereabouts. I guess all the details hadn't come out yet at that point. Then Baxter stopped talking to them, but they kept hearing on the street about him being seen here and there around the Border Cities, and not like he was on the run but more like he was doing something. I think Charlie Baxter is our best lead here. Find Baxter, and you might be on to something."

The boys each took a swallow of their Cincinnati Cream in an effort to wash all of this down. None of them, including Shorty, were quite sure what to make of it. They'd have to have a conversation with Shorty about it. As far as Shorty was concerned, he wasn't just a little surprised at Jack's sudden interest in their enterprise. He wondered if it didn't have more to do with tracking down Baxter and less with a lost fortune. He felt like he needed to have another private conversation with the boss before they continued, to try to get a better sense of where exactly his mind was. But first he had to ask a more practical question. "But what about those other leads, Jack?" he asked. "The ones we were just talking about? And what about —"

There was a racket outside and the clatter of horseshoes on icy cobblestone. People sitting or standing near the windows of the bar rushed outside to find a commotion in the lobby of the hotel. The bootleggers got up and ran out onto the street, into the intersection of Riverside Drive and the Avenue.

It was a horse and a passenger — not exactly a rider. They could tell by the way the passenger's head was bobbing that he or she was likely dead. The horse was bareback and the shirtless body was draped along it like it was the horse's saddle. The arms were tied around the horse's neck, and the legs, straddling it, were tied around its belly. A constable working the intersection and who must have known a thing or two about horses managed to calm the beast and grab hold of its bridle. The passenger's right cheek came to rest against the horse's mane. The constable steered it toward the curb, right to where the boys were standing.

They all recognized the passenger. It was Three Fingers. Even in the dim light that came from the windows of the hotel they could see how battered and bruised he was. McCloskey walked up to Three Fingers and checked for a pulse. He turned to the gang and shook his head.

"The Guard," Shorty whispered to himself.

The cop asked McCloskey to hold the bridle while he phoned from the police box across the street outside the bank.

Shorty approached in a daze and, still staring at Three Fingers, said "They're real, Jack."

"Yeah, Shorty, killers are real. Killers do things like this, not ghosts or whatever it is you think they are." He looked again at the Huron. "What do these guys want, Shorty?"

"You know what they want, Jack."

Gorski overheard them. "I don't want it any more," he said.

"It's too late. We're in it."

Others from the gang chimed in, but they ended their discussion when the police constable returned.

"A detective is on his way," he said.

About thirty minutes later the gang and the gawkers heard

first and then could see a figure coming toward them, on a diagonal from the other side of the Drive, taking big steps up and down through the fresh snow. The figure went straight to the constable and they exchanged a few words, though he still seemed to be trying to catch his breath, and then the figure turned to the small crowd. He looked slightly dishevelled; his overcoat wasn't done all the way up and it looked like he had been sleeping in his clothes.

"I'm Detective Campbell."

It could be freezing cold and late at night but people will still gather around in their pyjamas to see a dead body.

"Who was first on the scene?" Campbell asked, making eye contact with as many of them as he could.

Everyone in the gang looked at each other but no one spoke. McCloskey had heard about this man but had never actually met him, socially or otherwise. Apparently bootlegging wasn't in this lawman's purview.

Two young men who happened to be in the lobby at the time the horse arrived at the intersection stepped forward. Campbell called them aside and they had quiet words, and there was some pointing in a few directions. They must not have had anything interesting to say to Campbell, because they were quickly dismissed.

Campbell returned to the rest of the crowd and pulled the remains of an unlit cigar out of his mouth. He had paused at a couple of places en route from his apartment to try and get it going but was unsuccessful.

"Does anyone here know this man?" he said.

McCloskey had a feeling the question was being aimed at him and the boys. Sure, they were almost the only ones left standing at the curb — the cold and the late hour were draining the morbid fascination out of the gawkers, sending them back into the hotel — but the constable probably also told Campbell that he and Shorty hadn't hesitated to approach the body and that Shorty might have seemed a bit distraught.

Campbell walked right up to McCloskey and Shorty and then sent anyone else left on the curb, including the rest of the gang, packing. He then got down to business. It was too damn cold to stand out here and mince words.

"You're Jack McCloskey."

McCloskey didn't say anything.

"And who's your friend here?"

"Morand, Shorty Morand."

McCloskey looked down at his junior partner.

"I'd like to know what happened to your friend here," said Campbell, "and I'm sure you would too. Unless you already know who did this."

McCloskey wondered what the hell he could possibly tell Campbell.

"Mr. Morand, why don't you go home and get some rest."

Shorty looked up and McCloskey nodded. Shorty took off south up the Avenue, disappearing quickly into night. Campbell then took the bridle from the constable and told him he could return to his duties. The constable thanked him and then trudged off, probably to look for a warm doorway in which to spend the rest of his shift.

"Mr. McCloskey, I'd like you to walk with me."

McCloskey still wasn't speaking.

"Mr. McCloskey, you're not under arrest."

"Where are we going?"

"We're going to take this horse and its unfortunate passenger up to the creamery stables."

"Where?"

Campbell pointed in the general direction. "Pitt and McDougall. They're the nearest stables."

They started making their way east along the Drive. When they got past the hotel and last couple of buildings on this block, they could feel the wind from the north, coming from Lake St. Clair and along the Detroit River. They gripped the collars of their coats. Campbell had no free hand, so he aimed the top of his head directly into the wind. The only way he could tell if he was walking straight was by keeping an eye on McCloskey's feet.

"What was your friend's name?" said Campbell, almost shouting over the wind.

"He went by Three Fingers."

"Did you know him well?"

"Well enough."

"Did he have any family?"

"No."

"Where did he live?"

"With friends."

"It sounds like there wasn't much to know," said Campbell.

"What do you mean by that?"

"McCloskey," Campbell was dropping the formalities, "while I may not know the finer points of it, or all of its players, I do know what line of work you are — or were — in, and while I at least know that occasionally men die in your profession, they do not generally die like this. And the victim is usually is not such a minor player, like Three Fingers. This is different, strange, and violent, and it looks symbolic to me, almost as if someone were trying to send you a message. That's what I mean by that."

Campbell watched McCloskey's feet turn right up McDougall.

McCloskey knew Campbell was right.

"I really don't know what to tell you, Detective."

Now that they were on McDougall and sheltered in a

corridor of buildings, there was less wind. Campbell stopped and looked at McCloskey.

"Usually when people say that to me it isn't because they feel ignorant of the facts but rather because they can't decide which fact it is they feel comfortable sharing with me."

They stared at each other for a moment and Campbell looked ahead.

"Come on," he said, "I have people waiting for us."

McCloskey stopped in his tracks.

Campbell turned and said, "Don't worry, I won't give them your name."

Windsor Creamery was on the southeast corner, and the stables were directly behind, facing McDougall. They could see a light coming through the small windows in one of the sets of doors.

"Go knock," said Campbell.

A stable boy pushed one of the half doors open. McCloskey held it for Campbell, the horse, and Three Fingers, and pulled it closed behind them.

It was warm inside. To Campbell and McCloskey it felt like an oven. Laforet was already waiting, as was the creamery's proprietor, Gordon W. Ballantyne, who looked upon the horse and its passenger in horror.

The stable boy disappeared and those remaining introduced themselves. Campbell introduced McCloskey as "John," a witness from the scene.

"I've already phoned Janisse for an ambulance," Laforet told Campbell as he circled the horse. He had his camera with him, but before he got to that he was going to brush the snow off the animal and the victim.

In the light of the stable they could now see how badly beaten Three Fingers really was. There were parts of his upper torso that anatomically no longer made any sort of sense.

Laforet insisted on taking a few photos before they untied him. He and Campbell took notes. To McCloskey, this looked like the war; to Ballantyne, still standing there, slack-jawed in pyjamas and overcoat, this looked like nothing he had ever seen before.

There was banging at the door and it could only have been the ambulance. The stable boy reappeared, and this time McCloskey helped him with the other half of the door. They repositioned the horse so that the ambulance could back into the stable. The driver got out for his instructions but froze when he saw his parcel.

"Don't worry," said McCloskey dryly, "the horse stays."

The stable boy fetched a knife and McCloskey and the driver cut the ropes and he and Campbell gently lowered Three Fingers onto a stretcher and into the vehicle. Laforet left with the ambulance.

Ballantyne approached Campbell. "I don't want to be reading about this in the *Star* tomorrow," he pleaded.

"We'll do the best we can, sir. I appreciate your cooperation in this very serious police matter."

And then, with his hand cupped at the side of his mouth, Ballantyne pointed his thumb at McCloskey and said, "Can we trust this man?"

McCloskey looked away and pretended to be studying the straw on the floor. Campbell was layering it on thick; he didn't want to ruin his play. The detective then broke away from Ballantyne and turned to the stable boy.

"Is this one of your horses?"

"No, sir."

"Do you know who it might belong to?"

"No idea."

Campbell thanked Ballantyne and the stable boy for their services and walked with McCloskey back out into the bitter cold. McCloskey stopped Campbell at the street corner.

"Where are they taking him?"

"They're taking him to Grace, where Laforet will continue his examination. He'll get to work immediately. I'll touch base with him in the morning. Should I let you know if he finds anything of interest or significance?"

"Yes."

"And you'll contact me if you have any valuable information on the case?"

This was a bargain, and McCloskey hated bargains.

"Yeah," he said.

"Where can I reach you?"

"You can leave me a message at the British-American."

There were polite nods. Campbell was first to break away and head back to his apartment, only a couple of blocks away, leaving McCloskey standing on the sidewalk, or wherever the sidewalk happened to be under this ice and snow.

When he could no longer make out Campbell through the blowing snow, he stopped to look around. It was a different city, again. Buildings went up, buildings came down. People moved in and out — but mostly out these days. He reflected on how when he came back from the war, after being away for years, what he came back to was a different city in every way imaginable. There are events that change cities, like when Prohibition started or the auto industry exploded. And then there is when something happens inside of you, and suddenly you see the same city, but differently.

He started walking through the wind and blowing snow toward his apartment. It was in a three-storey terrace of townhouses just up on the corner of Chatham and Dougall. Not quite the farmhouse out in Ojibway. He crossed the Avenue and continued west on Pitt Street. The streets were empty.

Why did it have to be Three Fingers?

McCloskey had first encountered the Huron in the street in Sandwich. He had been bouncing between that town and various other places between there and Amherstburg. He picked up farm work in the county during the growing seasons but always found himself out of work in the season in between: winter. McCloskey knew what that felt like. He remembered bringing Three Fingers to the British-American and getting him a room. It was the next day that he introduced him to Shorty.

McCloskey turned left up Dougall. At least he was out of the wind now. He looked up and could see his apartment — top floor, right at the corner. He had left a light on, and it was like a beacon. Every other window in the terrace was dark. Crossing diagonally, he climbed over the pile of snow at the corner and made his way carefully up the wooden steps, now caked in ice, to the door that opened to the foyer. The door to the second-floor apartment was immediately to the right, and the stairs leading up to his apartment were right ahead.

His feet were heavy.

— *Chapter 15* —

SPRAYS, WREATHS, AND RYE

Tuesday

"Jesus, where did you come from?" Lavish pressed his hand to his chest and pleaded for a moment to catch his breath. Yes, he would freely admit, he was the nervous type. Morrison had called out to him from behind this morning's edition of the *Star*. The detective had been waiting for him in one of the two wooden chairs meant for customers here at Wyandotte Garden Florist. A curious sort of waiting room for people anxious about their roses.

"It's been two days, Lavish, and I've heard not a peep from

you." Morrison folded his paper and pulled himself up out of the chair. It was at least two sizes too small and begging for mercy.

The girl behind the counter looked a little nervous too. Lavish figured Morrison had something to do with that. Lavish approached him. "You know we can't talk here," he whispered. He was here to check on shipments for some arrangements he was going to be working on. "And it has not been two days."

"Yes, it has."

Morrison was now rolling up the folded newspaper, like he was about to swat the nose of his naughty dog.

"How do you figure?"

"C'mon, let's cross over to Whittakers," said Morrison. "We can talk there."

"But —"

"You can come back and finish your business when we're done." Morrison held open the door and they took baby steps across the ice on Crawford Avenue, trying to outpace a car turning from Wyandotte that looked as if it might be losing its grip on the road. A snowflake hits the pavement and suddenly everyone forgets how to drive.

"So you're still doing these funeral arrangements?" said Morrison.

"People like my work. I get compliments, repeat business."

"So then why are you still bootlegging?"

"The flowers don't really pay. It's more of a hobby."

They paused outside the door.

"It's been two days, Lavish."

"I still can't figure that."

They entered Whittakers, a stove works joint. They'd been doing a brisk business, what with this arctic stuff happening lately, but this morning things looked a little slow.

"I ran into you Sunday morning," said Morrison, "and this is Tuesday morning."

"Don't I get till tomorrow morning?"

"No. You had all day Sunday and all day yesterday. That's two days."

"The way I see it, I should have until tomorrow morning. Two full days."

"Is this your way of telling me you don't have anything?" Morrison asked, and then he turned and hello'd the boys behind the counter before asking them if anyone was in the stock room. They said no. Morrison had worked here when he was a kid and continued to maintain contact with some of the staff. He always liked to say, *You can't know too many people.*

Lavish followed Morrison into the stock room and Morrison closed the door behind him. It was a big space, as large as the front area. Without missing a beat, Morrison swatted the side of Lavish's head with the rolled-up newspaper, knocking his hat off.

"Ah, crap ... was that necessary?"

"What can I say? I got off to a bad start this morning. Now get your head out of the long stems for a minute, Lavish, and tell me what the fuck Shorty Morand is up to, or I'll trade for that brass poker over there."

Lavish bent down to pick up his hat. "All right, all right." He held his hands up. "It's sketchy. It doesn't make any sense. I was hoping I would have had today to try and piece some if it together for you. It's like someone threw the pieces of different jigsaw puzzles together in a box."

"What are you talking about, Lavish?"

Lavish sighed and took a moment to collect his thoughts before he began, glancing around the stock room. "It's like this," he started. "Shorty and the rest of his boys are doing their own snooping around. I don't know what they're looking for, but they've been asking questions at their old pool hall, and get this, poking around Davies's old place in Riverside. They also botched an across-the-ice shipment to some boys in Rouge over the weekend — Sunday morning. And a colleague of yours, Detective Henry Fields, tried to do some follow-up on that caper yesterday morning in LaSalle and came up with nothing."

"I talked to Fields last night," said Morrison, "and he never mentioned anything about that."

"With all due respect, Detective, do you tell Fields everything you're up to?"

"All right. Tell me, when you hearing this stuff about Shorty Morand, did Jack McCloskey's name ever come up?"

"Nope. I didn't think he was in the game anymore."

"That's because he isn't. At least I don't think he is."

"Should I ask?" said Lavish.

"No, don't bother. What else have you got?"

"This is the shadier part: those boys from Montreal might be back in town, and they're doing their own investigating."

"What boys from Montreal?" said Morrison.

"The ones that were seen in town after Davies got taken down. You heard about the train the other night? The near-runaway train? Well, they were on it."

"Anyone seen them?"

"Not in town, but I know people who know people who rode on the same train."

"And what are these characters supposed to be after?"

"I don't know. Like I said, I was hoping I would have had today to piece at least some of it together for you."

"This is interesting stuff, Lavish, but —"

"I got more."

"What?"

"You know that murder on Maiden Lane?"

"I understood it was a suicide," said Morrison.

"I'm hearing it was a murder. And that's one of Campbell's? You should ask him."

"We don't talk much."

"Yeah, you and Fields neither."

"That's why I have to talk to people like you," said Morrison.

"You're not the only detective on the force, Morrison."

"I'll pretend I didn't hear that, Lavish."

"All right, all right, don't take it the wrong way. I was just saying. Anyway, that's the latest, and it's the stuff that's not making the papers, or your desk, apparently. Can I have my shipment back now, or at least what might be left of it?"

Morrison was rubbing his chin, letting his eyes wander over the racks of stovepipe, the andirons, potbellies, hardware, and whatnot. "I don't know, Lavish. It's a bit thin."

Lavish didn't think so. He was thinking he could have pieced more together if he'd had until tomorrow morning. He was thinking Morrison drank all of his rye.

Morrison started pacing the aisles. It was a maze of shelving units. Lavish stood where he was and let the detective ruminate.

"This Maiden Lane thing just sounds like a few foreigners airing their differences. Let Campbell sort that out. There's nothing for me there. Shorty botched a job. He and his boys were a little careless. Daring, but a little careless. But keep them in your scopes. I'm sure they will have to pull something else off in order to make it up to their partners on the other side of the river. Revisit these boys from Montreal. If it's true they're back in town, they sure are going through a whole lot of trouble." Morrison reappeared in front of Lavish. "Is there more?"

"You remember them, right?" said Lavish.

"I remember the stories. I never actually saw them. Come to think of it, I can't think of anyone I know that did."

"That's because if they did see them, they wouldn't have been around to tell you about it."

"But you said you know people who were on the train who saw them."

"Yeah, but they weren't getting in these boys' way. Now, you know how the rest of the story goes, don't you?"

"Give it to me in a nutshell," said Morrison, "I gotta be somewhere."

"Those boys from Montreal foiled a drop-off that a few bootleggers had organized for somewhere in the county. They didn't jump off the train to avoid the law. They were thrown. Now, those three, I'm guessing, got in the way of our Montreal boys." Lavish was feeling like he had Morrison hooked now.

"Like I said," repeated Morrison, "it sounds like they're going to an awful lot of trouble. What are they doing here? What do they want?"

"Davies's money," said Lavish with his arms extended.

"That again?"

"That's what we heard all along."

"I don't know. I'm thinking they want to set up shop down here. Isn't that why Davies came to the Border Cities?"

"I guess so."

"Okay," said Morrison, "I want you to leave these Montreal boys to me. I want you to keep your ears open with regard to Shorty Morand and his boys."

"And McCloskey?"

"I still think he's out of the picture. He's washed up."

"And my rye?"

"Find out what Shorty's next job is, the one that's going to make up for his little mishap, and you can have it all back when we make our standing engagement on Friday afternoon."

"But you said —"

"Or none of it, Lavish."

Morrison followed Lavish out of the stock room, thanked the boys behind the counter, and headed back outside to the cold.

"Good luck, Lavish."

The stick was getting longer and the carrot was getting smaller. Lavish sulked all the way back to the florist.

THREE

TUESDAY, FEBRUARY 6

Chapter 16

MERCURY RETROGRADE

Early afternoon

"I've been doing some reading."

"You are smarter now?"

"I'm not sure."

Zahra rose from her chair. "Do you want tea?"

"Thank you," said Campbell.

She seemed different. He watched Zahra pass through the beaded curtain into the tiny kitchen still stacked with pots and saucepans and tea things. He was wondering who should speak next. Zahra solved that.

"What are you reading?" she asked.

"Um ... a variety of things," said Campbell. He was busy noticing other details in the décor. And then he could hear the samovar.

"But you have more questions," she said.

"Yes," he said after some hesitation.

She came out of the kitchen with two tiny cups of black tea and set them down on the same little table they had shared yesterday morning.

"Is this good?"

Campbell looked down into his cup. "It's fine, I mean it looks good."

She returned to the kitchen and came back with two small tumblers of water. She caught Campbell sniffing his tea and tried to hold back a smile.

"So you've been reading," she said.

"Yes," said Campbell, "and like I said, I have some questions."

She sipped from her cup. "If it helps."

Campbell took some water. It cut the bitterness of the tea. Then from his coat pocket he pulled out a notebook larger than the notebook he usually carried around. For this case it would serve as his primer.

"When we spoke yesterday, I have to admit I wasn't really prepared to talk about ... what it is you do. Would you call yourself a medium?"

"Yes." She nodded politely. Her elbows were resting on the elbows of the chair.

"And because you said you were in a trance, this means," he glanced down at his pad, "you don't practise physical mediumship?"

Zahra smiled. "No."

"Did I say something wrong?"

"When I immigrated here, I came through London. I was there only short while. I went to see other spiritualists, other mediums. It is true, the English are very theatrical. I saw dolls floating on wires, flashing coloured lights, puppets, and cut-outs — pictures of dead I recognize from old paintings." She smiled again. "And sounds that were supposed to come from beyond, from the astral place, but I could hear scratches on the gramophone."

Campbell started wondering about half the things he had just spent the night reading about. But now he had some perspective.

"Your séances are much simpler?"

"Like I said, I take what I do — what I am — very seriously."

Campbell looked around. "I don't see a crystal ball either."

"No," she said, "no crystal ball. Would like more tea?"

"Please."

She took his cup and went back into the tiny kitchen. While she got to work, Campbell flipped ahead in his notebook. He was enjoying this. His world was opening up a little. She returned and saw him looking at his notebook.

"You have more questions," said Zahra as she set the cups down.

He looked up. "And what about tarot?"

"My mother read the cards. She taught me. I was very young. I could read them, but while I was practising, while she shared other things with me, she saw I possessed other skills, things that couldn't be taught."

"Like channelling," said Campbell.

"Yes. Where I come from, there's more money in that than the cards. She knew what it meant to be medium; she saw them at work. She helped me develop."

"You said she saw these skills in you. How did she see them?"

He was becoming more and more curious. Having grown up

in a conservative, Catholic, and academic household, this was all so foreign to him. She was right when she mentioned gypsies in Hollywood movies, newsstand magazines. She saw the fear and prejudice, and she also saw both the demonizing and rendering silly and trivial everything her people might believe in and hold dear.

"My mother had vision, a sense."

"Your mother was psychic?"

"Yes, she was."

"I read that mediums often or usually carry psychic abilities. Do you possess them as well?"

She hesitated. "All of these abilities, these gifts, they have run through our families — our mothers, and our mother's mothers. But different women had different strengths."

"When you are in a trance, when the séance is in progress, what are the others seeing, hearing?" Campbell had asked the Yarmoloviches a similar question already, but he wanted to hear how Zahra put it. "Would Mr. Kaufman have heard his wife's voice?"

"No. He would have heard mine."

"Your words, or his wife's words?"

She hesitated again. She knew what Campbell was getting at. She also knew he would have asked the Yarmoloviches the same question. He could also ask any one of her previous clients. "Mine," she said, "but not clearly."

"Explain."

"They hear mutterings, murmers, sometimes just noise. My voice, but they cannot make out the words. They are not meant to hear them. The spirits know this is private conversation. Participants like Yarmoloviches are there to help open the door wider, to increase the energy, and sometimes to make it more confortable, more familiar for the spirit."

"I see. And as you've already told me, while you are in a trance, you do not know what it is you are saying, what words you are speaking. Is that correct?"

"Yes."

Campbell wasn't sure he enjoyed where he had to go with this. He needed to give her a rest. He also needed to maintain her trust. He thought he'd change the subject, shake things up.

"What's your sign?"

She blinked, genuinely confused by the question. "I beg your pardon."

"Your astrological star sign. What is it?"

"I ... I'm not sure."

"You don't practise astrology either?" He found that hard to believe, and if it was true, rather interesting.

"I don't concern myself with stars and ... myths." She noticed his surprise. "You think because I am who I am and I do what I do, that all of these is the same to me, that I am following or believing all of it. That is not true. I am who I am. What I do, I do naturally. I am no different from you, Detective. We are who we are."

"When is your birthday?"

Little did Campbell know it, but he was merely exchanging one flavour of awkwardness with another.

"It was last month."

"Really? Even if you don't practise astrology, have you ever come across a phenomenon known as Mercury Retrograde?"

"No," she said.

"Well, apparently at certain times of the year — hang on a minute," said Campbell as he opened his notebook again and looked for the page, "at certain times of the year certain planets can appear to be travelling backward through the zodiac?"

"I didn't know that."

"And that there is speculation that astrological events like this might explain certain events and behaviours. Mercury, if we could see it through this cloud cover, would appear to be moving backwards, that is, against the Earth's orbit."

She smiled. "You mean like full moon?"

He smiled back. She was relaxed now. "Yes," he said, "like the full moon."

He folded up his notebook and thanked her for her time, and the tea.

"And once again, if I have any other questions, I'll be contacting you."

He stood up and threw his coat around his shoulders, touched the brim of his hat, and headed back down the hole in the floor.

There was much more to think about. He needed to sound some of this off someone. Laforet was supposed to contact him this afternoon about last night's dead horseman, the Indian, an alleged member of Jack McCloskey's gang. This one was most definitely a homicide. Campbell decided he wouldn't wait for Laforet's call; he'd reach out to him first, and he wanted more than a simple phone conversation. Campbell would ask for a sit-down with the doctor. They now had plenty to talk about.

Mercury Retrograde, thought Campbell.

Chapter 17

YOU PICKED THE WRONG POCKET

LIQUOR SENT IN DISGUISE
Called Electrical Goods; Police Seize It

Between 150 and 200 cases of whisky, shipped from Montreal and disguised as electrical equipment, was discovered Wednesday night by License Inspector M.N. Mousseau and provincial police officers in the village of St. Joachim. The whisky is the property of John Reinke, William Lavoie, and

Stanislaus Painsonneault, all of Belle River, the police believe.

The above three men were charged in Windsor court today with unlawfully having liquor for sale. They were remanded for one week on bail.

The whisky seized is the best of Scotch whisky, the King George brand, and the value of the seizure at bootleggers' prices would run in the neighbourhood of $1,500, it is believed. This brand of whisky sells at between $6 and $7 per bottle at a dispensary.

The license department today refused to give out any information concerning the seizure, but it is known that the whisky was but recently shipped from Montreal in packing cases as electrical goods.

The plan sounded a bit too familiar. It gave McCloskey some pause for thought, but only a short one. He folded up the morning edition and tucked the loose edges under the lip of his lunch plate.

Shorty and Gorski were late. They were supposed to have met him here at the British-American over an hour ago. They were on a reconnaissance mission, meeting with a couple of irregular business associates that might know the whereabouts or where-the-last-seens of Charlie Baxter.

He was tired of waiting. McCloskey wrapped himself up and headed out to see if he might intercept them at the ferry docks. Passing through the swinging door of the bar into the hotel lobby, McCloskey was met by a bit of a ruckus. People — not guests, more like commuters seeking temporary shelter from the cold — were gathering, but sticking close to the entrance and the windows along Ferry Hill. He tried to get a read on what was going on. Lazarus, the bellhop, was on board and trying to maintain some semblance of order, trying to make sure actual guests were being taken care of.

"Lazarus."

"Jack."

"New hat?"

"Fella has to keep warm. I'm outside most days."

"I get you."

McCloskey looked over at the tall glass showcase that housed the fully dressed model of the nineteenth-century French-Canadian fur trapper who stood guard in the lobby. He was missing his chapeau. McCloskey wove his way through the chaos and found his way out the door. From the top of the hill, he could see what it was all about: two of the ferries were locked in the ice.

He made his way down, bouncing between people moving in both directions; people stranded; people giving up on the idea of a safe and timely passage; others freezing from waiting to connect with friends or family in the cold.

That's why.

McCloskey got to the shelter where he had a more direct view and thought, *That's not how I'd want to go.*

Of course, it wasn't the first time this had happened. You might pretend, but the truth is you never get over it. In winters like this, you'll always think twice about boarding one of these paper hats. McCloskey shouldered his way deeper into the crowd to get a better look. He saw the two ferries stuck mid-river, and the de facto icebreaker, a locomotive ferry the size of a city block, struggling as well just a few hundred yards downriver, smoke pouring out of its stacks. Man's iron muscle grinding away, attempting to break, push, crush the layers of ice. It was awesome. Pity the little wooden ferries.

McCloskey looked around him, examining the crowd. They couldn't take their eyes off the scene, all except for one man who appeared to be watching the drama unfold on the river but wasn't really. McCloskey sized him up: slight build, not too tall, not too conspicuous. Eyes furtively dodging about, not just back and forth but a lot of up and down. McCloskey moved closer to him. Thin leather glove on one hand, the other one bare.

With his eyes on the river, McCloskey loosened his overcoat, dropped his bait. The man's profile imprinted in his mind, he kept him in his peripheral vision. He sidled close to him, and the man appeared to be doing the same. He moved in for the kill. McCloskey kept his eyes on the ferries. He knew what was coming; he knew what to look for, though he would feel it as much as see it.

McCloskey craned his neck as if to get a better view of the ferries.

There.

The cuff of his shirt, a sliver of white between his coat sleeve and glove. McCloskey grabbed his hand and crushed it inside his own paw, his fighter's mitt, until he felt something snap. The man was silent in agony, his face crumpling. He couldn't even manage a whimper. McCloskey pulled him through the crowd with the same hand to where it thinned out, but still beneath the shelter. He took the man's hand and bashed it repeatedly against a support beam. The man wailed this time, but it was right in synch with the whistle of the locomotive ferry, which was now approaching.

"Nothing worse than a fucking low-life pickpocket. You're out of business now, fingersmith. Cheap son-of-a-bitch."

"Jesus Christ! You've fucking crippled me!"

"Sorry, caught me at a bad time. In one of my moods."

McCloskey was hearing more and more about these guys slithering through crowds at the docks and the train stations. He raided the man's pockets, emptying them.

"I'll give this to the orphanage."

"You'll probably drink it."

"I drink for free in this town. Now, you better get that looked at."

The fingersmith ran off, the broken tools of his trade tucked under his arm. McCloskey walked back up to the hotel to leave a message for Shorty, saying that whenever he got back he could reach him at his apartment.

He started feeling some remorse at what he had just done. Then he wondered if he wasn't starting to get soft. It was something else to think about.

— *Chapter 18* —

I'LL HOLD THE LADDER
FOR YOU

It was a quiet afternoon at Copeland's, not that Vera Maude was complaining. She was still adjusting to being back home. Back home in the Border Cities, but with one foot still in New York City. Her mind kept wandering.

She tried to stay focused by continuing to familiarize herself with the layout of the store, its selections, and the business procedures that Mr. Copeland had outlined for her. She kept some cheat sheets in her skirt pocket.

A few customers came to pick up the latest bestseller, their special order, or St. Valentine cards. Others came in just to browse and warm up. She could always tell the browsers. She was pretty sure the male customer, the one who seemed to be following her around the store, wanted to be her Valentine. Every time she turned around, he was standing right next to her, pretending to be reading something. *At least the book is right side up*, she thought.

"Vera Maude?" It was Mr. Copeland. He was bundling up. "I have to run an errand across the street. Lew already knows."

"Sure," she said.

"It's pretty quiet and I won't be long; I'll think you'll be fine," he said and then headed out. The bell that hung above the door gave up its little jingle.

She then turned abruptly, on purpose, and caught her Valentine staring at her. She didn't smile or change her expression. Best not give him any encouragement. He was old, maybe forty, with a thin moustache, not narrow but thin and wispy. Some guys just couldn't grow moustaches and had no business even trying. Blushing, he stuck his nose back in his book.

Yech.

Her co-worker, Lew, was nice. Not boyfriend material, but a decent fellow, a hard worker, and he knew his stuff. Vera Maude guessed he was about her age. She didn't think he had a girl. He had a sense of humour and could talk, but he was very private. She wondered.

"Excuse me, I was wondering if I could have a look at that book up there — that one there." It was her Valentine, pointing at a large volume of historical maps of medieval Europe.

Here we go.

"Um, sure, just let me …" She reached for the rolling ladder and pulled it across the front of the bookcase, set it in place and started climbing up. Valentine moved in, eager to lend a hand.

"May I hold the ladder for you, miss?"

She thought about accidentally kicking him in the face but reconsidered.

"No, thank you. I've got it." The book was really wedged in there, so she had to ease it out from the top of the spine, angling it, careful not to tear it. Once she could wrap her hand around it, she pulled it right out. The weight almost threw her off-balance. She clutched it to her chest with one hand while continuing to grip the ladder with the other.

"Can you take it?" she said.

Valentine shifted his attention from Vera Maude's calves to the tome that was about to be dropped on his head. When she bent down and her view was in line with the front window, she could see a figure standing outside looking at their display. She could have sworn it was Jack McCloskey. Valentine was babbling something about the Crusades while she was trying to quickly climb down off the ladder without breaking her neck so that she could get a better look at the man.

Jack McCloskey, I'll be gosh darned.

Her feet finally reached the floor and she rushed up to the window.

"Vera Maude, could you give me a hand for a moment?"

She halted. "What?"

It was Lew. "I need to do a gift wrap."

Jesus McGillicuddy.

"Sure," she said, and left Valentine and Jack McCloskey, who was now out of sight anyway, to their own devices.

"Unless you'd like to wrap," said Lew, trying to get out of it.

"I can't fold a napkin and I can barely tie my laces."

"So that's a 'no'?"

Vera Maude got out her dimples. "I just know you'd do a much better job."

Lew rolled his eyes. "All right; I'll take care of it. Can you help this lady with her purchase?"

"Certainly," said Vera Maude. "Will that be all today, ma'am?"

A notebook and a copy of the King James Bible.

I guess I can look forward to your annotated edition.

She bagged the woman's purchase and handed her the change. After that, she followed the lady out the door.

"Vera Maude?" said Lew.

"I'm just checking the window display."

Once outside, she looked up and down the Avenue, trying to see if she could spot McCloskey. He was nowhere in sight. Sufficiently chilled, she returned back inside the store.

"Everything all right?" asked Lew.

"Yeah," said Vera Maude. "Everything's fine."

All the way from the ferry dock, McCloskey had been debating walking up to Clara's instead of going straight home. He paused before going any further, staring blankly into a storefront window. It wouldn't be a pleasant walk in this cold. He supposed he could take a streetcar. No, later, he thought, he'd drive up to her place with the Light Six. Maybe he'd take her someplace for dinner, hit a roadhouse. He did an about-face, hung a left at Chatham Street, and faced the wind all the way to his apartment. Shorty would soon be looking for him there anyway, and he was anxious to hear what he had to tell him.

His mind still kept turning to Three Fingers, the idea of him beaten to death, the image of him tied to that horse. The Guard? No, someone else, someone gone underground, someone like Charlie Baxter. He caught himself about to look over his shoulder and stopped. *That's not me*, he thought, *that's not like Jack McCloskey.*

Chapter 19

"TROUBLES OF 1922"

Afternoon

Shorty and Gorski met with their contacts, Moishe and Ozzie, in Detroit at one of their speakeasies up Michigan Avenue near Navin Field. The two liked to brag about how Ty Cobb once entertained some friends there. Shorty found that hard to believe. First, because Cobb didn't have any friends, and second, because he probably had his own cellar. Name-dropping aside, the two had a reputation for being able to keep their ears to the ground and their noses out of trouble. But most importantly, they could be trusted. McCloskey still occasionally did business with them and their gang, and that spoke volumes.

The two gangs had exchanged favours in the past. Shorty was hoping they might have seen Charlie Baxter or heard something to do with his whereabouts. He might not exactly be of particular interest to them, but words, stories, and names can get around. Shorty was sure to leave out the part about Davies's lost fortune. He just said his people had heard rumours that Baxter had been recently seen in the Detroit area and left it at that. Moishe and Ozzie figured Shorty's interest in Baxter had something to do with McCloskey looking to exact some sort of revenge for trying to send him to an early grave, after what went down with Davies and all. They said they didn't like giving guys up just like that, even for someone like Jack McCloskey. They hoped Jack would understand. Suspicious these guys might actually know something about Baxter's whereabouts, perhaps even hiding him, Shorty assured them it wasn't anything like that. He gave them his word.

"You know Jack. He's not that kind of guy."

"All right," said Ozzie.

"But if you run into Baxter, or hear anything about where we might find him, let us know, because Jack would like to have a friendly conversation with him. It's strictly business. And if you want, if it will make you feel better, you can talk to me first. You know how to reach me, right?"

"You still at that hotel near your dock?"

"The British-American. That's where I pick up my messages."

"So you've seen him?" asked Gorski. He was picking up the ball.

Moishe leaned back in his chair. "Last summer, I assume it was right after the thing with McCloskey. We didn't know all the details at the time. He came knocking on our boss's door.

He wanted to flop with one us for a while, said he wouldn't stay long but would appreciate anything we could do for him. No questions. So the boss gives him a spare room in one of our joints, I don't know why, and doesn't Baxter rob it and then light out of town. Son of a bitch."

Now they might be getting somewhere.

"How long did he stay?" asked Shorty.

"I don't know," said Moishe. "Maybe two nights. Our boss made some phone calls, got pieces of the story from his contacts in the Border Cities. It was hard to put it together, sounded like things were sort of falling apart."

"Well," said Shorty, "we're putting it back together again."

"Good," said Moishe. "McCloskey should sit down with our boss sometime soon then."

"Any idea where Baxter went after that?" asked Gorski.

"No idea," said Moishe. "We had other, more important things on the go. Of course we were concerned about Jack and his well-being, but we really had no interest in Baxter. From what we heard, he was just a goon."

The four had a few drinks and a light lunch, Shorty and Gorski said thanks and they all agreed to stay in touch. They got into the Packard, and Moishe and Ozzie took them down to the ferry dock at the bottom of Woodward Avenue. When they reached customs they saw the little wooden ships wedged in the ice and the icebreakers struggling to reach them. When Moishe and Ozzie, who had stayed to see them off, also observed the situation they recommended that Shorty and Gorski wait it out someplace nice and warm. Shorty automatically assumed they would be returning to their speakeasy, where they could shoot a few racks and throw back some shots. But that wouldn't be the case. Ozzie had an idea.

"Hey — there's a vaudeville playing not too far from here," he said, "a good one."

"Yeah," said Moishe, thrilled with the idea. "By the time it's over, things'll be sorted out on the river, and we'll get you back to the dock."

"A vaudeville?" said Shorty. He was trying his best to hold back his shock and disappointment.

"I know, I know," said Ozzie, "but apart from the big laughs, of which I guarantee," he said, holding up a gloved hand, "because we've seen it twice and laughed harder the second time — there is this line of chorus girls who are to die for." His tone softened when he said that.

The more he gushed about the show, the more Shorty thought he might actually be an idiot. He looked over his shoulder at the ferries and the icebreakers, and then at the long faces standing at the dock, blowing snow accumulating on their hats and shoulders, stomping their feet on the wooden platform, and supposed he and Gorski could still probably do a hell of a lot worse.

"Sounds good," he said. "All right, let's go."

"Great." Ozzie checked his wristwatch. "We have plenty of time to catch the two o'clock, and in this weather it probably won't be too crowded. We'll get good seats."

They brushed the snow off the windows of the Packard, a big one, the single-six hard-top, and then once more piled in with Moishe at the wheel, driving slowly up Shelby to Lafayette. There was some greasy slush under the new snow and the tires weren't liking it. Neither was Moishe; he was borrowing his boss's car.

The Shubert Theater was on the southeast corner: a tall, handsome, almost cubic pile of brick, with ribbons of lighter stone running up and down and fancy trim at the top. Shorty and Gorski gaped and goshed as they entered.

The show was George Jessel's *Troubles of 1922*. Ozzie liked the tunes; Moishe liked the chorus line. He had a favourite that he liked to imagine he was exchanging private winks with. Truth was, she winked at any fellow who winked at her.

Shorty also spied a girl in the chorus line. He noticed her because she bore a striking resemblance to Charlie Baxter's paramour and Richard Davies's trophy girl: Pearl Shipley. She wasn't a blonde any more, and she was styling her hair differently, probably so that it matched the other girls'. Shorty said nothing to Moishe and Ozzie, but at the first intermission, he spoke to Gorski in the men's room.

"Impossible."

"I'm telling you it's her," said Shorty.

"Maybe that means Baxter is in town."

"And maybe these guys do know but they're not sharing with us. I've had a bad feeling about them ever since this whole vaudeville thing. Do I look like I go to those things? Don't say anything. I mean to Moishe and Ozzie about Pearl."

"I knew what you meant," said Gorski.

They went back into the theatre and took their seats. The next time the chorus line came out, Shorty looked, and then glanced discreetly over at Gorski, who saw in his peripheral vision and nodded slowly. At the final intermission, they left the building, grabbed a taxi, and had the driver race down to the ferry dock.

"What about Ozzie and Moishe?" asked Gorski.

"Honestly, I don't know what Jack sees in those two."

They had to get this information to McCloskey. Even if Baxter wasn't in Detroit, Pearl was likely the last person to have seen him or spoken to him.

Chapter 20

THERE'S NO ONE HERE BY THAT NAME

Late afternoon

The store closed at five, but apparently Mr. Copeland always stayed behind to close the register, count the receipts, and do a quick balance of the accounts. He wasn't one of those types who liked taking his work home with him.

"Well, Miss Maguire, how was your first full day?"

"I thought it went well, Mr. Copeland." She hoped that was the right answer. She knew it was at least an honest one.

"I did too," said the old man, smiling. "Have you any plans for tonight?"

"No, not really. I thought I'd do some more catching up with my uncle and then read for a while."

"Very good." The old man nodded and smiled. "I'll lock the door behind you when you're ready."

She started wrapping the layers on and had to pull the muffler down from her mouth to wish Copeland a good evening. She heard the bell dingle one last time and the door latch behind her. What Vera Maude had left out in her plans for the evening was the side trip she would be making to the British-American, where she would inquire about a certain Jack McCloskey.

She shuffled across the icy sidewalk down the Avenue and distracted herself by looking into the shops and checking which were still open and which were closed. Most of them were closed by now. It had occurred to her that she had no idea what Jack's reaction might be, or what she would even say to him. Maybe she never heard from him because he wanted nothing to do with her. Or maybe he was just the out-of-sight-out-of-mind type. He had his life and she had her new one, and maybe that's the way it was meant to be. But it might not be what she wanted. She wasn't sure. She'd only find out if she got to talk to him.

Is that why I'm walking through the freezing cold to the British-American, an alleged criminal meeting house? Er, maybe that was a little dramatic.

She crossed Riverside Drive, stepped over the snow accumulated at the curb, and paused at the entrance of the hotel. She really didn't know what to expect from the place. Sure, she had been living the last several months in New York, but this was a little different. For one thing, this was her hometown. But it wasn't like she had a reputation to uphold, or at least she didn't think she did. *And besides*, she thought, *no one would know me from Eve in this place.*

She entered. There was a different kind of a buzz and

commotion in the place, different than what she had experienced in other hotels. Maybe it was unique to the British-American. It was certainly nothing like the Prince Edward. There were the denizens, the ones checking her out, and the travellers, just searching for a room for the night. Salesmen and businessmen, most likely, people who knew nothing of its reputation — unless the B-A happened to be a regular stop on their circuit. Not many tourists visiting the Border Cities this time of year. She must have looked a little lost because a bellhop came up to her and asked if he could be of any assistance. She had no bags, she wasn't heading for the bar, the doors into which were right in front of her, and she was pretty sure she didn't look the working type. She thanked the bellhop and walked up to the desk.

She gave the bell a gentle slap, and after a moment or two, the desk clerk put down the pen he was using to dot i's and cross t's in the giant registration book. He seemed to be in no hurry.

"May I help you?"

He had droopy eyes, a thin moustache that matched his thin lips, and his jet hair was slicked back.

"Yes, I'm looking for Jack McCloskey." Vera Maude could swear the desk clerk's moustache twitched, but it could have been her imagination.

"Sorry, miss, there's no one here by that name."

"Are you sure?"

"Yes, miss. Now if you will excuse me." He started fussing with some unseen objects behind the countertop.

"Well, was he here? I mean did he recently check out or something?"

"No, miss. His name doesn't ring any bells at all, and I make it a point of meeting everyone who comes through here."

He kept moving further along behind the desk, but Vera Maude continued to follow him.

"See, I met Jack once, a while ago mind you, but he told me at the time that if I ever needed to reach him, all I need to do was drop by the British-American or leave him a message or something. Could I at least do that?"

"I don't see how that would be of any use."

"Are you new?"

She didn't mean to sound snide, but she was sure it must have come out that way.

"I beg your pardon, miss?"

Is this guy for real? He's snowing me, probably running interference for McCloskey.

"Forget it," she said and headed for the door. The bellhop was quietly standing there, probably watching and listening. She briefly considered asking him about McCloskey but then thought it might get him into trouble. He smiled, touched his hat, and helped her with the door.

"Thanks. I like your hat."

She stood on the street corner for a while, cooling off and collecting her thoughts. She looked up and down the Drive, back at the doors of the hotel, down toward the ferry docks where she had met McCloskey last summer, and then up the Avenue. The points of a compass. And then she looked behind her again at the doors of the hotel.

No, we're done for today.

Cold and hungry, she decided to just head back to her uncle Fred's. She wanted to avoid running into Copeland on the Avenue, so she walked west along the Drive to Dougall Avenue and then up to London Street, where she caught the streetcar. She didn't want to risk having Copeland see her on the street at this hour, not after what she had told him. She couldn't mess this job up, not like she messed up at the library. Copeland's was a good job. And she had to demonstrate how women could hold their own, or so she thought. She always felt she had something to prove. Maybe it wasn't necessary. Maybe that's just the way she was — a little worried all the time.

She was more tired than she thought and doing a continuous head bob in the streetcar as it rumbled along toward McEwan. There weren't many passengers at this hour, maybe a dozen, so it was cold inside, not like it was when the car was packed with bodies. *Okay*, she thought, *it's cold, but at least it doesn't smell.*

She let her mind wander: *I saw Jack McCloskey today. I know I did. Or was it a ghost? No, the desk clerk knew who I was talking about. I could tell. I bet the bellhop did too. But if I'm not going to get anywhere with the staff at the British-American, what's my next move? Maybe I could stake out the hotel? A girl hanging out in a hotel lobby — this hotel lobby — or worse, the bar. Yeah, that'd go over well. Then again, it might be worth a try. I just have to time it right. My next day off, Thursday. That'd give me time to come up with some sort of plan. And if that leads to nothing, if that's another dead end, then what? Who can I talk to? The police? Interesting angle, but how to play it. They'll look suspiciously on me. And again, I can't be screwing things up at the store. And then there's Uncle Fred. I have to think about him too. Winter's different along the Detroit River, different than in Montreal or New York. The ice, the snow, the wind, everything. Different under my feet, different in the air. And despite that, the Border Cities never really seem prepared or it. This is a summer place. Great. Now I'm feeling lost again. I'm like the sailor who crossed the ocean only to find that China wasn't there, where the mapmakers said it would be. And yet I feel like I have to bring back something from the new old world. I'd bring back a potato, but that's been done. Maybe I'll just bring back a disease. I know I saw Jack McCloskey. I also know it was that bitch I shared the apartment with in the Village who stole my copy of* Ulysses. *What's worse, she probably sold it. Gosh, I'm tired.*

Chapter 21

SHOOK'S SYNCOPATED ORCHESTRA

Early evening

Laforet was first and foremost a surgeon, and it showed as he gently and precisely cut into his sausage-stuffed quail. He closed his eyes and leaned over it as the aromatic vapour escaped. He breathed it in deeply, and then scooped a shred of the tender meat along with a bit of the stuffing into his mouth. Campbell could tell by the look on his face that it met with the doctor's approval. His favourite thing about dining with Laforet was watching him eat and listening to him talk about food.

"Sausage?" said Campbell.

"Oh, not just sausage." The doctor was dissecting the morsel of stuffing he still had in his mouth, staring ahead somewhere across the dining hall. "Cranberry, chestnuts … thyme and sage, and … I think I'm getting some nutmeg in there … lemon. Wonderful. How's your prime rib?"

"Tastes like prime rib."

"Probably a better plate than what you're accustomed to being served at those roadhouses."

Campbell was used to this. It was the other side of dining out with Laforet: the occasional scene in a restaurant as he complained about the food; being teased about his profession; his so-called life (unmarried); his taste in clothes, etc., etc. But Campbell always took it in stride, not because he was some sort of masochist, but rather because he actually liked the man and greatly respected his work. Otherwise, he would have pushed him into traffic a long time ago.

"You always assume I frequent the roadhouses, like they're my home away from home," said Campbell.

"Well, aren't they? I thought they were where all you dicks hung out, where you got your information."

"We've been through this before," said Campbell.

It was Laforet who had proposed the Prince Edward when Campbell contacted him about meeting over dinner. True, it wasn't exactly Campbell's style, but neither really were the roadhouses. And he knew he'd never get the doctor to join him in some chow mein over at Ping Lee's. They were having the table d'hôte. It was Laforet's favourite way to dine at the Prince Edward; he claimed the food tended to be of better quality and a little more adventurous when it came off the fixed menu. He also took great pleasure in coming up with just the right combination, given the limited selection.

Laforet flagged down the beverage waiter. Campbell braced himself, but all the doctor wanted was a top-up on their lemon cordials.

"Thank you."

"Maybe I'll take you to a roadhouse one day," said Campbell. "Somewhere nice, like the Island View out in Riverside."

"Is that a threat?"

"We'll wait until the weather turns around."

"The weather. It seems to be all anyone ever talks about these days. You wished to discuss your Maiden Lane case?"

"If you wouldn't mind," said Campbell.

"Not now," said Laforet. "Let's wait until dessert. Eat those vegetables."

Laforet was using his fork to point at the braised carrots, butter peas, and seasoned roast potatoes so far untouched on Campbell's plate.

"Yours look better than mine," said Campbell. "Would you like to trade?"

"Now that wouldn't really make any sense, would it?"

They could hear the band warming up below them on the mezzanine floor. Shook's Syncopated Orchestra was a regular at the Prince Edward. Laforet wasn't really much of a jazz fan, or of this type of arrangement, but here on a special engagement were Dorothy Curtin, violinist, and Dorothy D'Avignon, pianist. The orchestra was to assist with their solos, and it was something he had been looking forward to since he saw the notice in the *Star*.

"We should order our dessert," said Laforet, and he gave the waiter a nod, who in turn signalled another waiter. They both descended on the table; one began removing the dinner plates while the other handed each of the gentleman a dessert card.

"I'll have the pineapple sherbet."

"And I'll have the vanilla ice cream."

"Any toppings, sir? Caramel? Chocolate?"

"Just the vanilla ice cream, thanks."

"Coffee?"

"Yes."

"Yes, please."

The waiter scurried off with his orders and Laforet gave Campbell a look.

"What? I like vanilla ice cream. Why ruin a good thing."

The coffee arrived first.

The truth was that Campbell did not have to bribe Laforet with dinner at the Prince Edward to get him to come out on a frigid winter evening; Laforet was intrigued not just with the Maiden Lane case, but last night's as well.

"All right, what can you tell me about our night rider?"

"Extraordinary. A severe beating, as anyone can plainly see, but there are no hand, fist, or any kind of weapon-shaped bruises on him."

"What about the rope used to tie him down?"

"It appears only to have been used for that purpose. I know what you're thinking, and there were no rope marks around his neck."

"And how did he die?"

"Severe internal hemorrhaging. Most terrible thing is, Campbell, there is evidence that he died on the back of that horse. Did you find out where it came from?"

"Belongs to a boy in Sandwich."

"It rode in all the way from Sandwich?"

"Looks that way. I'm going to be speaking to McCloskey further on this. I have a feeling he knows more than he is telling."

"Simple gang warfare?"

"Possibly," said Campbell.

The dessert arrived in chilled silver cups.

"Now, the Maiden Lane case."

"I'm not sure what to make of it, of her."

"Go on."

"Well, first off, from what I know of the subject, I don't know how much of an occultist she really is. While I'm still skeptical about all of this astral plane stuff and channelling the dead through these séances, her comments about other aspects of the occult seem, to me at least, a little inconsistent. Do you know much about the occult?"

"A little, mostly from friends and acquaintances. And Mrs. Laforet once attended a lecture. It was all I heard about for a week."

"All right, tell me your thoughts on a medium who, for instance, does not believe in astrology? Or possess a crystal ball?"

"So she specializes. So do most of my colleagues."

"I never would have thought the occult could be so compartmentalized. I mean, isn't the idea that these people, these individuals, are supposed to be open, connected — that it's all — on some level the same? It wasn't that she didn't practise these other ... crafts. She didn't believe in them. She was critical about how other mediums practise their crafts. She doesn't go for the theatrical stuff; you can see she's no vaudeville act."

"So what is it she does, exactly? I mean, how does she make it work?"

Campbell got into it and Laforet signalled the waiter.

"They sit around a table, touching hands. No crystal ball, like I said, just a candle in the middle of the table. No props, no light show, or sound effects. They close their eyes, and she simply opens, or rather, as she put it, becomes the spiritual door."

The waiter brought over two fresh lemon cordials and took away the dessert things.

"And is she one of these mediums who speaks in the voice of the dead?"

"No she isn't — and that's another thing. Zahra says it's the words of the spirit, but in her voice."

Laforet looked up from his glass. What did the other couple have to say? The Yam ..."

"Yarmoloviches. They said that when they do this sort of thing, and it's successful, they hear Zahra's voice but not the words. Just murmuring. Zahra said the same thing. Interesting. She says the spirits treat it as a private conversation."

"So it's not a party line," said Laforet.

"I guess you could put it that way."

"Did she tell you anything else about her background?"

"She did," said Campbell. "She told me she comes from a long line of spiritualists, people — all of the women on her mother's side — each endowed with certain gifts. Her mother was primarily a tarot reader and psychic; she began to cultivate and hone these natural skills in Zahra at a very young age."

"Interesting."

"I'm going to continue reading up on it."

"Is it going to help you solve the mystery of Kaufman's death?"

Campbell hesitated, staring across the room at the other diners, watching the waiters flit about like fireflies in July. "I don't know," he finally said. "I feel like somehow it might. The truth is: I'm not quite sure how to continue with this case. Speaking of Kaufman, what have you learned from the autopsy? Anything useful?"

"You observed how the body was contorted?"

"Yes," said Campbell.

"Well, I would have to agree that Kaufman did turn at some point in mid-air, probably very close to impact."

"But he landed face down."

"And?"

"I've pretty much concluded that he propelled himself out of the window — dashing straight into it. Could he have turned more than once?"

"I suppose it's possible," said Laforet.

"A very fast, agitated fall. Like he would have been writhing in mid-air."

"Difficult to imagine."

"If only I had looked up in time," said Campbell.

"It was a natural reaction."

The sounds of the orchestra warming up began to make their way into the dining hall.

"I had a wild idea," said Campbell, before he could be drowned out. He was saving this for last.

"What?"

"I'd like to bring Zahra into your morgue, have her see Three Fingers's body."

"What do you hope to accomplish by doing that?"

"It's an experiment. I want to see what kind, if any, of a reaction we get from her."

Laforet sat back in his chair and started drumming the fingers of his right hand slowly on the linen. "All right," he said. His natural curiosity was working for Campbell. "We can arrange a time in the morning. I plan on being there early."

"Thanks."

"And let's try and keep this low-key. I don't want people thinking I'm turning the morgue into some sort of sideshow venue."

"Got it."

— *Chapter 22* —

BORDER CITIES AMATEUR
ATHLETIC CLUB

Tuesday evening

Shorty and Gorski split up after the ferry finally delivered them
to Windsor. Gorski went home and Shorty hiked straight over to
McCloskey's place as instructed by the note he had found at the
B-A. But in approaching the terrace he could see his apartment was
dark. He walked up and into the building and tried McCloskey's
door, just in case. No answer. He figured McCloskey must have got
tired of waiting around. He'd have to hunt him down now, or he'd
hear about it in the morning. Shorty went to Clara's apartment first.

"No, I haven't seen him all day."

"Are you expecting him?" asked Shorty.

"Nope."

Shorty's concern was rubbing off on her; he could tell.

"I'll find him," said Shorty. "He's around."

They worried quietly about this man. But despite the conversations they were recently having regarding McCloskey's health — both mental and physical — he was actually in better shape than they thought. His little sabbatical following his convalescence had actually done wonders for him.

After a couple other stops, Shorty followed up on a lead and finally tracked him down at the Border Cities Amateur Athletic Club — one of McCloskey's other new homes away from home — on Pitt Street, right next to Royal Lunch. It was a big studio, fully equipped with weights, kettle bells, Indian wands, a medicine ball, mats, towels, and plenty of sweat. There were about a dozen other guys working out here tonight. Nothing much else for these fellows to do this time of year.

McCloskey was shirtless, punching a bag, making it look like a down-filled pillow. Shorty could see the scar from the bullet hole just below McCloskey's left shoulder and noticed the asymmetrical pattern to his shoulder muscles. Shorty guessed he was working on evening that out.

McCloskey stopped swinging when he spotted Shorty standing there still with his hat and coat on. "Where the hell have you been?" He kept punching away.

"We got stuck in Detroit on account of the ice and went to a vaudeville."

"You blew the afternoon at a vaudeville?"

"And you'll never guess who we saw on stage."

"Who?"

"Pearl Shipley."

McCloskey stopped mid-swing, almost throwing himself off balance. "No."

"It was Pearl, I swear. Just ask Gorski."

"You're sure?" said McCloskey.

Shorty nodded, eyes closed.

"And Moishe and Ozzie didn't notice?"

"They said nothing."

"And you didn't tell?" McCloskey was pointing at Shorty with a taped fist.

"No, we kept it to ourselves."

"Okay, let's back up. So Moishe and Ozzie had nothing on Baxter?"

"No — I don't know. Sometimes I think it was just too much of a coincidence that they'd be taking us to this vaudeville with Pearl in the chorus line."

"Like they were leading you to her? Or to Baxter somehow?" McCloskey reached up for his towel. It was looped through the leather straps suspending the punching bag. He wiped his face with it and then draped it over his head. "Wait a minute. They wouldn't know who she is. She left for California while Baxter was still being spotted on both sides of the river, right?"

"That's right," said Shorty. "I forgot."

"Too many questions. Is the show playing again tomorrow?"

"Same time."

"I want you to go back tomorrow and talk to her."

"Gotcha."

"And go alone," said McCloskey.

"Without Gorski?"

"Without Gorski."

McCloskey then asked to see the key again. Shorty handed it to him and McCloskey turned his back on the studio and re-examined the key, still looking for some kind of clue, some hidden meaning. As it got passed back and forth and jostled, buffed in coat pockets, it became shinier. Maybe it was worth something. He handed it back to Shorty.

"Talk to Pearl."

"Will do. Oh, Jack, you might want to check in with Clara. I stopped by her place when I was looking for you. You don't want to get her all worried on you now, do you?"

Shorty wanted to say, *because she's been taking good care of you.*

"Thanks."

"Hey, I've been thinking we should do something for Three Fingers."

"I've been thinking the same thing," said McCloskey. "Next time we all get together we can talk about it."

"The police are working on the case?" said Shorty.

"Yeah, a Detective Campbell. Seems like a decent guy. Don't know all that much about him. I should tell you, I don't think he's interested in us."

"He's not into bootleggers."

"I guess we're just not his type," said McCloskey. "Maybe he prefers blondes."

"Anything else? Anything new on the wrecking and salvage front?"

"I've got someone going through the inventory sitting in the yard on Mercer. Getting rid of some dead wood, clearing some space for another garage. It's going to have quite the cellar, let me tell you."

Shorty smiled. Now this was more like it.

McCloskey went back to the bag, working that left. He appreciated that Shorty left the Guard out of the conversation.

FOUR

— *Chapter 23* —

THERE WILL BE MORE

The tires on Campbell's Essex had a knack for finding any bare patch of streetcar track along London Street, and when they did, he would always lose control of the vehicle for a split second. It made Madame Zahra want to reach for the dashboard.

"Do you drive?" he asked when they were stopped behind one of the streetcars as it dropped off a few of its passengers. He knew what the answer would be before he even decided to ask it.

"No," she said.

She was wearing a long coat and had her neck and shoulders

wrapped in a heavy shawl covered in what looked to Campbell to be some sort of Oriental print. There were patches of leather in her fur hat, and strings of small beads, some silver, some stone, hung in loops on the sides and back. Her hair must have been pinned up under the hat. Her hands were tucked into a muff. Despite all this, and the fact that it was rather snug in the front of the Essex, especially with all of the winter garb they were wearing, she looked like she was freezing.

"Isn't it at least this cold in Belorussia?" He wanted to impress her with his fresh geographic knowledge. Earlier he had dropped by Copeland's again to see what they had in the way of atlases. They had a copy of the *Times* atlas published last year. There was no Belorussia; the artificial lines dividing people in the world had once again been redrawn. The maps contained in the atlas clearly identified the new political boundaries of Lithuania and Russia. He recognized the names of the places Zahra had mentioned to him, leaving Campbell with only his imagination to draw a picture of Belarus. He wasn't satisfied with that. Now it was the bookstore sending him to the library. There he found a few older atlases where her homeland was clearly marked. People had always told him how visually oriented he was.

"Colder. And I always hated cold."

The streetcar got moving again. They were approaching Crawford Street now and Campbell looked for a break in the snow banks along London Street, or anything that would indicate a safe entrance into the hospital's circular drive. He slowed to give himself some distance between him and the streetcar; glancing left, he could now make out the gap and carefully made the turn. The cinder drive was covered in packed snow and he immediately thought how much more convenient it would have been had the cinders been on top of the icy surface rather than locked below it. It was a wide drive; hugging the curb, he parked just beyond the front doors.

"Hold on a minute," he said to Zahra.

He climbed down into a ridge of shovelled snow that was as high as the running board and had to continue through it, taking high steps until he got to the front of the car where it was clear. He stomped the snow off his galoshes as he walked around to the passenger side, and once he got there he opened the door for Zahra and helped her step down.

Her boots navigated the front steps of the hospital better than his galoshes. She paused at the door and Campbell held it open for her. This was going to be quite an entrance, he thought.

Inside, it was quiet as a church. Campbell made his way toward the reception area just to the left while Zahra waited, standing in the middle of the lobby, looking not a little uncomfortable. Passersby almost walked into each other as they stared. It was warm inside, even a little humid. She loosened her shawl.

Campbell peeled off his gloves, pulled his identification from his breast pocket, and showed it to the nurse. "Detective Campbell here to see Dr. Laforet." The nurse was looking around Campbell at Zahra. Campbell noticed and shifted his position so that she could get a better view. "He's expecting us," he said.

The nurse picked up the phone. It must have rung several times. "Yes, Dr. Laforet? Detective Campbell and —"

"Madame Zahra," said Campbell.

"— Madame Sarah are here … very well." She hung up. "He'll be right up."

The detective and the medium shuffled around the lobby, trying to stay out of people's way. The chairs were occupied, so they stood. It wasn't long before Laforet surfaced.

"Sorry for the wait." Laforet smiled and gave Zahra a very continental bow. "Please, follow me."

More heads turned as the doctor led them to the elevator, bringing them to the basement. The new wing had been open only for a couple of months now, and the administration was still deciding on how to allocate a few vacant spaces in the building. Apparently they wanted to see how the building functioned in full operation before making any of those final decisions. While Laforet's laboratory had a temporary feel to it — coming from the fact that he was only using about a third of the space and there was furniture piled in a corner — it was still far better than the conditions he was used to working in. He had a feeling the space might get further carved up. The doctor entered first and held one of the swinging double doors open for his visitors.

Zahra froze as soon as she entered, and Campbell almost walked into her.

"Are you all right?" he asked.

She looked white.

"Yes," she said and proceeded slowly, seemingly with caution.

When Laforet didn't hear any footsteps, he turned around and saw his tour group was lingering at the gates, likely due to Zahra's unfamiliarity with such an environment. He looked at Campbell, standing behind her but to the side, and Campbell nodded and raised his hands slightly, as if to say, *It's all right; let's just let Zahra set the pace.* Laforet took Campbell's cue and walked over to his desk.

"This is probably where I do half my work," said the doctor. "Not very exciting or particularly interesting. Coffee?" He had a drip coffee maker standing on one half of a dual, coil-element hotplate, the footprint of which was no larger that the tall, white-enamelled table it rested on.

"No, thanks," said Campbell. "Zahra?"

She shook her head. It occurred to Campbell that she had not said a word since entering the building. The detective and the doctor kept glancing at each other.

"Madame," said Laforet, "may I take your things?"

She handed the doctor her muff and then unravelled her scarf from her neck and handed him that too. She left on her headgear. She unbuttoned her coat slightly. It looked like it might have taken a major operation removing it. Campbell left his hat on a coat rack that stood just inside the door.

Zahra couldn't seem to take her eyes off the mortuary tables at the end of the long room. While she was hesitating, she at the same time appeared drawn to them. Meanwhile, the doctor needed to keep things moving along. His work was piling up, as it were.

"Shall we?" he said, extending an arm toward the tables.

Campbell touched Zahra's shoulder and the trio moved forward, past a couple of countertops, one empty and the other covered in lab equipment — some as yet to be unpacked; stacks of wooden stools and a chalkboard perhaps meant for instructional purposes. Their footsteps on the tile floor echoed through the mostly empty space. It wasn't Campbell's imagination; the room actually got colder the nearer they got to the tables. There were five of them, on wheels, standing side by side. Four of them were occupied, the bodies covered by a sheet, one of which Campbell and Zahra could see now was stained.

The two men let Zahra break away as soon as she started moving quicker toward the bodies. Laforet had arranged them in no particular order. It could be a sort of shell game. They silently watched her move between one and the other. Campbell did not know which was which, though he had a pretty good idea where Three Fingers was resting.

One of the bodies, the one to the far right, held no interest or fascination for Zahra. She returned to the one that was second from the right, the one with the stains. She gently pressed her hand on the torso and then the head, and then turned to Laforet.

"May I?" she said.

Laforet looked at Campbell, and Campbell gave him a look that must have said, *That's what we're here for.*

"Let me help you," said Laforet, and he walked around the other side and positioned himself between the wall and the head. Campbell followed and stood opposite Zahra.

"Are you sure you are all right with this, madame?"

She looked at Campbell, and Campbell suddenly remembered what she had told him about how she had practically run through battlefields to escape her country. Campbell gave the doctor a nod, and Laforet folded the sheet down until it was at the bottom of Three Fingers' ribs.

Campbell watched her reaction the whole time. She didn't flinch; she didn't even blink. It was as if she knew exactly what was under the sheet before it was even lifted. Her reaction came the moment she stepped into the room.

"Zahra?"

She looked up at Campbell. "No one touched him," she said. The two men looked at each other.

"Is that what you're telling us?" Campbell asked.

"Not with their hands," she said and then moved around to the next table. They followed Zahra's lead. She seemed unable to settle between this table and the next. She stood between them for a moment with her eyes closed, but that somehow seemed involuntary. There was an unmistakable shiver, and then her eyes opened, and when they did, she was staring straight at Laforet. He would say later to Campbell that the sensation he was experiencing right then was of someone speaking directly to him, but without moving their lips. *It was something in her eyes.*

Zahra then removed the sheet from the body next to Three Fingers, turned, and removed the next. Campbell would have never thought it possible, but these guys looked even worse than

Three Fingers, and not just because they had been sitting around a couple more days.

"These men ... they did not know. But they were wrong to be there."

Campbell knew these to be the two bootleggers that were thrown from the train outside of town on the weekend. They were carrying identification and Laforet was still waiting for instructions from the next of kin. The police had a hard time tracking them down. These bootleggers weren't from the Border Cities.

Zahra glanced back over at Three Fingers.

"Is there a connection between the first body and these two, Zahra?"

She was looking a little overcome, like this was something she never expected, and something she had never felt before. Campbell looked over at Laforet, who remained as stoic as ever, and then went over and gently pulled Zahra away from the bodies. As he did this, the only other thing she said was, "Kaufman is not with them." Campbell glanced back at the fourth table and then at Laforet, who was pulling the sheets back over the other bodies.

The farther they got away from the bodies, the warmer it became in the room. Campbell noticed for the first time the electric space heater in the corner behind Laforet's desk, the bars glowing dimly. He pulled out the chair and swivelled it around.

"Zahra, here, why don't you just take a moment and sit down, warm yourself up?"

He wanted to catch any image, thought, or sensation she might be holding within her before it was lost or buried. She slumped down in the wooden office chair, her fingers loosely folded together and hands resting on her lap. She was staring blankly at the floor. He squatted in front of her and gripped each arm of the chair, trying to lift her eyes with his. He spoke softly.

"Now, tell me, Zahra, what did you see? What was it you were feeling?"

It was clear to Laforet that Campbell's interest in all of this was becoming something more than of an investigative nature, more than just clinical. He maintained his distance but observed closely.

"What did you see?" repeated Campbell.

"There will be more," said Zahra as she looked straight into Campbell's eyes, "more will die."

"Who?' asked Campbell. "Who will die?"

"They are searching for something."

"Not someone?" said Campbell.

"No, something."

"But you said 'there will be more, more will die.' Who is being targeted?"

She looked drained, like there was almost nothing left in her.

"All right ... what is it they're searching for?"

"I do not know."

"You can't tell me anything about what this 'something' might be that they are after?"

"No ... it's not what it appears to be."

Campbell took a breath. "You said 'they.' There's more than one of them?"

She took a short breath. "Sometimes."

"Sometimes?"

"I see only shadows," she said and slowly shook her head. "I see only shadows."

"I asked you if there was a connection between the first body and the other two. Is there?"

"Yes and no," she said.

"But *they* did it," said Campbell.

She was fading. That was enough for Laforet. He moved in.

"Campbell," he said almost in a whisper.

The detective seemed to be in his own kind of trance, or possessed at least by this tangle of mysteries in his head.

"Campbell, I think you should take Madame Zahra home."

Campbell snapped out of it. He looked over his shoulder at his friend, standing there in his glowing white lab coat, the white tile walls, over at the empty, glass-door cabinets, and up at the scoop lights hanging from the ceiling.

"And then," continued Laforet in the same tone, "perhaps you yourself should also get some rest."

Campbell straightened and looked down at Zahra, who did appear slightly disoriented. He wondered if he looked the same. "Yes." He blinked. "Yes."

"Are you all right for driving?"

"I'll be fine," said Campbell. "Zahra, we should go." He helped her up while the doctor fetched her things.

"I'll show you out. I'm sure the brisk air will do the both of you some good."

Up in the lobby, as Zahra once again prepared herself for the cold, Laforet took Campbell aside.

"Are you sure you're all right?" he asked.

"Yes," said Campbell, not a little defensively. "Of course."

"Good. This time it will be me contacting you. But not until you've had a meal and gotten some sleep."

Zahra was coming back around, but still quiet. The colour was returning to her face.

"It was a pleasure meeting you, madame."

She smiled and took the doctor's hand. Laforet helped them with the door and watched them make their way down the steps. After he had witnessed them drive off, he re-entered the building and noticed the look he was getting from the nurse at reception. He cleared his throat and headed straight back to the elevator.

"You know where to find me, Gladys."

Chapter 24

OTHER PEOPLE'S DESTINIES

"I didn't come here to talk about Jack," said Clara, "I came here to talk about you."

They were at Henry's place, once their family's place. It had been left to her brother. It wasn't much, just a little clapboard house on Glengarry. Clara was saddened to see it becoming a bit run-down looking. Kind of like Henry.

"Oh," he said as he hung up her coat.

She parked herself on the chesterfield in the front room. All the same furniture she grew up with.

"Really, Henry, how are you doing?"

He went to draw the curtains to let in some light. She wanted to talk and he looked as if he wished he had something to tell her. Or maybe he just didn't know where to start. He would start to say something, hesitate, and then try to start again, but he couldn't seem to find the words. He looked out the window at the postage stamp–size front yard that spilled down sharply onto the sidewalk; it had barely enough space to pile all the snow. His arms hung loose, but he was grinding his fingertips into the palms of his hands. He turned and sat down in the bucket chair adjacent to the chesterfield, his good ear facing her.

"I'm fine," he said.

"You're not fine, Henry. I can't begin to tell you in how many ways you are not fine. First, tell me about your ear. And are you still getting those headaches?"

He looked at the floor and remained quiet for a moment, and then he surprised her by admitting, "It's getting worse."

"Your hearing or the headaches?"

He went back to grinding his fingertips into the palms of his hands. "Both," he said.

"Are you still seeing a doctor?"

"Yes."

"And?"

"He tells me there's nothing more he can do. He explained it all to me. Superior temper gyro something or other. He just keeps giving me painkillers, headache pills."

"Maybe you should be seeing someone else, a specialist of some kind, someone with more experience with this sort of thing."

"I'll ask him," he said.

"Meanwhile, is there anything I can do? What can I do to help?"

"Nothing," he said. "Thank you. I'm sure I'd feel ... at least a little better if I could just close a case. I want to make ..."

"Henry?"

"I feel useless," he said.

"Maybe you just need some time."

"I just want to close one case."

Clara felt she was going to get nowhere with him, at least not at this moment, not with how he was. But she had to start the conversation. Right now she would go along with him and offer as much support as she could.

"Okay," she said. "Do you have any leads? Is there something you're currently working on?"

"I have Corbishdale trying to work some up for me. He can be pretty good at that, and the experience will be good for him. I also try to get information from others in the department on items they might be too busy to follow up on."

Table scraps, Clara thought to herself. None of this sounded good. This wasn't how detectives were supposed to work. She suspected her brother already knew that.

"Henry, don't take this the wrong way, but do you enjoy doing what you're doing? I mean, do you enjoy being a detective?"

She knew he heard that clearly by the look of concentration on his face.

"I don't know," he said. "I enjoyed being a constable — and I thought I made a damn good one — but I was working for that detective's badge. That was what I really wanted. But not without the experience, not without having really earned it. And not without the respect of my fellow officers."

It was hard for him to get that out. Clara thought now she was getting somewhere. He continued.

"It's not the way I wanted it to happen, and I wouldn't have wanted it if I were … damaged. But I took it anyway. Now I know I shouldn't have. But I can't step down; I can't demote myself. I'm not going out that way."

That sounded a bit better.

"Close that case, Henry." She stood up. "And let me know about your doctor and a referral."

"Can I give you a ride back to your apartment?"

"No, thanks. I could use the walk."

He went to get her coat.

"What made you think I came here to talk about Jack?"

"I don't know," he said. "How's he doing?"

"Better." She wasn't going to go into any details. Her brother didn't have to know how much better McCloskey was doing than he was, that he was probably going full tilt back into the bootleg business, and that the two of them still spent a lot of time together. The less he knew about McCloskey the better.

She kissed her brother on the cheek. "Take care of yourself, Henry. And let me know if you need anything. Don't forget I know people at the hospital."

After he closed the door, he went to the window to watch her walk away. His little sister.

Fields pulled a folded newspaper clipping out of his trouser pocket. He re-read it for the umpteenth time then crumpled it into a ball and threw it into the corner.

THREAT TO BUMP OFF MOUNTIE HEAD

Sergeant Birtwhistle Too Active, Anonymous Letter States

With death as a penalty, if his activities against moonshiners of a certain creed in the Border Cities are continued, Sergeant Archie Birtwhistle, in charge of the Essex County detachment of the RCMP, today received a threatening letter postmarked Detroit.

The letter complained that recent arrests were made against members of a certain creed, solely, and that the RCMP detachment had maintained a system of persecution against this creed for some time. The only arrests that Sergeant Birtwhistle could connect with the letter was in regard to several peddlers of foreign extraction who had been caught smuggling moonshine whisky from across the river. The letter fairly bristles with horrid means of getting rid of Sergeant Birtwhistle's detachment and concludes with the statement that if there is any more interference, Sergeant Birtwhistle is to be "bumped off."

The sergeant received the proposal of his demise with considerable amusement and states that he is not taking the matter seriously. The handwriting in the letter was disguised, and there was no clue that would lead to the possible identity of the writer. The Detroit police, however, were notified, purely as a matter of form.

Chapter 25

A PEARL OF GREAT PRICE

Afternoon

Shorty had been trying to reach McCloskey by telephone at the hotel, and then, just as he was about to hang up for the third time on the switchboard operator at the British-American, his boss came walking in the front door.

"Shorty? Where are you?"

"No names. Listen, I'm in a drugstore across the street from the theatre, and I've got her with me. She wants to have a conversation."

"So have a conversation."

"With you."

"Has she told you anything?"

"No."

"Should I meet you?"

"No, she wants to come to you."

"So bring her over," said McCloskey.

Pause.

"We might have a problem," said Shorty.

"Oh?" McCloskey's wheels were turning. There was another pause. "You know who to go to, right?"

"Yeah, I just wanted to bring you up to speed and clear it with you first."

"All right then, just do it. I'll wait by the phone."

Click.

Through his own bootlegging activity with his old boss, Lieutenant Green, McCloskey would occasionally have to do business with a fellow in Detroit who hired out girls for special occasions, and sometimes these special occasions were in the Border Cities. White girls, negro girls, big and small girls. Leander Hartshorn (if that was his real name) of East Jefferson Avenue ran a house where he operated not so much as a madam but as a talent and booking agent. Not only did he have wigs, dresses, hair, and props, but since his business expanded to the Border Cities, catering to the bootleggers, auto executives, and liquor barons, he had to get into another trade, that of false identification and what he called "transportation."

McCloskey's business was to either supply Hartshorn directly with liquor, or if the special occasion happened to be on this side of the river, he would make sure it was a wet one. McCloskey and his boss were never involved with the girls. They were simply the caterers, so to speak. There were a few roadhouses involved.

Shorty and Pearl's ferry kissed the Windsor dock at around four. They timed their arrival for dusk. They sweated a few beads at customs and then cooled as they shuffled up the hill to the British-American.

"Where's Jack keeping tonight?" asked Shorty. "He's expecting us."

"He's in 2C," said the girl at the desk. She knew Shorty; she didn't know the girl.

Pearl was just starting to warm up. She unbelted her coat and folded down the fur collar. But she kept her hat down low, still afraid of being seen. Shorty asked if she was all right.

"Yeah, I'm good."

"You'd tell me if there was any real trouble, right?"

"Yeah," she said, "I'd tell you."

You're lying.

Shorty still wasn't entirely sure what he was dealing with. Pearl wouldn't talk, not in big words at least — just little ones that were easy to shuffle across the playing board. He knocked on the door of 2C and tried to look solid, like the boss's number one. McCloskey opened it wide but said nothing as they stepped into the room. Pearl removed her chapeau.

"Is that really you, Pearl?"

"Yeah, it's me."

No one knew what to say after that. And then Shorty spoke up. "It was a good show."

And then Pearl blurted out, "I'm real sorry Charlie tried to kill you, Jack."

McCloskey smiled. "Let's just sit down," he said.

It was one of the nicer rooms. Simple and with newer furnishings, but nothing like the Prince Edward. This was your father's Prince Edward Hotel. There was a round table with four chairs in the corner near the window. McCloskey would have the occasional meeting here, when he required more privacy than the bar or to have a card game with a few of the boys.

"Talk to me, Pearl."

Sitting, she pulled her coat off her shoulders and let it drape over the top of the chair. She looked like she'd just stepped out a movie picture, but worse.

"I'm in some trouble, Jack."

"I figured that."

"Ever heard of a guy named William Taylor, William Desmond Taylor?"

"He in our line of work?"

Shorty just watched the volleys.

"No, not exactly. He was in pictures, a director."

"This is back in Hollywood, I guess."

"Yeah."

"He making trouble for you?"

"Well, no. He's dead. Here, let me finish."

Pearl told the story about how a year ago Taylor was murdered in his home in Los Angeles. There was an investigation, sloppy at first and inconclusive, which only got the morality squad fired up. People were demanding Hollywood clean up its act, so to speak. Newspapermen came from all over the country, looking for vice and scandal, only making it worse for the industry and even worse for the investors. They got to the studios' heads and persuaded law enforcement to call off the dogs.

"And then something happened," said Pearl. "I guess the lawmen decided to approach the problem from a different angle. In the early part of the investigation they uncovered a lot of drugs going around.

"That became a more effective way of getting to the problem. So police turned over that rock and found all manner of worms, parasites, and vermin. It was a whole new ball game. The case reopened in December when a raid in New York uncovered connections to what now appeared to be a nationwide dope ring.

"Taylor was trying to get these guys to stop selling drugs to the actors," said Pearl. "They think that's why he got killed."

McCloskey, halfway through his cigar, leaned forward. "And what's this got to do with you, Pearl?"

Shorty was feeling the heat, but he was trying not to show it. Maybe he should have dragged his boss across the river rather than bring Pearl, a.k.a. Nora Sullivan of Plum Street, Detroit, into their territory.

"There were some drug raids ... back in Los Angeles. Some of my girlfriends got picked up. These guys — the cops — they're crazy. They're like a dog with a bone. Like the Prohibition officers here — only worse. They're serious and they mean business, Jack. I swear, if you're in the business — the pictures, that is — all you got to do is have shared a dressing room with someone or worked under this or that director, and you get hauled in. I don't need trouble like that, Jack. I got scared, and I just wanted to come home."

McCloskey looked at Shorty, Shorty looked back. He knew McCloskey didn't need any of this, none of it. It would get neither of them any further ahead. But here they were.

"What makes you think you might be in some kind of trouble?"

Pearl started playing with the long string of beads hanging around her neck.

"I may have been at a couple of parties ... known a couple of girls ... I got tipped off by them, you know, that the investigators might come calling. It got quiet ... I was getting a lot of work when I was out there. And then nothing. No one would talk to me, no one would return my agent's calls — or so he said. It was like I was going to get hauled in next — but I didn't do nothing, Jack, nothing like that. You know me, right, Jack?"

Yeah, thought McCloskey, *I know you.*

"Jack," she said, "I just wanted to come home. Now I know all that stuff's not for me."

"So what are you going to do now?" he said.

"When I left Hollywood, Los Angeles, wherever, I worked my way east with touring vaudeville companies and revues. I learned a lot from being in the pictures and working in shows. I was thinking I might start my own little club, you know, me and a few girls providing the live entertainment, and someone like you supplying the booze."

"Sounds like you already got it all figured out. Except for getting across the border."

"When I saw Shorty, that's when I really got to thinking. I guess he kind of saved me."

"You're not saved yet, Pearl. Enough of your sob story; I had Shorty bring you here so that you could tell me something about Charlie Baxter. First of all, where is he?"

"Honestly, Jack, I don't know."

"When's the last time you saw him?"

She sunk back in her chair, threw her head back, and searched the ceiling for an answer. Better this than the interrogation room at the Los Angeles or Detroit Police Department. She faced McCloskey again. "Got anything to drink?"

"When's the last time you saw Charlie Baxter?"

She started making little circles on the coffee table top with her finger. McCloskey was about to slap her hand off her wrist when she said, "The night that everything happened, you know, at Davies' house, Charlie and I were out on a riverboat cruise with some friends. This was after Davies sent me back upstairs to the suite at the hotel. He only wanted me to decorate his arm while he talked business over dinner with these guys from Detroit. I don't know who they were and it didn't matter to me. Anyway, earlier, Charlie and I had agreed to meet up for this cruise." She smiled. "It was fun." She was sitting with her hands in her lap now, staring at the smeared tabletop. "We were back on dry land well before the storm started. We didn't want to say good night, but we didn't know if we could go back to the Prince Edward. We got in Charlie's car and just drove around for a while, thinking of hitting a roadhouse, maybe in the west end, you know, out of sight. We wondered together if Davies had put two and two together yet. Maybe he didn't really care about me, but he might care about being made a fool of by the likes of Charlie, an ex-lumberjack. We never knew. Maybe someone had already seen us and it was too late. We were getting careless. Even if we couldn't go back, we had no idea how to move forward.

"I guess we weren't quite ready to cut with Davies. It was still pretty cozy, you know? Anyway, Davies had given Charlie the night off, so it was just me that needed a story should he come back to the suite and I wasn't there. I planned to tell him that a couple of my girlfriends, bored, called up to the room and were asking if I wanted to come out and visit some new blind pig in the west end. I'd probably use Daisy, who had been on the boat with us, as an alibi. I'd telephoned her as soon as we got to the Dominion House.

"That's about when the storm started, so we hunkered down over a plate of chicken wings and beer. It seemed like it would never let up." She looked at McCloskey. "Remember how bad it was?"

McCloskey grinned. He remembered almost drowning in it.

She continued. "It was late when it finally cleared. We stayed at the D-H for a bit longer, and then we could see people were starting to head home, like it was all clear. And then this guy comes in with a story. He made money running beer, real beer, between roadhouses, and got caught in the storm at Wolfe's, way east. When the storm cleared, he left, and on his way back to Sandwich he passed what looked to be some sort of crime scene. He said all kinds of police were outside this house on Riverside Drive. When he slowed down to ask one of the cops what was going on, the uniform was too busy trying to keep people away. All the cop said was that Richard Davies had been killed. End of story, get lost. The guy, who was stopping in at the D-H for a nightcap, told anyone who would listen the story.

"Charlie immediately drove me to Daisy's place downtown, saying he was going to lie low, maybe make some queries, and contact me in the morning if it was all clear for him.

"When I didn't see or hear from him in the morning, I figured there was some kind of trouble. Then nothing in the afternoon. I didn't leave Daisy's place or make any phone calls. Daisy stayed put too — no, she ducked out to get a newspaper.

"Then Charlie appeared at the door, not long after five. He looked awful. Shaken. He said we had to leave town, but he didn't say why. That's when I reminded him about my dream of living in California, of making a go in the pictures. He liked the sound of that and told me this was probably our cue to leave.

"But then he said he didn't want to go all the way to California. He said he still had some business to take care of in the Border Cities. By 'get out of town,' I knew he meant across the river, over the border somewhere. He also said he would eventually have to get back into the Border Cities again somehow, but only when the time was right. I kept asking him what he was talking about, but he said he didn't want to get me into any trouble. He said going to California sounded like a great idea, that I should go and he would catch up with me. He said we could stay in touch through Daisy. I told him I had no money, no means. He took care of that; he had some cash on him and said he might be able to wire me some more. We said our goodbyes and our see-you-laters, but that was the last I ever saw or heard of Charlie. I heard nothing through Daisy and I never heard from him while I was on the Coast.

"Daisy and I did stay in touch. She's the one that told me in a letter that witnesses saw Charlie shoot a man at Michigan Central Station, here in town, and that man turned out to be you. Apparently, you were a goner, but somehow you pulled through. I'm glad you did, Jack, and like I said, I'm awful sorry Charlie did that to you. I have no idea why he did it. Do you?"

"No, I don't. So Daisy never mentioned anything else about Charlie? She never saw him after that?"

"She didn't, but there were always rumours."

"Rumours like what?" said McCloskey.

"Rumours like people spotting Charlie here and there in the Border Cities. But she didn't know Charlie or anyone he hung out with, and she was sure none of these people spreading the rumours did either, so she never knew what to believe."

"What did they say he was doing when they saw him? Where was it exactly they saw him?"

"I don't know. None of it really meant anything to Daisy so she had no details. And to tell you the truth, I was over him so stopped asking. Jack, that was months ago, what's the big deal all of a sudden?"

"It's a little complicated, Pearl. Listen, I can't let you stay here. Have you been in touch with Daisy?"

"Yeah, she's been to see the show, and we've gone shopping a couple times together."

"Been over there long?"

"No," she said. "The company arrived only two weeks ago, and the show only started last week."

"I'll drive you over to her place right now. Do you think she'll be home?"

Pearl thought for a moment, trying to remember what day it was. "Yeah, she should be. But can't I phone her first?"

"No, I don't want to take any chances."

Chapter 26

FIRE AND ICE

The night watchman was just finishing his rounds when his wandering flashlight lit upon a body half-buried halfway up one of the several coal chutes that emptied onto the floor at shipping and receiving. He telephoned the police immediately from the emergency box outside the office.

After the incident at Maiden Lane and the one involving the Indian and the dairy horse, the call didn't get dropped into just any constable's lap; it got forwarded straight to Campbell. They reached him at his apartment, and Campbell in turn left an urgent message at the British-American for Jack McCloskey. He had a feeling about this one.

It was a distance, so he took the Essex this time, plowing fresh snow and skidding through slick intersections. Windsor Ice & Coal was a sort of neighbourhood landmark. The complex was south on McDougall, in the heart of the city's factory district. The massive ice barn standing on cinder blocks, its basement sunk deep in the earth, was right at the corner, and the eight silos that spelled FORD COKE were lined up directly behind it, parallel to the road. Campbell slowed before he lost control and turned left onto Shepherd, dumping the Essex in a snowdrift he could only guess was somewhere near the curb.

He stepped down from the car and shuffled through the dark over slush and snow collections — it was yet another overcast sky and there were no surrounding homes throwing any stray light to guide him. Several times he almost tripped and fell. It partly had to do with his legs moving faster than everything else attached to them.

Wake up, wake up. Too often he was yelling at himself inside his head, but outside it was a different dead quiet than what he was used to; it was factories asleep between shifts in the middle of a harsh winter. He scanned the industrial landscape and spotted some fresh snow covered in an amber glow on this side of a doorway in the middle distance. He shuffled over hastily and banged on the door with a gloved fist. When a face appeared in the frosted glass he produced his badge.

"Detective Campbell."

He had become used to shouting over the wind, but there was no wind tonight. It was now a force of habit. Campbell thought for a moment about how one becomes conditioned to certain things, and then he looked down and noticed he was only wearing one glove. He searched his pockets for its match, but before he found it another personage, whom he could only assume was a night watchman appeared, opened the door, and allowed to him enter.

He felt the need to repeat his half-delirious claim, if only to provide himself with some kind of an anchor. "I'm Detective Campbell." Unable to find the match, he removed his one glove and stuffed it in its overcoat partnered pocket.

"Well," said the night watchman, "you really wouldn't be anyone else now, would you?"

Campbell, even after the breakneck drive with the window down, was still struggling to come to his senses. If anyone, the night watchman in particular, had asked him how he got here, he would have had to struggle for an answer.

You wouldn't be anyone else now, would you?

Campbell knew he was coming around because it suddenly struck him what a philosophical question that might be coming from a person covered in coal dust and pigeon shit.

Pigeons?

"No, no it wouldn't be anyone else," he said. "You found something?"

"Someone, more like. The name's Reg."

Reg held out his hand and Campbell took it and gave it back.

"Nice to meet you, Reg. Can we ..."

"Yes, yes this way." Reg started hobbling along. "I see you brought your own torch."

"Flashlight?"

"It's over 'ere."

"What is?"

Reg looked over his shoulder. "Our interloper."

They were nearing their destination when there was another knock at the door. The two looked at each other; Campbell turned his head sharply but the rest of his body followed at a slightly slower pace.

Note: Need to be eating and sleeping more. Everything's becoming disconnected.

"I think I know who it might be," Campbell said out loud.

Reg duplicated Campbell's about-face while Campbell leaned on the walkway railing. The detective pretended to play with his boot for a moment while he regained himself and then they proceeded.

"Let me get this," he said as he opened the door. "Reg, this man might be able to assist us in this matter."

McCloskey brushed the snow off his arms and shoulders, then removed his homburg and gave it a few gentle shakes until it seemed presentable again.

"What's the story?"

"Reg here," Campbell said, "has something to show us."

They followed the watchman's flashlight through the bowels of the coal facility until they were standing on the main floor of shipping and receiving. The only light in the space was coming from a bulb that hung over the desk behind a framed, soot-smeared glass partition.

The night watchman's flashlight was pointing at the side of a head. There was also a hand. The body appeared twisted under the coal rubble. "I found him 'ere," said Reg, "just like this. I didn't touch 'im. Well, I couldn't get to 'im."

"There isn't a conveyer?" asked Campbell.

"No," said Reg.

Campbell handed his flashlight to McCloskey and climbed the standing river of dusty coal. He wasn't going to wait for Laforet this time, though the doctor was already on his way.

"Can I have some more light up here?" Campbell was working in his own shadow. McCloskey and the night watchman closed in and held their flashlights up at arms' length, aimed at Campbell and his efforts.

Campbell pulled at the exposed hand and the body easily came loose, sending both him and the body tumbling backwards down the chute and onto the apron of coal that met the shallow pit at the bottom. The detective stood up but his footing was still unstable and he fell backward onto the chute. Reg gave him a hand and he managed to right himself and drag the body by one of its arms onto the concrete floor. He flipped it over and McCloskey shone the flashlight on its face.

"Lapointe," he said.

He knelt down at one side of Lapointe's head and Campbell knelt down at the other.

There was a banging on the door.

"Just in time." Campbell looked up at Reg. "That will be my colleague, Dr. Laforet. Please, would you show him in?"

The night watchman followed the request.

Campbell waited until Reg was out of earshot. "Lapointe is another friend of yours?"

"Yes," said McCloskey, unable to take his eyes off the body.

"When was the last time you saw him?"

"Monday night ... downtown at the hotel."

Footsteps could be heard.

"We need to talk," said Campbell and then he stood to greet Laforet.

"Doctor."

"Campbell. I can think of better habits to form other than meeting you at scenes like this in the dead of night in winter." Laforet set down his case and peeled off his gloves, exchanging them for another pair from his case. "What do we have here?"

"His name's Lapointe," said Campbell. "Another acquaintance of our friend here." Campbell still wanted to help maintain McCloskey's anonymity.

Without looking at McCloskey, Laforet said, "You're a

dangerous man to know," and then he crouched down over the body.

Laforet shined his flashlight up and down the length of the body and then settled on Lapointe's face. It could have been his imagination, but even with Lapointe's eyes closed, he could have sworn he saw a look of horror in it. Lapointe's jaw was open slightly and his throat was rigid. It looked like it might even be distended. Laforet gripped the jaw and turned Lapointe's head slightly toward him so they were facing each other.

"Hold this." He gave his flashlight to Campbell, who set his own down.

Laforet pried open Lapointe's jaw.

"What is it?" asked Campbell.

"It's filled with coal," said Laforet, and then he felt Lapointe's throat. He opened his coat and shirt. He couldn't tell for sure, but he thought Lapointe's ribs looked cracked. There were bruises under the grease and coal dust.

"Coal dust under his shirt?" said Campbell.

Laforet gently felt Lapointe's chest and torso, and then he stood up.

"The ambulance is on its way," he said. "Let's not move him again until they get here." He turned to the night watchman. "Can they back into here somehow?"

Reg looked toward the two garage doors that led to ramps up street-level. "They dug them out this morning; they might still be clear enough."

"All right," said Campbell, "go out to the corner and flag them down. They'll have no idea where they're going."

Reg complied. They waited until they heard the door slam. Laforet took Campbell aside, safe enough from McCloskey's ear but not clear enough for him not to get the gist of the conversation.

"I think I'm pretty much through with taking a clinical, bemused, semi-professional stance with all of this, Campbell. Bodies are piling up in an unfinished morgue like we're seeing some sort of natural disaster. Is that what it is? Tell me what's going on."

Campbell looked dazed.

"Wake up." Laforet was coming too close to slapping him, and as much as he wanted to, he couldn't because he knew that McCloskey was watching them.

"I don't know," said Campbell. "I don't know what's going on."

They paused for a few moments of idle chatter, some space, and a chance to decompress before returning to McCloskey. Something was wrong with all of this, thought Campbell. But no one was talking. Why? He would have to speak with McCloskey first thing tomorrow, privately.

McCloskey watched Laforet bundle himself up and then make his exit. Campbell approached McCloskey.

"The doctor has to make another call. I'll wait for the ambulance."

McCloskey nodded and Campbell continued.

"We're going to have a conversation, first thing tomorrow morning."

"All right," said McCloskey, probably thinking the same thing, but with some reservations. "Where? The British-American?"

"No, not there."

"Your place?"

"You mean my apartment? No, not there either."

"And I'm not going to be seen with you in any of the local diners or roadhouses."

"I have to pick up a book tomorrow at Copeland's. Meet me there at ten."

"Copeland's? The bookstore on the Avenue?"

"Yes, in the Victoria Building," said Campbell.

"Okay. I can go now?"

Though he suspected there was no threat of this happening, Campbell had to say it anyway. "Just don't leave town."

Whenever they needed to communicate with someone, it was through verbal messages passed from strangers in the street. Someone you wouldn't recognize would stop you, and it was never the same person twice. You knew where it was coming from, though. You knew it was coming from them. There were certain words these strangers used that always tipped you off. Not exactly a code, more of a vocabulary, with some personal fact thrown in just to let you know they had the right person, that they knew who they were talking to. And then you would never see this person again. Ever. But you would hear from the Guard again, through someone else.

He had been stopped in the street a couple of days ago. Was it Tuesday? A man was walking toward him. He had been exchanging words with a friend, he could see that, and then they were saying their goodbyes, waving at each other as they separated, and the man was smiling, like he was recalling some old joke they had shared. And then he was looking at nothing, nothing but snow-covered sidewalk and shop windows, still smiling to himself. He remembered liking the man's face. He was about to pass this stranger and then the man raised a hand against his shoulder and stopped him. He looked down. The man wasn't smiling any more.

Soon, he said, *you won't hear anything but the ringing.*

What do you mean? he said. *Who are you?*

They had reached inside him, and somehow he knew they

would not let go. Last night they had come to him in his sleep.

They told him to meet him here, in the car barns at the Hydro Electric Railway hub on London Street. They said they would be waiting for him. He did not know who they were or what exactly they wanted, but he was being compelled. They, whoever they were, were real, but it was a reality that could not be fully explained. He kept it all to himself.

And here he was, standing among the idle streetcars. He wandered between them, looking for someone or something. But he heard them before he saw them, more than one, more than two voices, and they were speaking in unison. And he only heard them in his head.

What do you have for us?

He wondered if they could in turn hear his thoughts.

I don't know what you want, he replied.

Yes, they could. They sent him an image. It looked like a key.

It was last in this man's possession.

What followed was like a short kinescope reel playing in his mind's eye. He recognized the man. It was a face no one who ever came across him could easily forget.

He's dead, he said, *lost.*

Not lost, said the voices.

They were shadows. He thought there might be three, maybe four of them. He wasn't sure.

No, they said, *not lost. He was found.* He knew now that he couldn't hide anything from them.

The barn began to hum. He felt it first in his feet, and then in his fingertips, and then the trolley buses started vibrating, and then they shook. There were small bolts of pale blue lightning, twitching spider legs of energy climbing and descending the connections to the overhead lines. He felt the hair on the back of his neck. It was like a burn.

Who has it?

I don't know, he said. *But I'll find out.*

You are close.

Am I? he said. *But if you know all this —*

You must hand it to us. We cannot take it. That is all you need to know. Someone must hand it to us. You are going to do that.

Hand it to you …

They closed around him. They said nothing, but he understood. They were inside his head now. He was their instrument.

I'll find him … I'll find it.

They turned and dissolved in the darkness. Fields waited until he couldn't feel their presence any longer and then he collected himself and headed out. There wouldn't be any more sleep tonight. Perhaps ever.

— *Chapter 27* —

YOU'RE NOT TELLING ME SOMETHING

Thursday morning

Campbell had arrived at Copeland's a little early so that he could get his purchase out of the way first, but the shop was doing brisk business this morning so he had to wait to be served. McCloskey would be here any minute. The girl at the register was completing her sales transactions as quickly as possible while at the same time trying to answer other, less patient customers' questions. The only other staffer on the floor was a young man helping a woman in the poetry section. Judging by the expression on the young

man's face and his body language, Campbell had to guess he was
attempting to wrap things up and move on to his next customer.
The conversation looked, and from the snippets of it he was
overhearing, like it had become a waste of time. What started out
as a discussion about Elizabeth Barrett Browning had somehow
descended into a conversation about the woman's dog.

*That's very interesting, ma'am. I didn't know that about Cocker
Spaniels.*

Campbell heard the jingle of the bell on the door, turned,
and saw McCloskey enter, bundled up and his hat pulled down
low. *He must have walked a distance*, thought Campbell, and then
he wondered from where. He had to find out more about this
man. He could ask Morrison, but he really didn't want to get him
involved in this.

Fields might know something.

When he saw that McCloskey had picked him out, he
nodded at him.

"May I help you?"

Campbell turned his attention back to the sales counter. "Ah
— good morning. I understand another special order of mine has
arrived. I received a phone call."

"And your last name again, sir?"

"Campbell."

"Oh — yes."

The shop girl ducked down below the counter and Campbell
could hear her shifting around the piles of special orders.

"Here it is," she said. She straightened up and slipped off the
order form that was wrapped around it. She checked the title to
confirm it matched.

"*The Magus*?"

"That's the one."

"Will that be all today, Mr. Campbell?"

Campbell turned to McCloskey, who was browsing out of the shop girl's line of view. "Did you want anything?"

McCloskey approached the counter. "They carry the *Daily Racing Form*?"

Vera Maude, thinking she recognized the voice, looked up and over Campbell's shoulder. It was McCloskey. She froze for a moment.

Campbell, knowing what the answer was going to be, decided to be polite and ask anyway. "You wouldn't happen to carry the *Racing Form*, would you?"

"Uh … no, no I'm afraid we don't."

"Thanks," he said, noticing her preoccupation with McCloskey. Campbell figured he was used to that sort of thing. "I guess that'll be it then."

She rang it through, and she had to concentrate on hitting the right keys.

"That'll be $2.75."

"Steep."

"Yeah," said Vera Maude, "rare book." She bagged Campbell's purchase and handed him his change. Campbell checked it before dropping it in his trouser pocket.

"Do you mind if we continue browsing a little?" he asked.

"No" she said, "please go right ahead. And let me know if you need any help."

"It's Vera Maude, right?" said Campbell.

"That's right: Vera Maude." She said it loud enough that McCloskey could hear and watched his face for a reaction. Nothing.

"Thanks again, Vera Maude."

The two men stepped away from the counter and then Campbell said to McCloskey, "There's a little alcove around the corner; we can talk there."

Vera Maude watched them relocate to the children's section.

It was packed with books, some of which faced out on easel-type shelves eye level to a six-year-old. There were also two tiny chairs.

"I thought it might be time for us to lay all our cards on the table," said Campbell, "so to speak."

"That sounds just fine," said McCloskey, "but trust me, I'm not holding that many cards."

"First, I haven't heard anything from Laforet yet about your friend Lapointe. I'm heading over to see him as soon as we're done here, but I don't know if he'll have anything. He's got a lot on his plate right now, as do I. Now let's back up a little. Whoever did this to Lapointe, is it the same people or person that did in your other friend Three Fingers?"

Campbell had McCloskey in a corner, literally and figuratively.

"I can only guess," he said.

"Still no idea who it is, or at least who it might be?" Campbell wasn't going to tell McCloskey about the bootleggers that got tossed from the train on the weekend and what Zahra had to say about that, mostly because he wasn't exactly sure what Zahra was trying to say about that.

McCloskey was hesitating.

"When I'm working multiple cases, one of the first things I look for is a common denominator. So far, McCloskey, you're it." He studied McCloskey's face. "Whoever it is, they're after something, or someone. Is it you?"

McCloskey looked down and noticed an illustrated edition of *Treasure Island* on the easel-shelf.

"You know, if you're becoming some sort of liability to your own crew, it might be in your best interest to bring me on your side. Do you want more of them to die like this for you?"

Campbell was trying to pry the door open.

"There's talk," said McCloskey, "just talk now, there's this other gang, from out of town, and they operate deep, very deep. I don't have names and I couldn't tell you where to find them. If I had any of that kind of information, I can tell you we'd be taking care of this business ourselves."

Campbell relaxed a bit and eased back a little off McCloskey. He believed him. "Okay, now, what is it they're after? What are they trying to accomplish? Is this some kind of gang war?"

"Can't really be a war if you don't even know who your enemy is, can it?"

"Well, you might not know them, but they certainly seem to know you, or at least your crew. Let me ask you again, what do they want with you and your boys?"

Yes, thought Campbell, *these are also your boys, and you're responsible for them, and you know it.*

"It might have something to do with Richard Davies," said McCloskey.

"Richard Davies? But all of that happened months ago. This other gang, did they know him? Did they work for him?"

"Again, we don't know."

Again, Campbell was believing him, at least about what McCloskey was telling him. But instinct was also telling him that McCloskey was leaving something out. What was he hiding? The detective just looked at him, trying to see if he could silently squeeze anything else out of this man. For a former pugilist, a veteran of the war, and a somewhat notorious gangster who survived what should have been a successful attempt on his life — he had been reading up on McCloskey — he was looking a little uncomfortable, if not a little nervous. Something was wrong; this was something new for McCloskey.

"Detective, I really can't bring you on side right now. Don't ask me why, because it's nothing I can fully explain — yet. I hear everything you're saying. Trust me, all we're doing is playing defence. If we need your help, I know where to reach you. I know you have to investigate these two deaths, and I won't stop you, but I'm telling you right now, you won't get very far."

"So I should just let these two cases go cold?"

"You know I can't tell you how to do your job."

"If there is one more incident like this involving one of your boys, I'm bringing Morrison in on it. I think you know Detective Morrison."

What McCloskey knew was that Morrison would like nothing more than to ride him and his gang, all his contacts, his whole business, even the one he was right now just trying to get off the ground, until the whole thing was in tatters, and it would be just for the fun of it.

"Yeah," said McCloskey, "I know Morrison."

"Hmm. You know, I think we're beginning to understand each other."

It was McCloskey's turn to relax a bit. It felt good to get at least a little of this off his chest, though it still felt sometimes like someone was standing on it.

"You always use this for your interrogation room?"

"I got places all over town," said Campbell.

They stepped out of the alcove and started heading for the door. McCloskey wasn't even going to do up his coat.

When she saw them, Vera Maude walked around the counter and up to McCloskey, tentatively, straightening her cheaters, dropping her hands at her side, swaying a little, nervously.

"Jack? Jack McCloskey?"

McCloskey looked down at Vera Maude and then over at Campbell. "Um, yeah," said McCloskey. She looked harmless enough.

She paused to let him take a longer look at her, and then said, "It's me, Vera Maude. Remember? Last summer?"

McCloskey looked at Campbell again, and then back at Vera Maude. "No, you must be mistaken."

"But you are Jack McCloskey, though, right?"

"Yes, but …" He was slowly shaking his head.

Vera Maude thought he looked a little uneasy. Maybe he remembered, but this wasn't the right time, not with Mr. Campbell standing next to him.

"Um, sorry then," said Vera Maude. "Thanks … have a nice day." Not wanting to make any more of a scene, she turned and walked back toward the counter, bumping into its corner as she rounded it.

"Do you know her?" said Campbell.

McCloskey was already searching his mind. "No … I mean, I don't think so … I don't know."

Well, thought Campbell, *I guess you can't be expected to remember all of them.*

"Let's leave separately," said the detective.

"You first," said McCloskey.

Campbell looked back at Vera Maude and then said to McCloskey, who was still studying her, "Is it all coming back to you?"

"We'll talk later," said McCloskey, still distracted.

Campbell headed out. McCloskey waited a few minutes then proceeded up the Avenue in the opposite direction. He needed to talk to Clara again.

Mr. Copeland appeared from behind his desk. "Oh, did I miss the detective?"

"Detective? That was just Mr. Campbell."

Copeland smiled. "Detective Campbell, Miss Maguire, of the Windsor Police."

Well, that explains a few things, thought Vera Maude. *Wait — with Jack McCloskey? Jack McCloskey.*

"Are you all right, Miss Maguire?"

"Fine, just fine, thank you."

"What's the matter? What's wrong?"

"I'm not sure," said McCloskey.

"Did something happen?"

"Yes — no — I'm not sure." He stopped pacing the room and looked at Clara, seated in her reading chair. "I'll have that drink now."

"What drink?"

"Not the ginger ale."

"Sit down, Jack."

Clara went into kitchen and poured him a rye.

"Here. Sorry, I'm out of ice."

"That's all right."

She sat back down in her reading chair. "Now let's start again. Where are you just coming from?"

"Copeland's."

"Copeland's? The bookstore? You were not."

"What's that supposed to mean?"

"Forget it, I'm sorry. Go on."

"A guy I know called a meeting there."

Clara was biting her tongue. McCloskey continued.

"Anyway, there was this girl there, a shop girl, and just as me and this guy were leaving, she stops me, to say hello or something, I don't know."

"So?"

"So she knew my name," he said, and then finished his drink.

"I still don't get it."

"It seemed like she really knew me from somewhere, and I have absolutely no idea who she was. Her face didn't look familiar at all."

"Was she cute?"

"Well, yeah."

"Would you like another?"

He held up his glass.

"Keep talking," she said.

"That's not all. You know what the kicker was?"

Clara returned and handed him his glass. "What?"

"She mentioned last summer. She said we met last summer."

It took Clara a moment for it to dawn on her. She leaned forward in her chair.

"You think she really recognized you from somewhere?"

"I'm convinced. She was really sweet. Didn't look the type that would be trying to pull one over, I mean, just a girl in a bookstore, right?"

"Did she tell you her name?"

"Yeah, yeah, it was two names … Vera something … Vera Maude. I kept repeating it to myself after I left the shop."

"Do you think this has something to do with this gap in your memory?"

"I don't know." He sat back. "Might be a piece to that puzzle."

"So she didn't mention the hospital or anything like that?"

"No, nothing else."

"Well, why didn't you ask her for more details while you were there?"

"At first I thought it was nothing, and then I thought it was a bit too strange. And then I started to wonder."

"Why don't you go back and ask her for more details?"

"Oh, I don't know."

"Jack, come on. A few days ago you were in here anxious and confused about this gap in your memory that's suddenly bothering you again, and here's someone practically fallen into your lap that might be able to put it all together for you. Why won't you just go talk to her?"

"I'm telling you, I don't know, it's just that —"

"Why, Jack McCloskey, you're afraid, aren't you? Killer McCloskey, afraid of a little shop girl."

"I'm not afraid, especially of no little shop girl."

"Well then, what is it?"

"Maybe … well maybe, now that door's opened a little, I might not want to see what's on the other side. I mean, everything's just fine right now, right? So why ruin it?" He looked up from the carpet and saw Clara's disapproval. "What?"

"Everything's not all right, Jack, and you know it."

They took a break. Clara knew she couldn't push him too hard on this because he would just close up again.

"So who was this guy you had the meeting with?"

"You won't believe me if I tell you."

"Try me."

McCloskey finished his drink. "A police detective."

Clara's jaw dropped and she leaned forward. "Oh, this just gets better and better. You're having casual meetings in bookstores with police detectives now. Does he know who you are?"

"Of course he does."

"Is he dirty?"

"No, no, I don't believe he is."

Clara was squinting at him. "What's his name?"

"Campbell."

"Nope, don't know him. I'm sure Henry does, though. Do you want me to ask Henry about him?"

"No. I just want to keep this between me and Campbell."

"What was the meeting about?"

"I can't tell you."

"Are you in some kind of trouble?"

"Not the kind you're thinking of, I'm sure."

"What kind then?"

"I said, I can't tell you. I'll fill you in when it all shakes out."

"Which will be when?"

"Soon, I hope."

"Is it bad?"

"You read about the body on the horse?"

"Yeah."

"You read about the body at Windsor Ice and Coal?"

"No."

"Probably didn't make the morning edition. Anyway, those were two of my boys."

"Oh, Jack. Who did it?"

"That's the thing, we haven't got a clue. I'm not saying any more."

"Okay," said Clara.

He stood up.

"What's the hurry?"

"I just remembered I've got some furniture being delivered to the new office shortly. I promised I'd help the guys move it in."

"How's the shoulder?"

He was walking toward his coat. "Right as rain."

She got up to unlock the door for him.

"Take care of yourself, Jack."

"You bet. Thanks for the drink."

Chapter 28

A DARKNESS FROM WITHIN

Laforet greeted Campbell at reception; he started talking when they got inside the elevator.

"I opened up Lapointe. His entire digestive tract, his lungs, were packed with coal. You have to see this. I haven't finished cleaning him up yet, so your timing is perfect."

Campbell drew back the brass scissor gates, and then the heavy brass door. He closed it up behind him and Laforet moved quickly toward the swinging door into his lab. The doctor was already tying his apron behind his back by the time Campbell caught up.

"How is that even possible?"

The room was dim except for where Laforet was working.

"Come."

The mortuary table that Lapointe was on stood apart from the other tables, near one of the long counters. Two very bright surgical lights stood over the body, shining down on it. A smaller, white enamel table, also on wheels and positioned an arm's reach away, had a top no larger than the tray that was resting on it. There were a few instruments on it as well as Laforet's rubber gloves. He stretched them back on, pulling them up to his wrists.

The doctor had indeed opened up Lapointe. He was cut from his Adam's apple to his pubic bone, his ribs cut laterally and chest plate removed. Campbell was leaning over the body cavity, his hands behind his back.

"I never would have believed it unless I saw it for myself. The physical evidence suggests the coal coming from the inside of the body out, as if it expanded from within him, rather than it being stuffed into him at either end."

"The physical evidence?"

"The way the organ tissue was stretched and torn, the rib damage." Laforet was shaking his head. "The victim's tongue should have been jammed down his throat — it wasn't. His stomach, his esophagus, his throat, everything I'm looking at is consistent with a body producing internally a foreign matter that found the paths of least resistance, forcing itself out."

Campbell was letting his eyes rake over the sooty organs. Without looking up, he said, "Based on what you're telling me, I'm surprised the coal didn't just burst through his abdomen."

"So am I. But there weren't any particularly large pieces. What I've pulled out of him so far is in that washbasin."

Laforet gestured toward a medium-size basin over on the countertop. It was almost overflowing with coal. Campbell hadn't noticed it in the dim light. He walked over to have a closer look.

"You'll notice there are no pieces with sharp points or jagged edges. None are much bigger than a walnut. A lot of it's like gravel, some of it's like sand. That's why it's taking me so long."

Lying next to the basin were Lapointe's chest plate and his other major organs, everything but his lungs and gastrointestinal tract. Campbell gave them a cursory glance.

"Nothing else unusual?"

"Not that I could see. An otherwise healthy specimen."

Campbell came back around. "I know this will sound like a stupid question, but you know I have to ask it: How did he die?"

"Choked or suffocated. Take your pick. Whatever it was, I think it started slowly, and then finished him off quickly."

"What's your report going to say?"

"I don't know yet. I'm not finished. I was about to remove the stomach and bowels and attempt to flush them out."

They were already small slits in them.

"One more time, Laforet: How is this possible?"

The doctor rested his hands on the edge of the table and leaned forward, out of the dim light of the room and into the surgical light.

"I don't know," he said. "It just isn't possible."

"And yet ..." said Campbell, looking down again at the body splayed open in front of them. "Now you know how I feel."

Laforet knew what Campbell was referring to. "I'm sorry about last night."

"Now you have an idea where my mind is right now."

"Not entirely," smiled Laforet. "You have to leave at least some of yourself to mystery."

"It's only natural," said Campbell. He paused. "You're the

one who pulled that bullet out of Jack McCloskey last summer, weren't you?"

Laforet stiffened a little. "Yes. He's lucky to be alive."

"Point blank range, from what I understand."

"He lost a lot of blood."

"The other night, at the stable, was that the first time he'd seen you since then?"

"Yes, well … it was a long recovery. I was concerned, and I visited him a number of times after the surgery to follow up."

"It looked like he might not make it?"

Laforet gave a sigh. "Oh, I knew he'd make it, physically. Once he fully regained consciousness, I spoke with him. He had no recollection of the event that brought him to me, the trip to the hospital or the surgery, or his recovery. There was a convalescence … I always thought he was recovering from more than the bullet wound."

"He's a vet, isn't he?"

"Yes," said Laforet, "as well as a few other things."

Campbell glanced over toward the other tables, still parked at the end of the room. "And his other friend over there, the one they call Three Fingers, his wounds, don't you find them as curious to you as this man's?"

"They are."

"Remember what Zahra said yesterday morning? 'There will be more'?"

"It's been echoing in the back of my head all morning."

"I just met with McCloskey. He doesn't have much to say about all of this — not yet, at least."

"If you don't mind my asking, is he hiding something?"

"Definitely."

"Does he know who the assailant or assailants might be?"

"He says he doesn't, and I believe him on that point."

"But you have other questions?"

"Yes."

Laforet knew that when Campbell started with the one-word answers he should quit with the questions. He gave Campbell some breathing space, and then he opened up again.

"I wonder if when Zahra said there would be more Lapointe was all she meant. I don't need to tell you this, Laforet, but I'd rather none of the details about his and Three Fingers's deaths leave this room. I'll only share them with McCloskey if I think it will get him to open up."

Laforet nodded.

"I'll show myself out."

Chapter 29

BETWEEN TWO WORLDS

Vera Maude was glad she didn't have to wander too far in this weather to grab some lunch: Andros Brothers' Confectionery was on the same block, just the other side of Woolworths.

Winter wasn't half over, but she was already getting tired of bundling up and burying herself under layers; all she did before heading out was tuck her hair into her red suede tam, give it a peak, and throw on her coat without bothering with the belt. And nix to her gloves and muffler. When she got outside, she shoved her hands deep in her coat pockets and folded one and then the other panel across her front.

There was a wind, but it wasn't bringing any snow, at least not yet. Of course she had to bump into a few shoppers going in and coming out of the five-and-dime because she had her head down while they had their hopes up. She caught her beacon — the Andros Brothers' neon sign — just in time before passing it, and it signalled CANDY, SODA, AND LIGHT LUNCHES.

Andros Brothers' wasn't really much of a sit-down kind of place, not like the other Border City diners and cafeterias. For starters, it was too narrow, and it had no real kitchen. Inside the entrance and to the left was a cluster of small, marble-topped bistro tables with curved metal chairs. Patrons willing to brave the occasional gust from the open door occupied a few of them. The tin ceiling, painted white, reminded Vera Maude of a shop in SoHo she would visit when she needed to calm her raging sweet tooth. The candy and sweets also kept her off the cigarettes. To her right and after the space on the floor reserved for those kind and generous enough to take a number was the showcase featuring today's freshest, most eye-catching confections. While gawking, she was buffeted by bodies moving in all directions, making their lunch-break sorties. It reminded her she had better keep moving.

This showcase was joined at a right angle with the main display area and counter that ran the length of the place. The penny candy selection was an organized chaos arranged around the register, enabling the person attending it to keep an eye on any children with particularly sticky fingers. Next was the soda fountain station: a shiny, sweet version of the control panel on a locomotive; and then the lunch counter with its polished colonnade of leather-capped stools. The rear was close and humid, packed with patrons and insulated with the smells of hot lunch and damp wool. Even with the traffic moving the way it was, she wondered if she would be able to get a seat. When she turned around, prepared to eat her lunch huddled by the door, she noticed the first stool after the soda fountain was now available. Someone was heading toward it. She hustled, nearly sliding on the greasy slush that covered half the floor. She won the race, much to the chagrin of the young bank teller from next door.

"Hi," she called to the man behind the counter who looked as if he had been rolled into the apron he was wearing, "do you have any soup?"

"Of course I got soup. I got a nice beef barley and a French Canadian pea soup. I make both this morning."

"I'll have the pea soup."

"Sure."

"Oh — excuse me, are there biscuits with that?" He was already on the move and it was probably her last chance to place a bid before he was out of earshot. She upped and leaned into it. "And could I get a tea?"

I know how to get served. And I'm not talking court orders.

He turned and gave her a nod without missing a step as he made his way to the soup tureens. *This Andros brother knows how to get people on and off these stools*, thought Vera Maude.

He was back in no time with a piping hot bowl, as wide as it was deep, and a side plate with a couple buttermilk biscuits on it. Vera Maude immediately started stirring the soup, sending a few pieces of the salt pork to the surface. She blew gently on her first steaming, thick spoonful.

Delicious.

She gave it another stir and then started breaking up one of the biscuits, dipping the largest piece first. Relaxing now, she let her mind wander back to the most obvious issue at hand.

So, Jack McCloskey, what's your excuse? Do you really not remember me? I know it was only a few hours out of your busy bootlegging life, but really! How many girls are you going through in any given week? Or am I that forgettable?

The fellow sitting next to Vera Maude was attempting to pry himself from between her and the person sitting on the other side of him. Luckily, she was last on the row and could widen the gap a little. And good thing she wasn't left-handed or this spoonful of pea soup would have ended up on her blouse, leaving a stain that would be like a ticket inviting her male customers to stare at her chest.

She looked around as she continued to spoon the yellow goodness into her mouth, all the while trying to remain conscious of the time. She spotted the Ward's Orange Crush clock on the wall behind the soda fountain station. *Time enough*, she thought.

She turned toward the door to check on the conditions outside, and much to her relief it looked about the same, though now that she was all warmed up inside from the soup, she dreaded heading back out into it. She noticed the ceiling again. A different kind of light was hitting it at this end of the long room. She returned to her soup, thinking about New York again, about the Village, about him.

Out of sight, out of mind. I'm not even going to give him the satisfaction of thinking his name.

"Bill," she said out loud to her soup.

Damn it.

She put her spoon down and pushed the bowl away.

"More?" Half of the Brothers Andros suddenly appeared out of nowhere. He never seemed to stop moving back and forth behind the counter. It was like there a little conveyer belt on the floor back there.

"No, thanks." *I've had enough of him — it. I've had enough of it. He —* "It was delicious."

She managed to get out another "thanks," but he was already

heading back toward the sink where it looked like Mama Andros had her hands full. Vera Maude stopped her mouth with the last piece of biscuit before she embarrassed herself any further.

"Hey, George!"

That got everyone's attention. An older gentleman had just entered, calling out to none other than the Andros brother who'd been waiting on her. It looked like he was some kind of a regular. Next time she'll call him by name, and try not to behave like such a ninny.

Vera Maude slid down off the stool, made sure she still had her gloves and her purse, and headed down to the register. Before the girl totalled it up, Vera Maude asked her to add a dime's worth of Tootsie Rolls.

That should get me through the afternoon.

"Thanks."

Chapter 30

CAN'T FIND THE WORDS

As anxious as Campbell was to get back to Madame Zahra about yesterday morning, he knew he would have to give her some time to regroup, as it were. He also had to remind himself that she ran a business and wasn't at his beck and call, even though she was part of an ongoing "mysterious death" investigation. That's what he insisted everyone in the department refer to it as, though with these last two homicides most people had stopped talking about Kaufman. It was on to the next headline.

This was becoming routine now, and it concerned Campbell

not just a little: Sitting with Zahra in her attic apartment and talking over coffee or tea, his concern was that, especially with the Kaufman case, he might be losing his objectivity. On the other hand, he could feel himself changing, as a detective, that is, and he hoped it might be for the better. He remembered what Laforet had said to him in the past about his methods, his approach to certain cases. Maybe with what had been transpiring over these last several days a new dimension was being added to his skills.

"I'm not going to ask you to come back to the lab with me. I'm not even going to go into any details with you about this latest victim. I will tell you, however, that there are certain similarities between the two cases."

She had a fringed scarf tied over her head, but her hair was left hanging loose down her back. She was wearing no makeup. The blouse she wore looked heavy; there was a shawl wrapped around her shoulders. Her skirt almost touched the floor. One of her legs was folded under her. Sitting there like that, with her hot tea cupped in her hands, Zahra looked as if she was recovering from a terrible cold.

Campbell added, "You had said there would be more."

"Now you wish to know how many more."

"You can't tell me, can you?"

She took another sip from her tea. "No hands touch this body too?"

"There were no markings on it that would suggest that." He leaned a little closer to her. "Zahra, have you ever seen anything like this before?"

"Seen? No, I only hear stories. But where I come from stories … everything is made from stories. They are like water and air, you know?"

"I understand. But the person or people who are doing this, they are not just stories."

"You don't understand. Sometimes, Detective, there is no difference."

"But this is really happening. You've seen the bodies."

"Yes."

He leaned back. "Do you mind if I smoke?"

"If it pleases you."

Campbell lit up the unfinished cigar he had tucked into his breast pocket after breakfast.

"I'd like to share something with you. Something a little more tangible."

She looked sideways at Campbell.

"I spoke with someone this morning who might tie all, or at least some, of this together for us. The two victims that I'm most interested in right now — the one you saw yesterday, Three Fingers, and the one that arrived overnight, Lapointe — worked for him. He has other people working for him right now. That should explain some of the questions I was asking you — I've been trying to figure out if it's a *who* or a *what* this other gang is after. You seemed to feel that there is something in all of this, and I agree. I need to find out what, and I need to stop them before there are any more. I don't want any more to die because of whatever the hell it is. Will you help me?"

"Yes, I will."

Chapter 31

BITTER GROUNDS

They were sitting in a booth at White's Lunch. Irish Thom had picked the location; he figured he'd be safe there. It was crowded with the usual lunchtime patrons. Shorty got there first; he picked the booth.

"Keep your voice down," said Shorty.

Since there was all of this business to do with the key this week, rather than keep driving in from the county every day under these severe conditions, Thom and Lapointe decided to share a room at the Bridge Hotel on London Street in Sandwich.

It was just a little enough out of the way. McCloskey first drove to Shorty's to give him the news and then he proceeded to the Bridge. He knew the people who ran it, so the hour wasn't a problem. Thom didn't take it well.

"Jack gave me all the details," he said. "At first he didn't want to, but I made him. I'll tell Lapointe's folks, right after we're done here."

Shorty was sensing something in that. "What exactly are you going to tell them?"

Thom turned his attention to the window. It would be a long drive back out to LaSalle. Truth was, he didn't know what he was going to tell them. He also knew Shorty had his reasons for asking.

"They're going to see his body. I can't dress that part of the story up any." He turned back to his cold cup of coffee, and then faced Shorty. "I'll tell them it's still under investigation...."

"What else?" Shorty was trying to remain as sensitive as possible, but he knew what was coming and that he would be the one that would have to brief McCloskey.

"It was Lapointe's dad got him into this business, you know. He had a few close calls himself."

"Nothing like this, Thom."

"No, nothing like this. He got gun-shy after one encounter a couple summers ago and started scaling back his activities. Lapointe got his taste of it, though, and wanted more. More of what exactly, I don't know."

Thom paused to gather his thoughts and Shorty didn't rush him.

"You hungry?" asked Shorty.

"No. I couldn't eat."

Shorty signalled the waitress, and when she noticed, he pointed at his empty cup. She came right over with the carafe.

"Thanks."

She gave Thom another good look while he was staring blankly out the window. Not only did Thom look like he hadn't slept all night, he also looked as if he hadn't had a decent meal in a couple of days.

"Are you sure I can't get you boys anything?"

Shorty held his hand up. "Thanks, angel, we're fine."

Without taking his eyes off whatever he was looking at, Thom said, "I was actually born in the city, did I ever tell you that? Lost my older brother in the war. I always remember my father being old. I don't think he saw my tenth birthday. Mother died of cancer. I held her hand at Hotel Dieu until it got cold."

Thom was speaking as if he were in some kind of dream state. Shorty let him talk.

"That's when I got shipped off to my ma's parents' pig farm in the county. It sure was different. I guess I got bored. I met Lapointe at a church social one Sunday. That's where you went to meet people. There wasn't anywhere else to go, nothing else to do. Lapointe, he wasn't bored. He told me what kinds of things he and his family were up to. They lived right on the river, where there was always something to do, always something to get yourself into. I never told my grandparents about any of it. It was easy to keep it from them. But I'll have to break the news to them as well that Lapointe is dead. There'll be questions. I'll have time to arrange all the lies in my head while I'm driving out to their place."

"Thom, the police have probably already told Lapointe's family, told them everything."

Thom looked at Shorty. There was a slight look of panic on his face, and then he seemed to resign himself.

"I want to see him."

"No," said Shorty. "He's still with the coroner."

"Three Fingers too?"

"Yeah."

Thom looked around the diner. "Who's next, Shorty? Huh?"

"It's not like that, Thom."

"Is that what you're going to tell Mud and Gorski? Of course it's like that, Shorty. Of course it's like that."

"Thom, keep it down."

"It's the key, and that cursed —"

"Dammit, Thom, don't make it any —"

"I'm out, Shorty, I'm out."

That's what Shorty was waiting for. They both leaned back in their seats, and both took a pause in the action to watch the snow now blowing and swirling through Pitt Street.

"There's nothing you can say that can make me change my mind."

Shorty already knew that. This wasn't the kind of thing guys like Lapointe and Irish Thom signed up for. Actually, it wasn't the kind of thing that any of them signed up for.

"I'm sorry I'm letting you and Jack down."

Shorty was shaking his head. "Thom, you didn't —"

"Don't, Shorty, just don't."

"Thom, we'll call on you when all of this blows over."

Thom smiled, almost chuckled a little.

"No, I'm headed back to the hog farm for good. It was because of Lapointe that I got into all of this."

"All right, Thom."

"Well, I should go."

"I'll walk you to your truck. Where are you?"

"Around the corner, on Goyeau."

Shorty threw some coin on the table. The donned their hats, bundled up, and headed out.

Fields waited until he heard Shorty say his thanks and goodbyes to the waitress before he turned to try and get a look at them, and then he waited until they passed the window to get an even better look.

He was sitting in the next booth, his back to Thom. He didn't move or so much as clink his spoon against the inside of his coffee cup. He didn't want to miss a word of what they had to say. He had found what the Guard was looking for over a coffee at White's Lunch.

Chapter 32

PUNCHING AIR

Late afternoon

McCloskey had just come off a solid workout at the gym, and, feeling good, he thought he'd drop by the office and see if he still liked how he and the movers had arranged the furniture that was installed this morning.

"And at what number should I tell him to contact you, Mr. … what was that name again?"

"Upthegrove, Martin Upthegrove at Seneca 1008. You sure you've got that now? It's important."

"Got it. He'll get right back to you."

McCloskey could hear Campbell bounding up the stairs, and he met him at the door.

"You got my message?" asked Campbell.

"No, I didn't," said McCloskey and he closed the door behind the detective, locking it.

"I left you a couple messages at the B-A."

"Well, all right, but —"

"What's this about then?"

"I just got here about a half hour ago, I haven't … no one has been here since I was here this morning with the movers, but when I got here a short while ago … I found this."

McCloskey walked to the middle of the hardwood, still mostly exposed since not all of the furniture had been installed yet, and pointed to a crudely drawn outline of something scratched into the floor. It had to be ten feet long.

"A key," said Campbell. "Who did this? What does it mean?"

McCloskey started pacing.

"All right, McCloskey, time for full disclosure, or like I said, I'll just hand you and what's left of your gang over to Morrison."

McCloskey had his back to Campbell. The detective could see McCloskey reaching in his pocket for something. McCloskey turned, holding up the key.

"This, this is what they, whoever they are, are after."

He handed it to Campbell.

"A key? Is that what all this has been about?"

"There's more to it."

"Where did you get it? Did you steal it from someone?"

"No, well, not exactly. Let me explain, we … you're going to think this is crazy."

"Oh no, I won't. Now start your allocution."

"What?"

"Start talking — first, tell me how you came to be in possession of this key. Wait — let's stay on point and not get into any of your peripheral activities. Let me put it this way, was it in someone's possession?"

McCloskey had to think about that carefully; he understood what Campbell was doing. "No, it was not," he said.

"Good. Was it taken from a private property? Was it burgled in any way?"

"No on both counts. It was recovered from the river."

"When?"

"Last Sunday."

Campbell held his hand up. "Stop there. Now, there are people after this key. We can agree on that now. Do you still not know who they are?"

"We don't know their names, and none of us has ever seen them."

"But they want it. Why?"

"We're not sure."

Campbell studied it some more under the nearest ceiling light. "Perhaps it has some sort of intrinsic or historical value. It looks quite old and doesn't look like it's ever been used to open a lock. Why not just sell it? Why have you been hanging on to it?"

McCloskey was hesitating again and Campbell started slapping the key on the palm of his hand.

"C'mon, McCloskey."

"A few of the boys had an idea, they had heard rumours …"

"About?"

"Shit, Campbell, you're making things awful complicated if you want to keep throwing up all these, what do they call them? Chinese walls."

"You haven't tried to fence it. I'm not convinced it's meant to open any kind of lock. I think your boys had it backwards. I

think you should have just taken it to an auction house in Detroit
and —"

"We're fairly certain it belonged to Richard Davies and the
boys thought it was a key to unlock some lost fortune of his.
Those were the rumours they had heard, rumours that have been
going around since last summer."

"Ah-ha. And he's dead. So who's after this thing?"

"You might hear some people call them the Guard."

"You found this last Sunday?"

"The boys did."

"Hm. Tell me, honestly, do you know anything about those
two bootleggers that got thrown off the train outside the city last
Sunday evening — just a yes or no."

"No."

Campbell returned to the carving on the floor and, holding
the key, compared the two. "Almost an exact likeness, the
proportions at least. So, they know you have it."

"It sure looks like it."

"McCloskey, I've seen Three Fingers's body, spoken to
Laforet about his preliminary examination, and this morning
arrived in his lab just in time to catch Lapointe's autopsy while
it was still in progress. Laforet and I are still trying to come to
terms with what we are looking at. So far we have no rational
or scientific explanation for any of it. I don't need to go into
any of the details with you. You just need to know that what
was done to them was done without a hand or weapon laid on
either of them."

"What?"

"Just that."

It was Campbell's turn to start pacing, but unlike McCloskey,
he walked in circles.

"I'm taking possession of the key. Consider it police property."

McCloskey surprised himself when he didn't protest. He was glad it was out of his hands now.

"Are you sure you want it?"

Campbell tucked it in his inside suit pocket. "I've brought someone outside of law enforcement into this case. I'd like us all to meet tomorrow. I'll contact you in the morning when I've arranged a time. Likely in the afternoon, and at her place on Maiden Lane. Can you make yourself available?"

"Her? Uh, sure."

"You know, you may not have the key anymore, but that doesn't mean you're out of danger from whatever, or whoever this is."

"What do you think it is, Campbell?"

"I think you've stumbled upon something that's worth a lot of money, something that might not have even belonged to Davies, and whoever it belongs to desperately wants it back and they don't want to discovered so they are going about it as covertly as possible. And they are very good."

"But what you saw … Three Fingers and Lapointe?"

"I'll wait to hear Laforet's conclusions on that front."

Campbell turned to leave and then stopped himself. "One more thing, McCloskey, I'll agree to a don't-ask-don't-tell policy so long as you suspend all of your activities until this matter is resolved. Also, you should continue to contact me only through the department. They will relay any messages to me if I don't happen to be in my office. I'll continue to relay messages to you through the British-American. Agreed?"

"Agreed. Oh — who are we meeting with tomorrow?"

"Madame Zahra Ostrovskaya."

"She just off the boat or something?"

"I think you'll like her," said Campbell.

Chapter 33

ONE EXCITING NIGHT

Evening

"I know it might not be exactly your cup of tea, Mrs. Cattanach …"

Vera Maude's uncle Fred was pitching a movie idea, so to speak, to the woman. A copy of the *Border Cities Star* was open to the entertainment page on the coffee table between them. She had been lobbying for *Peg o' My Heart*, the new version, the one with Laurette Taylor. Fred was of course familiar with it, it having been first a popular song before the war, then a long-running Broadway play starring Miss Taylor, and then its first film adaptation just after the war. This was its newest cinematic incarnation.

"Does Peg not remind you of Vera Maude?" smiled Mrs. Cattanach. There may not have been a physical resemblance, but they were both definitely the rambunctious, spontaneous little Irish girl and all that.

"But the Maguires are no stodgy English family," retorted Fred.

"I know, but ..."

They each took another sip of their tea.

"So this is one of those gangster pictures?" she said.

"Mostly, yes."

Mrs. Cattanach glanced down at the newspaper. "I saw the advertisement, and I wasn't sure." She read out a few lines. "'*Brimful of love, laughter, and sensations. A frantic search for a half-million dollars. Stealthy figures and peering eyes. The funniest black-face comedian possible.*'" She peered over the rim of her glasses at the man seated across from her. "Really, Fred." She read on. "'*A tremendous storm scene as a gorgeous dynamic climax.*' Goes on to say it will make me laugh, cry, happy, sad, good, bad, sleep, dream, shudder, and scream." She leaned back in her chair. "I don't know what it's supposed to be, but whatever it is, it sounds exhausting."

"But it's a Griffith picture, so it must be good. See," he said, tapping the line in the advertisement, "'*smashing all records everywhere.*'"

Fred, fearing he might lose the battle and end up spending the evening with Laurette Taylor, put down his tea, leaned closer to the edge of the chesterfield, and gave Mrs. Cattanach a quick synopsis, hoping it might help her appreciate what he felt looked to be a work of cinematic genius.

"It's got everything — drama, mystery, and comedy. An

orphan girl — from South Africa, I think it is — is adopted by this wealthy, old Southern family in America. Her adoptive mother arranges a marriage to this Rockmaine fellow when she really loves another — Fairfax. Now that sounds interesting, doesn't it? Now Fairfax invites the girl, the mother, and Rockmaine to stay at his country estate — big and fancy, but it's been empty for a while —"

"Why, if it's so big and fancy, is it empty?"

"Well, I don't know. Maybe he's been travelling abroad, like the other family. You know what those folks are like. Anyway, but this is the thing, this is where it gets really interesting: these bootleggers have been hiding out there, and just before Fairfax arrives with his guests, the gang's leader is killed and a huge sum of money is hidden away."

"What about the body?"

"What body?"

"The gang leader's."

"I'm not sure."

"I was going to ask you if you saw this movie."

"No, I haven't. Honest. It was John next door saw it. I won't give away the rest, save to say a detective comes along to investigate the mysterious goings-on and, well, let me just say mysteries are solved and truths are revealed."

Fred relaxed and waited for Mrs. Cattanach's verdict. And she made him wait while she slowly sipped her tea.

"All right, this one it is. But if we do this again, I get to choose the picture."

Fred smiled, but not too much. He knew what a sacrifice the woman was making. He just wanted to see the picture before it left town.

"Right then." He picked up the tea things. It was the least he could do. "If we leave now, we might be able to catch the vaudeville."

Mrs. Cattanach folded up the paper and was already plotting her revenge. She noticed an ad for an upcoming picture. *Miss Lulu Bett.* She had read the book and was now anxious to see Fred squirm through the film adaptation.

Fred came back in the room.

Mrs. Cattanach was checking her watch. "And where's Vera Maude?" she asked without looking up from it.

"Oh — she telephoned to say she was running a little late. Had to help Copeland sort a shipment of special orders, or something like that. We'll probably just miss her."

"Well, I don't have anything for her."

"She'll manage. Let me get your coat."

In truth, Vera Maude was talking advantage of her uncle being out so that she could continue her search for Jack McCloskey. As soon as her shift was done, she headed straight up to Lanspeary's, where she was now enjoying a ham sandwich with a hot chocolate on the side. She also grabbed some reading material from the magazine rack — the latest edition of *Black Mask*.

She remembered the name of the police detective McCloskey was with in the store today: Campbell. Her plan, so far, was to take a walk over to police headquarters and ask to speak with the detective. What she hadn't figured out yet was under what pretense she should be asking for a bit of his time. She thought she might get inspired along the way.

When she was finished, she wrapped herself back up again, pulled her gloves out of her coat pockets, and stuffed the rolled-up magazine into one of them.

There was a light snow, pretty in the streetlights. Lots of swell-looking people coming in and out of the Prince Edward

Hotel, people for whom the dark, the cold, and the snow meant little as they climbed in and out of their big cars. Vera Maude crossed the Avenue and continued along Park Street toward police headquarters.

She gripped the handrail up the steps and entered the handsome new building. Constables were coming and going, one of them wrestling with someone in handcuffs. Time to sober up. In the morning he'd wake up trying to remember how he got there.

What am I going to say? she asked herself. *What?* She was standing in the lobby right now, looking around for a flicker of inspiration.

"Is there something I can help you with?"

It was the duty sergeant.

"I'd like to speak with Detective Campbell."

"He's not at his desk at the moment. Is this an urgent matter?"

"No, not really."

"Is there something I can help you with then?"

"I don't know. Maybe. I'm looking for someone."

"Someone's lost? Is this a missing person?"

"Um, not exactly," said Vera Maude.

"All right, who is it you're looking for?"

She paused, looked around the lobby, heard the switchboard going off, telephones ringing in the distance. She turned back to the duty sergeant.

"I'm looking for Jack McCloskey."

He leaned across the desk, thinking he may have heard incorrectly, and asked, "Who?"

"Jack — Jack McCloskey."

"Do you know Jack McCloskey?" The sergeant was squinting at her now, giving her a bit of a once-over.

I'm in it now, she thought.

"Well, not personally," she said. "He cost me a few bucks on last Friday's ice race down at the Devonshire track. He was getting pulled by Moscow Donna, or maybe it's vice versa … anyway I been looking for this sulky bumper McCloskey because I think it was fixed and he owes so I want to know where he is so I can get my money back."

The desk sergeant took a whiff. "You been drinking?"

"Only hot choc-a-lit."

"You know what, miss? I believe you."

"So you can't help me?"

He shook his head. "Nope, talk to the racing commissioner."

"I will do that."

Vera Maude did an about-face and marched back out of police headquarters, trying to maintain the appearance of a dainty lunatic. She walked back over to the Avenue and caught the first northbound streetcar to come along.

What next?

That's what she kept asking herself all the way to the transfer at London Street. She stayed on.

The British-American.

She disembarked in front of the bank at the corner of the Drive. When she stepped onto the sidewalk, she paused and took a long look at the old hotel. She had never set foot inside it in all her years in Windsor. Parts of her hometown were still undiscovered to her. There were very few people in the street. She crossed the Drive. The wind was whipping this way and that through the intersection. As she approached the entrance, the building enlarged and Detroit's illuminated skyline dropped behind it.

Her first thought was, *This place has clearly seen better days*. But its history echoed still, even through the lobby. It wasn't grand; there was no marble, and no chandeliers. There was a simple hardwood desk, a well-trod and occasionally stained carpet floor, and staff that looked like they were around to lay the cornerstone. The desk was to the left, running parallel to Ferry Hill, and the swinging doors into the bar had been straight ahead. She passed through them and found a table at one of the big windows that overlooked the Drive.

She removed her hat and set it on the chair across from her. She wasn't sure how to order, and just when she was prepared to approach the bar, a woman appeared.

"Good evening. What can I get you?"

"Just a tea, please."

The woman looked over her shoulder at some men at a nearby table who had some interest in these goings-on. They turned away.

"Right," the woman said.

She wasn't but a minute with the basic tea things.

"I'm sorry, I should have asked you how you took it."

Vera Maude looked around. More eyes.

"Milk is fine," she said.

"Very good. And I'll leave a bit more hot water for you here as well."

"Thank you."

Two cups would be nice, but all the same, Vera Maude thought it best to hold with the one cup. She didn't feel the desire to venture deeper into the British-American in order to find the lavatory. For one thing, she felt it might require a password.

It wasn't her imagination; everyone was looking at her sideways.

What's she doing here?

She stirred the milk into her tea and then set the spoon on the saucer and watched the brew become still again. She looked around. People were starting to clear out, leaving only a few bleary-eyed patrons and herself. There was a gentleman reading the *Detroit News* with his eyes closed, another with his face down on the little table he so elegantly inhabited. And then it got quiet as stars. The bartender disappeared into the kitchen and the swinging doors that led into the lobby stopped swinging and became still as well. Still as a snowflake careening toward the pavement.

Vera Maude gripped the edges of the wide cup between her fingers and brought it to her lips. Not too hot. It felt good inside her. She set the cup down again and looked around. There were fewer people and no staff about. She returned to her cup. The tea seemed to tremble in it. She thought she could hear the cup against the saucer. She felt it before she saw it. Vera Maude turned her head and instinctively fell to the floor.

They came charging through the main entrance. The treaty was broken. This was Morrison, burning down the British-American, figuratively speaking. He went storming up the stairs as if he had a specific target in mind. Officers from both the provincial police and the RCMP followed. The British-American's free ride was over. Either a patron had broken the B-A's unwritten rules or this was law enforcement tightening its grip, claiming some significant territory, the last bit of territory. Yes, it had to be all Morrison.

In the chaos, Jack McCloskey strolled into the lobby to pick up any messages at the desk. He looked around and could hear the stampede up the stairs. He met the faces behind the desk that said *Get out of here.* He turned around; the entrance and the street corner were closing. The night manager tilted his head toward the bar. As far as raids go, this looked like a sloppy execution, all last minute. This was careless, this was personal, and it was going to get ugly.

McCloskey went into the bar, froze inside the door, and scanned the room. He spotted a girl cowering under one of the tables near the window. She looked like she had no business being here. A guest maybe? Someone who had missed the last ferry to Detroit? He ran over to her.

"Hey," he said, "let's get you out of here."

She looked up and, recognizing McCloskey, said, "Hey, yourself."

He took a closer look.

"I know you," he said.

"Yeah, you do."

"So I find you under a table in a bar?"

"I don't get around much," said Vera Maude. "Do you know a back door out of this place?"

"C'mon."

McCloskey pulled up Vera Maude — "Wait, my hat!" — and then led her toward the kitchen. He spotted Grace on the floor behind the bar — "Hi, Jack" — and a few others taking cover in the kitchen — "Cancel my lunch reservation tomorrow."

"Jack — my arm," said Vera Maude.

"Relax, you got two of them."

He practically dragged her out the back door. They were now in the lane behind the hotel and he was still dragging her to Brock Street, overlooking the Canadian National Railway station and offices. The snow was blowing off the river and into their faces.

"Okay, slow down, just slow down a minute."

"This seems a little familiar."

"Okay, stop. You said in the bar, 'I know you,' didn't you?"

"Yeah."

"What's my name?"

If he had hesitated a second longer, she would have slapped him.

"Vera Maude, your name's Vera Maude."

"And you know me from where?"

"I'm working on that."

"You're working on that? What the hell is that supposed to mean?"

"Hey — it means I'm working on it. It's a little hard to explain, and I have to get you out of here."

McCloskey spotted a cab pulling up Brock out of the train station and he ran in front of it.

"You're going to take her to wherever she wants you to take her." He handed the driver some bills and Vera Maude climbed in.

"Where can I find you?" she said out the window.

"I'm between places right now."

"You're only making things harder on yourself, Jack."

"That's kind of my thing. Anyways, now I know where to find you."

"How was the movie?"

Fred was peeling off his coat.

"Terrible," he said. He unravelled his muffler from around his neck and hung it along with his hat on the rack that ran along the stretch of wall to the left of the door, dividing the entrance from the front room. He peeked around the corner and said, "That's the last time I listen to one of John's film reviews."

"John next door?"

"The same."

Vera Maude was lying on the chesterfield with a book on her lap. "What was Mrs. Cattanach's verdict?"

"I'll tell you, Maudie, I'm going to pay for this one. I'm going to bed."

"You don't want me to make you a tea?"

"No, thanks. I'm exhausted. The walk from the streetcar to Mrs. Cattanach's, and then the walk from her place to here did me in."

He was about to say good night but instead asked how was Vera Maude's evening.

"Not very exciting," she said.

"Ah well, it's not New York, I guess."

Vera Maude smiled. "It's just fine."

"You staying up for a bit then?"

"Yeah," she said.

"And are you working tomorrow?"

"I am. Another staffer sick with a cold."

"Best they stay away from you and the rest of them. Well then, I'll say good night."

"Good night, Uncle Fred."

Vera Maude opened her book and then closed it once Fred was upstairs. Who was she kidding? She was exhausted too.

So, Jack McCloskey …

This was his thinking chair. He faced the corner window that looked down over the intersection. He could see the skyline clearly from here.

This guy owned a restaurant over in Detroit. Strictly above-board, except for the liquor he got from McCloskey, or whoever happened to be representing him at the time, and which was only served to a particular clientele. It came about last fall, when McCloskey was still not quite on his feet yet. The restaurateur was adding a room to his establishment, a grand old house way up Woodward, just past the Majestic. He was ordering some furnishings, he had some money, and he ordered exotic pieces from New York and Montreal, but then he got smart and cut out the middleman and started ordering from abroad, direct from Paris and London. It gave him something to brag about. All said, he did have an eye and a certain penchant. He was being pitched some new lines by a London broker when he got carried away with a set of club chairs. Anyway, he over-bought and didn't know what to do with them. Two left over and bills still to pay to a few suppliers. He offered McCloskey the chairs to cover that particular balance. McCloskey had an eye too, though no one had any idea from whence it came. He took the chairs. Shorty happened to be with him and they carried them back — wrapped in canvas — home on the ferry. It was some kind of a picture. Right now both were in McCloskey's apartment, but one would end up in the new office space on Riverside Drive.

He had gotten into the habit of recounting small tales, experiences like that. It had become a sort of exercise, flexing that memory muscle.

So, Vera Maude whatever-your-name-is.

The chair wasn't working; he wasn't thinking. Right now his brain was doing all those other things it generally did when he wasn't really thinking.

I know you, don't I?

He gripped the chair leather and looked higher in the sky, to where the streetlights no longer caught the falling snow, and the flakes disappeared, flying upward as it seemed, into the darkness, like some sort of optical illusion. He then closed his eyes and tried once more to stoke his memory before finally drifting off to sleep.

FIVE

Chapter 34

GRIMOIRE

Friday morning

> *So great is the extent, power, and efficacy of the celestial bodies that not only natural things, but also artificial, when they are rightly exposed to those above, do presently suffer by that most potent agent, and obtain a wonderful life.*
>
> *The magicians affirm that not only by the mixture and application of natural things but also in images,*

seals, rings, glasses, and some other instruments, being opportunely framed under a certain constellation, some celestial illustrations may be taken, and some wonderful thing may be received; for the beams of the celestial bodies being animated, living, sensual, and bringing along with them admirable gifts, and a most violent power, do, even in a moment, and at the first touch, imprint wonderful powers in the images, though their matter be less capable.

Yet they bestow more powerful virtues on the images if they be framed not of any, but of a certain matter, namely, whose natural, but also specifical virtue is agreeable with the work, and the figure of the image is like to the celestial; for such an image, both in regard to the matter naturally congruous to the operation and celestial influence, and also for its figure being like to the heavenly one, is best prepared to receive the operations and powers of the celestial bodies and figures, and instantly receives the heavenly gift into itself; though it constantly worketh on another thing, and other things yield obedience to it.

Campbell was skimming through one of the books he had special-ordered, a reprint of Barrett's *The Magus*, when he came across this passage in the chapter describing "How Artificial Things (As Images, Seals, and Such Like) May Obtain Some Virtue From the Celestial Bodies." Leaving it open to the page, he pushed the dusty tome aside and started flipping through the other books in his growing stack. These words for some reason brought to mind an illustration he had seen, or thought he had seen, earlier in the week which meant nothing to him at the time. He hoped he wasn't just imagining it. His thoughts and dreams were lately becoming strange assemblages of everything he was absorbing from these books and his conversations with Madame Zahra, and they were indecipherable, most likely because they represented nothing more than fatigue. However, to someone like Zahra, these would be considered visions and would beg interpretation. To Campbell, fragments of wet tea leaves in the bottom of a cup would always be just that, and he could tell nothing about a person by the palm of their hand, except maybe that they should consider changing lotions.

And then there it was, in the last book in the pile: a sixteenth-century engraving depicting a ceremony or ritual of some sort being carried out by a high priest or mystic. Campbell wasn't entirely sure; his German was a little *rostig*. However, among the many symbols and objects arranged with an obvious significance along its border was a key — one that all too closely resembled the tumbler-tickler sitting here next to his coffee mug. With new eyes, Campbell then backed through his little library and started marking every relevant passage. His mind soon drifted to Richard Davies and what he had learned about him and his group's activities, and then it came together: This was not a key designed to open a door, a locker, or anything of the kind — nothing worldly at least. It was a talisman, but for what purpose or end he had no idea, and it would be impossible to figure out. That group would have assigned the object its own meaning, its own purpose, that no one outside of their circle would be capable of understanding, let alone put to work.

Make of it what you will.

Campbell rose from the table and looked out the window and across the river. Small dots of white light here and there, sometimes a short string of amber beads along the shore. He folded his arms behind his head, arched his back until it cracked, and then wobbled back toward the kitchen. He felt the pot of the Flavodrip. It was still warm. He poured the last dregs into his mug, unfastened the drip container from the contraption, dumped the spent grounds into the sink, and gave it a rinse.

Returning to the table, he slid the key off the edge and held it right up under the shade of the floor lamp. Sure, he was examining the object for the umpteenth time, but he was seeing it differently now. The loops at the end; the colour of the glass in each loop; the odd number of teeth and the queer shape to them; and probably the key's length and the type of metal from which it was forged — all of it would have meant something to them.

Yes, Zahra, he thought, *she might have some knowledge of these things, these talismans.*

He could go up to her place with the key and a couple of his books and they could put their heads together. He looked at his watch. Definitely too early to be phoning her. No matter; he needed to shower, shave, and ought to check in at the department. He would do all of that first and call her from his desk.

Campbell went over to his unmade bed, lay down, and fell dead asleep. He was awakened about an hour or so later by the phone. The ringing sent shockwaves through his system. He reached over and unhooked the earpiece. It took him a moment to get his mouth going.

"Campbell ... all right ... what time is it?"

There was also a clock at his bedside table but his eyes weren't working yet either. It was the switchboard at police headquarters. Still holding the phone, he sat up, swivelled his feet onto the floor and blinked at the big rectangle of grey early morning light that filled his window.

"So he hasn't left yet? ... Yeah ... No, wait — give him this number and tell him to call me here directly right away.... Yeah ... I'll be in shortly."

It was a vague message from McCloskey saying that he could no longer be reached through the hotel and he would explain later, and that he would be leaving to run an errand in the next fifteen minutes but that he and Campbell should meet up soon, real soon.

Campbell leaned out of his bed and got his legs moving back to the kitchen. He emptied the last of the fresh grounds into the Flavodrip and got it going. He'd have to stop at the M&P before the end of the day to pick up another pound of Courthouse or Old Government, whichever they had in stock. He wasn't picky. He thought they both tasted the same.

Odd names for their blends. When can I expect Customs and Excise?

When the thing started gurgling away he returned to the table to organize his books and notes. Before the coffee was ready the phone rang again.

"Campbell ... Okay, I need to talk to you, too ... When? How's one o'clock? ... Actually, I have something else in mind. I want you to meet me at this place on Maiden Lane, just west of the Avenue. ... Let's just say I need to get my palm read.... All right ... I'll try to get there ahead of you.... Yeah, I'll be parked outside."

It was going to be a busy morning.

What McCloskey was unable to share with Campbell was that a short while ago he was contacted by the now off-duty night desk clerk at the British-American. Apparently, in the raid last night all of those badges missed something: Pearl Shipley. So the raid really was as disorganized as it looked, thought McCloskey. She was in one of the rooms upstairs at the time, doing something she shouldn't have been doing in this neutral territory, something that was probably the reason for the raid. When she heard the ruckus, she and her partner in crime, apparently a hotel regular who knew all of the good hiding places, went into hiding. McCloskey needed to get her out.

Goddamn, she's a handful.

The desk clerk told McCloskey in a whisper that he was sure there were at least two, maybe three, undercovers staking out the place. It was decided that Pearl would be given a chambermaid's uniform and an armful of dirty laundry and be escorted by a trusted staffer down the service elevator, through the kitchen, and out the back door, where McCloskey would be waiting for her in a cab with the motor running.

Minutes later she appeared in the alleyway with not just the dirty laundry but also her friend in tow. There wasn't any time for another act in this drama; from the front passenger seat McCloskey told the guy — he didn't even want to know his name — to get in and keep his head down. He said the cabbie would take him as far as the streetcar waiting rooms down the Drive near Ferry Street.

"I know your face, now get a good look at mine, because next time I run into you, it'll be the last one you ever see. Understand?"

The guy shrank back in his seat under the weight of McCloskey's glare.

"Yes, sir."

"*Sir*? Your type, you're all a bunch of fu —"

"Jack!"

McCloskey was climbing over his seat, ready to turn this guy's face into paste. He knocked the cab driver, who almost slid across the ice into an oncoming streetcar. The guy held up his hands for protection. McCloskey cooled down and said to the driver, "Forget the waiting room, let's just spill him here."

They didn't even pull over.

"Hey, it's snowing," the guy said, "and cold, and I left my —"

McCloskey got out, opened the rear door, grabbed the guy, and dragged him moaning to the sidewalk in front of the Crawford Hotel. "Last stop." He climbed back into the cab.

"Jack, you didn't have to —"

"Yeah, I did."

McCloskey took Pearl back to his apartment, where he told her in no uncertain terms that she couldn't stay. He'd have to beg another favour from Clara. A big one.

Chapter 35

CLARA FIELDS'S HOME FOR WAYWARD WOMEN

McCloskey and Clara were having a hushed conversation in her little celery-coloured kitchen while Pearl, still dressed in a chambermaid's uniform, leaned against the window frame in the front room and stared down blankly at the snow swirling in the quiet neighbourhood intersection. The cigarette dangling from her fingers was mostly ash.

"This isn't fair," said Clara. "You can't just saddle me with her like this."

"That's not what I'm doing."

She was arranging the dried glasses on a shelf in the cupboard, a tea towel slung over her shoulder. *Souvenir of Niagara Falls*, it said.

"How long has she been on it?"

"Probably since the day she signed her first movie contract. It either followed or chased her here. I don't know. And I don't know that I want to know. Clara, you've been reading in the paper lately about all the trafficking going on here: heroin, morphine, opium, whatever it is. I can't keep it straight. All I know is it's becoming a little too readily available."

"And encroaching on your bootlegging business too, right? You're going to have to keep up with the times, Jack."

"I keep up just fine. What I'm trying to say is the Border Cities isn't the best place to be for someone who's trying to kick a habit — any habit." McCloskey wasn't finished. "And as far as my business is concerned, I'm not going to be touching any of it, and neither will my boys."

"Don't think for a minute you can speak for all of them, Jack. Please tell me you're not that naive."

"C'mon, you know you can be a real help here. How was I supposed to know she'd come gift-wrapped in all her vices?"

Clara was enjoying seeing him like this.

"She's a good kid," he said.

"Kid?" She almost laughed. "She's no kid, Jack. She's a grown woman."

"Maybe on the outside. She's still a bit young for her age." He paused. "And what kind of path were you on last year?"

"I wasn't locking myself in hotel rooms and seasoning myself with heroin."

"Oh, so now that you're all straightened out you get to look down on people who might need a little help?"

"Hey, that's not me and you know it. What about what I've been doing for you, and for Henry? And the work I do at the hospital?"

McCloskey couldn't argue that. "All right, all right," he said and then paced a few paces before wedging himself into one of the corners adjacent to the sink. "Any other suggestions?"

"Get her to a nunnery."

"Clara, she needs help, not religion. Okay, so this is a little out of your league. Don't you know people at the hospital or at school in Detroit who might be able to point you in the right direction? Wait — thing is, though, it has to be something on this side of the border because —"

Clara held up her hand like a traffic cop. "The less I know. Just tell me this: does she have any friends or family in town?"

McCloskey shook his head. "No friends I'd trust her with, and as far as family goes, I don't think she has any. She's actually from Detroit. The story is —"

The hand went up again.

"Clara, this is something you should know. Nothing incriminating, I swear."

"All right." She braced herself just the same, and McCloskey continued.

"She was being passed around among a few auto executives in Detroit before one of them decided to give her to Davies as a gift. He must have done somebody a big favour."

"Or she was their sacrificial lamb."

"I don't know. Anyway, Davies kept her on a very short leash. Though she was well compensated, from what I understand she wasn't very happy. Her only happiness came from the little something she had on the side." McCloskey paused for effect. "Wanna know who it was?"

"I don't know, do I?" said Clara.

"Charlie Baxter."

Clara's eyes almost rolled out of their sockets. "Are you kidding me?" She took a quick peek around the corner to get another look at Pearl. At second glance, Pearl really made the dowdy chambermaid's uniform look like a burlesque costume. Clara turned back to McCloskey. "She really is a handful, isn't she?"

"Yeah," he said, "she is."

"Hey, were you two ever … friendly?" Clara was grinning at him now, teasing him like he was a schoolboy with a crush. *K-i-s-s-i-n-g.*

"No." He smiled back. "I know it might come as a shock to you, but she's not exactly my type."

"Oh, come on. Look at her, Jack. Even I'd show her the town."

"Is that what the girls are calling it these days?"

"All right, so how do you know her then?"

"We'd run into each other at a speak, exchange winks. This is before she and Charlie hooked up. She'd sneak out with her girlfriends whenever she could, but she didn't talk to anyone and no one talked to her."

"Lest they incurred the wrath of Davies."

"Yeah, something like that," said McCloskey.

Clara moved closer. "But when has anything like that ever stopped you?"

"I *can* control myself, you know."

"Pardon my giggle."

There was a short break while the two of them, used to this kind of sparring, caught their breath, and then McCloskey came back.

"So what do you say?"

It was Clara's turn to pause for dramatic effect. "I can't be with her all the time," she said.

"I know."

"She needs to be partnered with someone, that's how these things generally work, when they work at all."

"I'll cover any expenses," said McCloskey.

"Folding money," she replied.

"Absolutely."

"Okay, let me see if I can find someone at the hospital. If this is becoming a problem in the Border Cities, then maybe there's someone there who's already working with people, putting some kind of program together. Meanwhile, that is, *meanwhile*, she can stay here."

"Roomies," said McCloskey.

"More like sorority sisters."

"Are you guys done yet? I'm getting hungry."

It was Pearl standing in the entrance to the kitchen, still clutching that cigarette. Clara and McCloskey looked at each other. Pearl must have been used to overhearing people talk about her like this, people who were at a loss as to how to handle her, what to do with her — her parents and teachers, the street toughs, and later the so-called men of power and influence who must have been a big disappointment to her, thought McCloskey. Men like that had no idea what to do with a girl like Pearl. McCloskey would have to be on his guard.

"I think I can put something together for us," said Clara.

"Great. And where's the little girl's room?"

"Down the hall. First door on your right."

"Swell."

They waited until she was gone before finishing their discussion.

"So where's Charlie Baxter?" said Clara.

"No one knows."

"Lying low?"

"Real low. Maybe even six feet under."

"Seriously? Tell me," she said, "do you think about him a lot?"

"Not much," he said.

Clara was surprised and not surprised to hear that. Even with all the work she'd been doing with veterans and influenza patients at the hospital, and with the street violence that had been a part of everyday life for her late husband — and was still for her brother-in-law — it was still difficult to understand. She could put at least part of it down to never having been a front-line soldier or a gangster who slept with a revolver under his pillow. The rest, she wasn't so sure. What no one could deny, though, was that death and dying were different now.

"I think more about the two guys I just lost."

That reminded her. "Say, how did your meeting go with the cop — what was his name? Campbell?"

"Good … I think."

"Still can't tell me what that's all about?"

"No, I can't," said McCloskey. "Trust me, the less you know about this thing the better. We're trying to keep this as closed as possible."

"Does Pearl have anything to do with it?"

"No, nothing."

"Good," said Clara. "Maybe one less thing for me to worry about."

"Definitely."

"Have you talked to your shop girl at the bookstore yet?"

"No, I've been a bit busy. We done with the interrogation?"

Clara felt like she hit the McCloskey wall with that one and decided she had better back off or he'd be bringing her more orphans from the storm.

"Yeah," she said. "Hey, she's taking her time in there; do you think she has anything on her?"

"She better not," said McCloskey. "After I leave, take her into your bedroom and show her some of your clothes. Play dress-up and get that uniform off and away from her, and let me know if you find anything. And check that she hasn't hidden anything in the front room or the bathroom."

"The bathroom? Where —?"

"You'd be surprised. Addicts can be extremely resourceful."

"I guess I still have a bit to learn."

"You'll be fine," he said. "Can you think of anything you need from me right now?"

"The ice box is leaking again."

"I know a guy; I'll send him over."

"Actually, Jack ..." She had her arms folded and was looking at the floor.

"What? What's the matter?"

"Jack, I'm really worried about Henry."

"Yeah? Is this new?"

"Don't kid. He's not well; he's lonely, isolated, frustrated.... Is there any mention of him in the street at all?"

"It's like he disappeared," he said.

"More like he's fading away. I saw him the other day. He kept going on about needing to solve just one case, if he could only have that. He almost sounded desperate. Now that's new."

"Yeah, that doesn't sound like Henry. So he solves a case — that'll put him right?"

"I don't think it's that simple."

"Could be a start. Would you like me to pick one of my least favourite people and throw him in Henry's path?"

"That's an idea."

"I'll see what I can come up with."

Pearl reappeared. "Staying for lunch, Jack?"

"No, I gotta run. I have to meet somebody."

"You and these meetings," said Clara. "You sound like a member of the Chamber of Commerce."

"I guess I sort of am. It's just not your dad's Chamber of Commerce. Well, you ladies behave yourselves. I'll drop by later with some groceries and maybe a bottle," he winked at Clara, "or two."

"You can show yourself out," she said.

— *Chapter 36* —

BLACK BREAD

Afternoon

McCloskey rode his accelerator all the way down Pelissier, taking advantage of the fresh ruts in the snow. Even under these driving conditions Maiden Lane was still only a few minutes away. The place wasn't hard to find, it being the only address on the block. McCloskey parked right out front, making himself as conspicuous as possible. He checked the neon sign in the ground floor window.

Madame Zahra's Astral Attic.

He didn't know from "astral," but it did sort of sound like it might be somewhere in the neighbourhood of palm reading. He lit up a White Owl, cracked the window, and sat back with one eye on the Avenue and the other on his rearview mirror. He started ruminating on any and all things potentially astral.

Cards with pictures — not exactly Jacks and Kings, though; fortune tellers; crystal balls. People looking for answers. But a police detective?

McCloskey was recalling a visit to the Michigan State Fair, just a little over a month after war was declared on Germany. A couple of his buddies dragged him into a tent where there was this guy in a shiny turban, wearing more makeup than most of the girls at the dance pavilion. He was sitting at a little table, hunched over a crystal ball that was slightly larger than a five-pin bowling ball, set on top of what looked to be nothing more than a fancy ashtray. He massaged this crystal with his long, knuckly fingers while humming in a low drone. And he wore a cape. It was all coming back to McCloskey now. He was remembering the poster: *Behold The Great Baseer!* They asked the man from the Orient — Turkey or Persia or somewhere like that — *Who is going to win the war?* McCloskey would never forget the mystic's reply: *What war?* This visionary in the dime store turban had probably never set foot beyond East Grand Boulevard or saw anything of the spirit world unless it was filtered through a splash of bathtub gin.

A car turned in from the Avenue, an Essex. It slowed and parked directly across from McCloskey. Through the frosted glass he could make out a man whom he thought could be Campbell. They both rolled down their windows. It was indeed Campbell.

"Is this the place?" said McCloskey, pointing his thumb over his shoulder.

"Sorry I'm late."

They killed their engines and stepped down onto the cobblestone made slick by the snow that was packed into every gap and crevice. McCloskey couldn't help but notice the bundle of books and the accordion file tucked under Campbell's arm and was about to say something but Campbell spoke first.

"I'll explain when we get upstairs," he said. "Hold on — on the phone you said there was something you wanted to talk about. Does it have to do with the key, or with any of your cohorts?"

"No, it doesn't," said McCloskey and he tossed the still-glowing butt of his White Owl into a snowdrift. "It can wait."

"Okay, then let's go. She's expecting us."

McCloskey looked up at the attic window and thought about The Great Baseer. "Do we need tickets?"

"We have what you might call a reciprocal agreement."

The detective led the bootlegger through the front door and up the stairs to the first landing. "Kick your boots off here," he said.

McCloskey did just that, unbuttoned his coat, and lifted off his fedora. It was warm up here, but the warmth seemed to be coming from inside of him. Even stranger, it seemed to have a smell, or was it a flavour? The two men continued up the last flight and through the floor into the little attic apartment.

"Detective," said Zahra, extending her hand.

"Madame Zahra," said Campbell taking it, or at least the finger portion. "This is Jack McCloskey."

McCloskey looked at him sideways. He never liked his name being thrown around, especially when his face was attached to it.

"Ah, Mr. Mikloskij," she said, smiling.

"Actually, it's McCloskey."

"Oh," she said, and the smile faded.

McCloskey was checking her out. He wasn't sure exactly why, but right away he had the feeling she wasn't some sideshow huckster or a girl in a rented costume working a stag party. Still, he wasn't entirely sure what to make of her or the décor. "Nice place," he said and left it at that.

"Please, make yourselves comfortable. I'll make tea."

Campbell set his books and folder down on the table and then took McCloskey's coat and hat and laid them on Zahra's daybed.

"Is she for real?"

"That depends on what you mean by *real*."

"Campbell ... is this detective work?"

The detective knew what McCloskey was getting at. "Purely," he said. "Let's just say I'm trying to extend this case's parameters."

"Am I here to get my parameters extended too? The last time I had my parameters extended was during an army physical, and I didn't much care for it."

"Just keep an open mind. I've been struggling with this too, but I'm willing to consider that there might be something in it."

"You a religious man, Campbell?"

"I sometimes like to think so.".

"Well, that's faith for you."

"And you?"

"I'm still recovering," said McCloskey.

Zahra reappeared with her tea service and set it down on the table. They took their seats. Coincidentally, no one sat in what had been Kaufman's chair. Campbell took the lead.

"We all know that lately there have been some unusual events in the city and I believe Madame Zahra might be of some help in approaching the situation from a different perspective, if you will, one that we might not have otherwise considered exploring."

McCloskey was already fidgeting.

"Now, hear me out," said Campbell, noticing McCloskey's discomfort. He pulled the key from his waistcoat pocket and set it on the table in front of Zahra. With her hands folded on her lap, she leaned over the object. She looked at Campbell.

"Where did you get it?"

"From him," he said, tilting his head at McCloskey.

"Where did you get this?"

"The river," said McCloskey.

"No," she said. "The river is a road. You took this from one of its travellers. That is the only way."

McCloskey looked at Campbell, and Campbell gave a discreet nod back.

"Well," said the bootlegger, feeling compelled to speak, "there was a body in the river. One of us took it off the body."

"Why did you take it off body?" She was holding the key now, examining it closely.

"It wasn't me," he said, still under her spell. "It was a friend, a colleague of mine."

"He is dead," said Zahra.

"You saw his body," Campbell said to her.

"What's she talking about?"

"I should tell you, I brought Zahra to see Three Fingers at the morgue."

"What the hell is going on here?" said McCloskey, and he leaned back, breaking their loosely formed triangle.

"Not one of us knows exactly," said Campbell. "But together we can …"

McCloskey let Campbell's voice trail off. He wasn't liking the sounds of any of this. And it was nothing he'd feel comfortable sharing with the gang, or at least what might be left of the gang by this time tomorrow.

The detective turned to the medium. "Zahra, I've done some research, but I'd like to get a clearer idea what this thing, what I believe to be a talisman, is and what it might mean to someone like you. Why would these people want it so badly?"

"Not people," she said.

"Yeah, people," said McCloskey. "They killed two of my men."

"They rode in last weekend on a train," said Campbell, "taking a few lives along the way — another was only just recently discovered. They're killers, but not like anything we've run into or heard of before."

"Not men," she said, in case they had failed to understand the first time.

McCloskey and Campbell sat back in their chairs, looking at each other.

"Then what are they?" said Campbell.

"*Padshiy ahngel,*" said Zahra.

"What?" said Campbell.

"Angels."

"Angels? These guys are no angels," said McCloskey. "We've all seen what they can do."

"Dark angels," said Zahra. "Fallen angels."

"Is that a gang?" McCloskey asked Campbell.

"Okay," said Campbell, "let's put that aside for a moment and go back to why they might want it so badly. I'm thinking it's something very valuable, an artifact of some kind that was in the possession of a man named Davies, and these men have been sent to retrieve it."

"So there is no lost fortune," said McCloskey. "There is no cash, no bonds hidden anywhere in the Border Cities."

"Money," said Zahra, "is for this world. This, this key," she was holding it up now, "is for the next."

That silenced Campbell and McCloskey for a moment. Each was trying to gather his own thoughts on that. The detective spoke first.

"All right, it seems to me we're stuck somewhere between this world and the next, somewhere between this key being a precious and valuable object, and the key being something that — its owners at least believe — carries metaphysical powers."

"Astral … metaphysical … I've heard about enough of all that stuff, but you two seem like you're only just getting started," said McCloskey. He turned to Campbell. "I came here because I thought you had a solution for getting these guys off our backs or make peace with them, but I don't think you have a clue."

"That's what we're working on," said Campbell. "A different perspective, remember?"

"Okay then, answer me two things." McCloskey was speaking to Zahra now. "First, how is it that these guys have managed to stay one step ahead of us the whole time, and second, why didn't they just take the key or talisman or whatever it is, away from us when they had the chance?"

Campbell was reaching for his resource materials. "Put your books away," said Zahra, "I know what is written in them." She had heard enough too. "I told you, Mr. McCloskey, these are not men. And they will not take talisman from you. You must hand it to them. Your men died because they either refused to hand it over, or *padshij* felt the talisman had been contaminated."

"Can't we just drop it in their mailbox?" said McCloskey.

"No. They need it handed to them by a living soul."

"Why didn't they just come and get it from me then? Or from McCloskey?" said Campbell.

"They also mean to frighten and cause pain any way they can. It is how they live. They make … mischief."

"Mischief?"

"You people," said Zahra shaking her head, "fairy tales, nightmares, daydreams, there is no difference."

"I thought the difference was that your friends don't die. Jesus, Campbell, where is she from?"

"Zahra, what can we do?" said the detective.

"I'll tell you what we can do," said McCloskey, "rally our gangs and corner these guys in the street, in our own territory. We take the fight to them."

"Give them the key," she said.

"How do we do that," said McCloskey, "when we can't even find them because they are too busy *making mischief?*"

"They will find you."

"That's what I'm afraid of," said McCloskey. "How do I know I haven't contaminated their talisman? Or if Campbell hasn't?"

"You don't," she said.

And with that, Campbell pocketed the key. "If they want it, they can come and get it," he said, "and that's how we will settle the matter. Thank you, Madame Zahra." The detective felt they had taken this as far as they could, for now.

"Nice to meet you, Madame Zahra."

She nodded at McCloskey without meeting his eyes. While the gentlemen exchanged a few hushed words, she fetched their coats from the daybed and dropped something into each of their coat pockets.

Chapter 37

THERE'S A NEW VICE
IN TOWN

Vera Maude found out about the lecture through a conversation she overheard while pretending to look at lobby cards in the Walkerville Theatre. The two men were discussing what they hoped to learn but were probably thinking more about how they could add their own two cents. She had been to enough of these affairs to know there would always be at least one person in the crowd who was only there to try to steal a bit of the spotlight, to show up the so-called expert.

As soon as her shift at Copeland's was over and done with,

she phoned the desk at the Prince Edward to confirm the details.

"And where are you off to in such a hurry?" asked Lew.

"To learn how to be a better crime-solver."

"That felt tricorn over there looks like a crime to me. Can you solve that?"

Vera Maude followed the direction of Lew's glance and saw the woman just leaving, tricorn set firmly in place, ready to do battle with the north wind.

"Shall we make a citizen's arrest?"

"I'm off-duty," said Lew. "Better call in the Boy Scouts."

"I hear they're busy patrolling the ladies' change rooms at Smith's."

"Have fun."

"I'll bring you back an autographed program."

James Murphy, fingerprint expert with the International Title Recording and Identification Bureau, was the special guest at this event sponsored by the Lion's Club. The lecture and slide presentation was to take place after the dinner, around seven. It was free of charge and open to the public so Vera Maude wanted to get there early. Instead of waiting for what would surely be a packed streetcar, she hustled up the Avenue to the hotel.

Once inside, she peeled off a couple of layers of winter wear and found the dining hall. This would be a first; she had never seen the room before. She positioned herself outside the closed doors, every so often looking behind her to take measure of the growing queue. Eventually, someone from the hotel staff had to poke his head out and ask the ruffians in the borrowed suits to keep it down.

As soon as the doors were flung open, Vera Maude moved in. Folding chairs had been set up along the perimeter; she started her hunt for the one that looked like it might give her the best vantage point. In her haste, she almost collided with one of the waiters still clearing dessert plates and refilling coffee cups.

"Sorry!"

She noticed a few tables reserved with place cards for members of the police department and the local branches of provincial and federal law enforcement. There were also places set aside for people from several of the Border City's major corporations, most likely their heads of security. Vera Maude watched these groups file in en masse, probably having just walked over from police headquarters after a brief meeting of the minds. She recognized one of them. It was Detective Campbell.

Vera Maude found a seat. Once everyone else had settled into theirs and quieted down, the club president, Kenneth Veale, started with the introductions. As a preamble, he described the plans that were taking shape for the Bureau's new Windsor branch. Much of the credit for the project was given to the Borders Cities own James Wilkinson.

"A veteran of the Great War, our man Wilkinson was a police officer in England for several years prior to joining the Windsor force. He has been a member of the department barely three years and is already making quite a name for himself.

"He returned to England and took a six-week identification course at Scotland Yard. He also trained with the Detroit Police and has attended numerous scientific conferences. His system of cross-indexing is known throughout the Continent, as well as at the Yard."

Wilkinson rose to speak and went into greater detail about his work, paying tribute to Chief Thompson and the entire Windsor police force. He then introduced the guest of honour, James Murphy.

"As a nationally known criminal and civil investigator, having been actively engaged in Secret Service work for the past twenty-two years, and as head of the Murphy Secret Service Agency, which he established in Detroit in 1906 ..."

There was a brief applause and then Murphy rose from the guest table. He thanked Veale with a handshake and then turned to his audience, launching into what turned out to be a sort of pitch or appeal.

"This science is not new," began Murphy. "We do not claim to be the originators of the idea of universal fingerprinting. We would rather have it known that we are simply doing our share toward bringing the importance of this movement to the homes and firesides of all the people. While we are the originators of many valuable systems of fingerprinting, to be used for commercial purposes, it is not our intention, or desire, to burden you with their many intricacies at this time."

Apparently Murphy had recently come to the realization that not only could fingerprinting be used for identifying and tracking criminals, but also identifying and tracking the movement of the public at large. In the United States alone, he claimed, there were many thousands of unidentified dead buried in unmarked graves every year. And if to this number, he stated, one added the thousands of missing persons and hundreds of kidnapped children, the figure would total over 100,000 persons. This number could be minimalized, he believed, through a thorough and effective fingerprinting program.

Vera Maude looked around the room and saw heads nodding. Not only was this not what she thought she had signed up for, but it left her feeling a little uneasy. What was this guy really on about?

And then one of Murphy's slides jammed. Two side-by-side images of the same print, one taken from a crime scene, the other from a file at the Identification Bureau. Crime solved.

"And if you look here ..." continued Murphy.

He looped back to the kidnapped children and then there was

a flicker and the lights went out. At first there was calm, perhaps people thinking it had something to do with the slide projector jamming again. But it stayed dark. There were murmurs, soon followed by uneasy conversation and even a bit of panic.

Why are people so on edge? Vera Maude asked herself.

Hotel staff entered the dining room with flashlights, telling everyone that the situation was under control and they were looking into the matter. A couple of blocks away, pipes were bursting at Avenue Market. Frozen, backed up, expanding, and bursting at the seams. The merchants' stalls were being flooded. And an accumulation of ice was weighing heavy on the electricity lines, pulling them down and cutting the juice being carried to places like the Prince Edward Hotel.

Staff pulled the curtains open to let in any ambient light from the street. Vera Maude stayed seated, her eye on Campbell's silhouette. She thought she might be able to take advantage of the situation. Feeling a little reckless, she checked her bag for her pack of cigarettes. Maybe should could wander over to Campbell's table and ask for a light. She got up and navigated a path between the shades of darkness.

"Any you gents got a match?"

The lawmen started fumbling through their pockets.

"I've got one."

Brilliant. It was Campbell who came through.

"Thanks."

She sat down in the chair next to him. The others around the table resumed their conversations. When the lighted match met the end of her cigarette, she glanced down at the place card on the plate in the empty seat.

"So where's Detective Morrison?"

"Hey — you're the girl from Copeland's. Vera Maude, right?"

"That's me."

"Morrison should be here shortly."

"Out cracking a case somewhere?"

"Or wandering around in the dark. What brings you here?"

"It sounded interesting."

The lights came back on.

"Well, I guess I'd better find my seat again," said Vera Maude. "See ya."

Campbell watched her walk away, turned back to the table, and found everyone else watching him.

"She's a bookseller," he said.

"Lavish?"

"Detective."

"Lavish, why do I have this feeling you got nothing? You know our deal."

"I know the deal, and you got the wrong feelings."

"So you got something?"

Lavish had been thinking. "Yeah, I got something."

They were standing in the front parlour at Janisse Brothers' funeral home on London Street. Lavish had recently been given a key to the place for the purposes of before and after-hour's deliveries, nothing in-between, and considering the recent tremors in the Border Cities, Lavish, ever the poetically minded, thought this might be the best place to have this week's conversation with Morrison, who, also for reasons known only to himself, agreed to it.

Lavish thought it was a shame the detective was so drunk, because chances were pretty good he'd remember none of this, what very well might be their last conversation, and Lavish wished it to be burned into his memory. To Lavish, this was going to be a gamble, but these days so was getting out of bed in the morning. Lately, he had been thinking about going straight, all the way. He had some ideas. On the one hand he saw a real future in the funeral business, and on the other he saw money in weddings. Black crepe and white lilacs versus scented linen and boutonnieres. Both a gouge, both a bit of a scam, but if one knew how to work the angles, it could pay off just as big as any bootleg operation. Then it occurred to him, right then, that maybe he could partner the three. He'd just have to figure out a way of staying out of Morrison's pocket.

"You know what they say, Lavish, *you can't have anything.*"

"I thought it was *you can't have everything.*"

"What's the difference?" said Morrison.

"You wanted to know about Shorty Morand and his boys," said Lavish.

"Yeah."

"Well, that's a dead end."

"I don't believe it," said Morrison. "They're hiding something. McCloskey's back in fighting form."

"I've been thinking maybe some things are better left not found. You been reading about King Tut's tomb?"

"What the hell are you talking about, Lavish?"

The coffins and urns in the room were smartly arranged. It was like the showroom at an auto dealership, just not quite as sexy, and there weren't any girls in flapper outfits draped across the hood.

"Extreme indigestion," said Lavish.

"All right," said Morrison. "Morand and McCloskey are a dead end. Then what is it?"

"H."

"What?"

"Heroin. You know it, Morrison. Cocaine, morphine, opium, the whole game. I want none of it."

"What are you talking about?" Morrison was leaning over an oak casket, one of the nicer ones, not one of the cheap ones destined for smoke.

"If you throw up in that, I'm done here."

"You got a lot of brass on you today, Lavish."

"The Border Cities are changing again."

"Yeah? Should I pick up my dry cleaning and get ready for the party?"

"Why is it everyone who has something important to say in this town gets laughed off; and when the shit finally hits, they say, *Gee, I never saw it coming*?" Lavish was studying the scissor legs of a coffin trolley. "I'm tired of this, Morrison, and I'm tired of you. I don't care what you might do to me. Maybe I'm not that smart, but it doesn't take some genius or street-wise cop like you to know which way the wind is blowing. It's getting hard and dirty. You have to know that. You also have to know that you're not that smart. I wasn't born a bootlegger or a snitch, so try and make me into one and I swear I'll kill you. Remember: I know people too."

Lavish wouldn't have said any of that unless he was sure that Morrison was passed out cold, which he was in a winged-back chair surrounded by ferns. He spilled Morrison out of the chair, dragged him out the rear door, and left him in a pile of snow between two parked cars. More snow was falling. Lavish did his best to cover his tracks on his way back into the funeral home.

He checked the arrangements already on display for the first service tomorrow morning. He watered them, straightened the tallest stalks, and braced the limp ones. The vase to the left of the casket was marked, destined for the address of a loved one on the other side of the river. Everything else appeared to be in place. He would check in with the organist in the morning.

And then the lights went out and everything was black.

"What the hell?"

Chapter 38

THE HIGHLAND PARK PAINT
AND GLASS SEXTET

Saturday

Locals referred to it as the McDougall Street Pen; it was an open-air rink on the southeast corner at Erie, and tonight the benches were stiff and cold. Vera Maude was sitting next to her uncle and watching a guy in cleats all by his lonesome push a glorified watering can on wheels in a tightening oval pattern around the ice surface, restoring its smooth as glass finish and counting on the frigid cold to then leave it diamond-hard.

The Windsor Monarchs were playing the Highland Park

Paint and Glass team in a hockey tournament for the *Detroit Times* Trophy. Despite the weather, it was a sellout crowd. Border Citizens were obviously becoming a bit stir-crazy and were willing to brave just about anything outside the cozy confines of their woolly domiciles.

"And which one's us?" asked Vera Maude.

"The black and gold," said Uncle Fred.

"I saw Gorski this morning, at the pool hall."

"Is that where you left him?" asked Shorty.

"Yeah," said Mud. "That's where I left him. Jack wanted me to meet some guys at Ford about car parts. How many places am I supposed to be at one time?"

"You should have brought Gorski with you."

In Shorty's mind there was safety in numbers, which was why he and Mud were freezing their cheeks off in the stands at a crowded rink. Their only comfort was coming from the Thermos they were passing back and forth.

"He's fine," said Mud. "Now, can you at least let me watch them drop the puck?"

The whistle blew.

"Is it over already?" asked Vera Maude. "Who won?"

"That was only the first period. And in case you were wondering, there's no score," said Uncle Fred.

"How is that possible? They were skating so hard."

"None of them put the puck in the net."

"That must be difficult," said Vera Maude.

She went back to watching a man who she figured was a sports writer for the *Star* feverishly jotting things in a notepad, pausing every so often to blow on his finger tips.

> *The first period was a smart exhibition of hockey with neither team being able to bulge the twine. Schreiber and Ulrich tore off some beautiful rushes but their efforts went for naught when Hammerleff turned aside their shots with monotonous regularity. Monarchs had a wide margin of the play in this period and should have been rewarded with one or two goals, but it was not to be.*

"You didn't go looking for him after you were done at Ford's?" demanded Shorty.

"Sure I did," said Mud. "The boys said he left an hour or so after me."

"Left for where?"

"He told them he was going to grab a sandwich and then probably spend the rest of the afternoon at the movies."

"Did you check his apartment?"

"Why should I check his apartment if he's at the movies?"

"What about after the movies?

"After the movies I'm sitting here next to you." Shorty was getting on Mud's nerves again. "You know, I'm all for getting rid of that damn key."

"We don't have it, remember?" said Shorty.

"I thought Jack had it."

"No, the cops have it now."

"When did this happen?"

"Late Thursday."

"Well then," said Mud, "it's out of our hands and no longer our problem, right? See, we got nothing to worry about." He sat back and took another sip from the Thermos. "Now let's enjoy the game."

"What's the score?" asked Shorty.

"How should I know?"

> Monarchs continued to attack when the second period opened, the Paints using a five-man defence in order to keep the Monarchs off the score sheet. Always there were five men for the puck carrier to pass to and it was not until Carl Schreiber tore off the prettiest piece of work of the game did the locals count. The fast Monarch defenceman grabbed the rubber behind his own goal, skated the entire Paint team dizzy, stickhandling his way through the whole works to drive the puck past Hammerlef for the first counter of the game, a minute before the period ended.

"So you were out with Mrs. Cattanach today?" said Vera Maude.

"She had some shopping to do. I helped her carry her things," said Uncle Fred.

"It sounds serious."

"There's nothing serious about Sunday dinner and a bit of baking."

"Sure there is. What's for dinner?"

"Roast."

"And what's she baking?"

"A raisin pie."

"You hate raisins."

"No, I never," said Uncle Fred.

"You do and you always have — see, it *is* serious."

Uncle Fred was starting to fidget. "Enough about me, Vera Maude."

Uh-oh, she thought, *here it comes. He's using my full name.*

"It's been a week now. You can see I'm fine. Aren't you missing New York?"

"Are you trying to get rid of me?"

"Of course not."

They were quiet for a moment.

"Well?" said Uncle Fred. "Are you?"

"Yes and no."

"Aw, you must be."

"And maybe when I was in New York I missed Windsor."

"Did you?"

"Yes and no."

"You're an equivocator, Maudie."

She went back to watching the sportswriter.

> *The Monarchs were feeling the results of the hard going when the third period started. Leaver and Schreiber were badly used up, while Ulrich was practically useless, the result of a nasty cross-check over the shoulder and throat. It was here that the Detroiters stepped out and ran in all of their goals. Shelby tied the point and Roberts put them in the lead a few minutes later and it was Shaw who put the game on ice with the third one. All two goals were the results of three-man combinations with only one man on the Monarch defence.*
>
> *Louis Martell worked like a Trojan in the third period while Wilson and Graham back-checked like fiends. However the two-goal handicap with*

the three stars just hanging on was just too much.

After outplaying the Highland Park Paint and Glass team for two periods, the Windsor Monarchs allowed the Detroiters to overcome a one-goal lead and defeat the local sextet 3-1.

"Uncle Fred?"

"Yes, Maudie?"

"I'm going to stay."

"You're young. You know you can always go back."

"I know."

"Shorty?"

"Yeah?"

"Let's go see if Gorski's at his apartment."

Chapter 39

MADE OF SHADOWS

Vera Maude had been looking forward to sleeping in, but it was apparently never meant to be. Her uncle Fred had conveniently forgot to mention that Mrs. Cattanach had plans for them today and they first involved arriving in time for morning service at St. Andrew's. Mrs. Cattanach liked to get there early so she could get a seat nearest the front. She felt she wasn't receiving the true and sacred word unless she could look Reverend Paulin straight in the eye. Therein lies the truth.

Vera Maude managed to stay awake through the service by

occasionally giving herself a pinch on the arm. It was already mostly purple.

There was a tea served afterward in the church hall. Vera Maude managed to talk her way out of that, and in return received a stern look from her uncle over Mrs. Cattanach's shoulder.

Now we're even, she thought.

She walked down Victoria to catch the London streetcar. The snow was back, again. It was almost a whiteout and the streets were empty.

McCloskey was winding his way back to his apartment after spending the night on Clara's chesterfield. He was still lending her a hand with Pearl. A quiet, snowy Sunday morning and he thought he had the streets all to himself until he saw a figure walking alone ahead of him. It appeared to be a woman.

When he crossed Park Street he could see four other figures; they seemed to appear out of nowhere and were about to converge on the woman. It looked a little suspicious so McCloskey picked up his pace.

He got closer. There was something strange about them; they were identically clothed, same height and build, and with no details he could make out, even though he could make out some of the lines and patterns in the woman's coat and hat.

It's them. It's the Guard.

McCloskey reached inside his coat for his revolver and started sprinting toward her. As close as he was now — about thirty feet or so — visibility was still poor, and if they reached her first, enveloping her like he'd heard they did, he would never be able to get in a good shot. They were almost on her now. He fired one and then another shot high into the air. Still not noticing her attackers, she froze at the sound of the gunfire that was echoing between the buildings. They looked as if they might now turn on him so he fired yet another shot in the air, and then, for some reason, they separated and disappeared, lost in the whiteout.

The woman stood still, and McCloskey walked around in front of her. She had her eyes shut tightly and her gloved hands covering her ears.

"Vera Maude? Is that you? It's me — Jack."

She opened her eyes. "What the hell was all that for?"

"Didn't you see those guys?"

"What guys?"

"There were four of them, moving toward you. I think I know who it was, I just don't know why they would have been after you."

"After me? What do you mean *after me*?"

He didn't want to take any chances. "Let's get out of here. My place is just around the corner."

"Your place?"

"I'll explain when we get there."

McCloskey realized he was still gripping his revolver. He looked around one more time, and without letting go of it he thrust his hand in his coat pocket.

"C'mon."

The door was shut, bolted, chained, and with a chair wedged between the floor and its glass knob. McCloskey had tested the length of the telephone cord and found it long enough to reach his feet. He thought he might hear from Shorty sometime soon and he didn't want to miss his call.

McCloskey was keeping a drowsy eye on Vera Maude and

occasionally roused himself with a jab to his thigh with the butt of his revolver.

Vera Maude was curled up like a treble clef on his loveseat that was parked below the street-side window. She had said she only wanted to put her head down for a minute. When he knew she was in a deep sleep, he went over and draped his heavy coat on top of her and then positioned himself in his thinking chair just a few feet across from her. Sometimes he did his best thinking while eating; other times he did it while watching a woman sleep.

Vera Maude.

The gap, those blank hours, were slowly filling up and pouring into him. He dropped his arms, dropped his fists. He relaxed.

It started choppily, like pieces from a film reel randomly spliced together or a deck of cards shuffled after a poker hand. McCloskey was trying to put it back into order. It was difficult, though; he didn't recognize some of the people he was seeing in his mind. There were no reference points; there was nothing to ground him. Maybe that was the problem.

Vera Maude stirred and McCloskey resisted the temptation to disconnect the phone. He wanted to hear from Shorty, make sure he was okay.

So this is the Guard, he thought to himself. *What now?*

The snow had stopped and he could hear people on the street.

"Wow, how long was I out?"

McCloskey checked her watch. "A few hours. I guess you needed it. Late night?"

"Long week. Heck, a long winter."

"And it isn't nearly over."

Vera Maude pulled his coat off her and sat up on the edge of the loveseat. "I should phone my uncle. He's probably wondering where I am."

"Just let him know you're okay," said McCloskey. "Don't go into any details."

Vera Maude noticed first the revolver on McCloskey's lap, and then the chair wedged under the doorknob.

"What's going on?"

"You were about to be attacked on the street."

She was remembering now. "Yeah," she said. "Attacked by whom?"

"It's kind of hard to explain," said McCloskey.

"Friends of yours?"

"Not exactly. You could say we —"

"We?"

"Me and some colleagues of mine had a few run-ins with these guys this week."

Nodding at the gun, she said, "I'm guessing it was serious."

"A couple of my boys didn't make it. You may have seen it in the paper."

"Again, what could this possibly have to do with me?"

"I don't know. I mean, I don't get it either. At first we thought they were after something. It started sort of like that, but we don't — that is, me and my colleagues don't — have the thing they wanted in our possession any more."

"Who has it?"

"The police. That reminds me." McCloskey picked the phone up off the floor and got an operator. "Windsor police."

Vera Maude rubbed her arms and looked around. Nice place, but it could use a few more sticks of furniture and maybe a pillow or two.

"Hello? Yes, I need to talk to Detective Campbell. Is he around?"

Vera Maude's ears perked up. *That's right*, she thought, *they were both in the store the other day.*

"Right…. No, this is Vanderbeke. He knows the name. Tell him he can find me at 305 Chatham Street West, and it's urgent…. Thanks."

"Detective Campbell?" said Vera Maude.

"Yeah."

"You were with him in Copeland's the other day."

"So I was. Look, I'm sorry if —"

"He's on his way over?" said Vera Maude.

"Hopefully. You said you needed to make a phone call."

"I'm thinking maybe I should just go."

"I think you should wait until Campbell gets here. Why don't you go ahead and make that phone call."

Vera Maude looked at the revolver, now on the floor where the phone was, and the chair wedged under the doorknob. He was handing her the phone.

"What should I tell my uncle?"

"Tell him you decided to visit a girlfriend, whatever, but you're not here — in my apartment — and everything's fine."

"Is it?"

"Yeah," he said and handed her the phone.

Vera Maude made the call. Not surprisingly, Uncle Fred was wondering about her whereabouts and if she would be home in time for the roast.

"I think so…. I'll call you back as soon as I know … we're just having lunch and catching up."

She hated lying to Uncle Fred. Sometimes it felt like that was all she had been doing since she arrived back in the Border Cities. But she hadn't last night when she told him at the hockey game that she wouldn't be returning to New York. She handed McCloskey back the phone and started pacing around the apartment.

"So when's Campbell getting here?" she asked.

"I don't know. They had to try to reach him at home."

"You got anything to eat in this place?" She wandered into the little kitchen and he heard her open the icebox. "There's nothing in here, just a fridge full of condiments and some bottles of beer."

"You hungry?"

"Yeah," she said.

"Want me to see if Campbell delivers?"

"Somehow I doubt it."

"Maybe we can go out after he gets here."

She re-entered the living room.

"You know some decent places around here open on a Sunday?"

"I might," he said.

"You want to split a beer?"

"Sure."

She went back into the kitchen and popped open the icebox. She came back with two bottles.

"I thought you said split one?"

"I lost count. Here — one for me and one for you."

"You didn't bring an opener."

"I was trying to stay out of your drawers."

"Give me that." McCloskey used his teeth.

"Thanks," she said, then took a sip and started pacing around the apartment again. "Nice place. A little spartan, but kind of nice."

"Spartan?"

"A simple décor."

"I don't do much entertaining."

She took another swig from the bottle. "So, when you were in the bookstore the other day with Campbell, and I approached you, did you really not know who I was?"

"No, not really. At least I didn't remember."

"Yeah," she said, "I guess it was a while ago."

"It's not like that, Maudie."

Maudie. That surprised the both of them, like it came from somewhere else.

"You wouldn't know," McCloskey continued. "It's really got nothing to do with you."

"Jack, before the detective gets here with more questions, can I get a few more in?"

He knew that didn't sound right.

"Only if I can too."

"Okay, you first," she said.

He took another sip of his beer. "Last summer …"

And he proceeded to explain to her, as best as he could understand, the situation with the key, Davies's lost fortune, and the Guard. He also told her about Madame Zahra.

Chapter 40

SNOW ANGELS

Fields woke with his cheek pressed against the bathroom floor. He reached for the edge of the sink and leveraged himself up. Catching his reflection in the mirror, he noticed how closely his pallor resembled the tile on the wall. And the howling was returning to his ear again. He tried to focus and centre himself by staring down the drain but it did little good. He opened the door to the medicine cabinet and found the brown bottle of painkillers between his safety razor and the box of cotton balls. He unscrewed the top and shook it over his cupped hand. It was empty.

"I'm getting cheated on these," he muttered. "I should have a word with the chemist."

And then he remembered. The Guard had visited him again, in his sleep.

The Guard — that's what everyone was calling them. There was talk. Word was getting around.

But he was the only one he knew who had actually met them. He touched his fingers against his temple and considered vomiting. Unable to recall the last time he ate solid food, he decided to put it off.

Some fresh air might do some good, he thought, *might clear my head*. He dressed and ventured out.

Campbell arrived at Maiden Lane about the same time as McCloskey and Vera Maude, shortly after nine. They stood on the snow-covered sidewalk and gazed up for a moment at the window of Madame Zahra's before heading through the front door and up the stairs.

Campbell told Zahra to cancel any appointments she might have had. In turn, he assured her that he would not be bringing any constables to her door. He was trying to control the situation as best he could. His plan was simple but still difficult for him to accept since it ignored all the basic rules of policing, not to mention the laws of physics: have Zahra "call" the Guard through one of her séances. He rationalized it by telling himself it might be an opportunity to better understand what had happened to Kaufman. His death continued to haunt him.

McCloskey had not heard back from Shorty, and according to Mud, Gorski was still nowhere to be found. McCloskey was trying not to overthink all of that. He was going to assume they were both safe and sound and leave it at that. What he couldn't seem to avoid thinking about, however, was how much he didn't like dragging Vera Maude into all of this. The Guard had some pretty good tricks, and he wished he could study their game more, better them at it, and then make them pay for what they did to Three Fingers and Lapointe.

Vera Maude kicked off her boots at the landing just below Zahra's apartment. She hadn't uttered a word since she and McCloskey left her uncle's place. She felt all talked out after the stickhandling she'd had to do through this evening's dinner conversation: avoiding subjects, dodging questions, and equivocating her answers. *Stickhandling*, she thought. *My gawd, I'm beginning to sound like Uncle Fred*. She was quiet also because she was feeling not just a little bit nervous about tonight's program. She was remembering conversations she had had at the bookstore in the Village with people who followed all of this stuff: these disciples of Blavatsky, occultists, and theosophists who bet their money on invisible horses. They always had this look in their eyes, and for some reason they always seemed to gravitate toward her. She looked up at the space in the floor. The phrase "etheric plane" suddenly popped into her head. "This way?" she asked.

"Yes," said Campbell.

She took the stairs slowly, stopped near the top, touched the edge of the opening, and poked her head up.

"Come, come," said Zahra with her arms outstretched to Vera Maude.

The medium embraced her like she was a long-lost relative and then gave her the tour. She could have done it from the middle of the floor, but she insisted on pointing out and describing to Vera Maude every detail of her studio. Meanwhile, McCloskey and Campbell stood in a corner, occupying themselves with an argument over their proposed strategies. The only thing they could seem to agree upon was that there might have to be some improvising.

McCloskey kept glancing over at Vera Maude and Madame Zahra. The two were sitting at the table now and really seemed to be hitting it off, connecting on some level. While they spoke, Zahra would occasionally touch Vera Maude's hand. And then they would lean close, like they were exchanging secrets. McCloskey couldn't even begin to guess.

None of this escaped Campbell's attention, though he was seeing it a little differently. He thought Vera Maude might be just the right ingredient in his experiment. Her mind seemed open, receptive, and she had already encountered the Guard. He wondered why they might be drawn to her. *Is she some kind of conductor?* Laforet would say that he was letting his curiosity get the better of him. "Let's start," he said to McCloskey and they approached the table.

"Is now a good time?" the detective asked Zahra.

"Yes," she said.

The two men sat, and Campbell reached in his pocket for the talisman and set it down in the middle of the table.

"What should I be doing?" said McCloskey.

"Take a deep breath," said Zahra, "and relax your body. Now touch fingertips. Good." She then asked for silence and closed her eyes.

Vera Maude closed her eyes too. The three waited patiently while Zahra hummed and swayed a little. McCloskey and Campbell let their eyes wander the room, anxious for a sign.

Footsteps could be heard coming up the stairwell. McCloskey and Campbell watched a shadow enter. It was followed by another, and then two more. Pitch-black silhouettes of hats, coats, and shoes, and profiles that seemed to melt in the darkness.

Campbell thought he could hear them speak, but it wasn't

exactly a voice. It couldn't be real. He told himself it was just his imagination assembling and twisting the anecdotal information he had been hearing about the Guard. The voices — yes, they were indeed voices now — were becoming louder in his head, more insistent, demanding. He struggled to block them.

The quartet moved swiftly about the room, and yet nothing seemed disturbed by them. Candles did not flicker, curtains did not flutter, and there was no creak in the floorboards. They were there, and yet they weren't.

McCloskey saw that the ladies still had their eyes closed. Zahra was breathing heavily, her teeth slightly clenched, and she appeared to be concentrating very hard. It was getting colder in the room but there were beads of sweat forming on her knitted brow. Vera Maude was sitting stiff and upright yet somehow seemed calm, almost serene. McCloskey got Campbell's attention again.

"Wait," Campbell mouthed.

"For what?" whispered McCloskey.

Campbell saw him reach into his jacket. "Not here," he said, "not now."

"Then when," demanded McCloskey, growing impatient, "and where else?"

"You're not alone here," said Campbell. "Look around you."

McCloskey glanced over at Vera Maude and then stood up and pulled his revolver. He wondered if the others would back off if he took one down. He tried to aim it at the intruders but they kept drifting together and then moving apart.

"Don't!" shouted Campbell. "Let's just give them what they want."

Zahra remained in her trance but Vera Maude's eyes popped wide open and she suddenly found herself in the here and now.

"Jack?"

"Don't move, Maudie." McCloskey kept his revolver fixed on the Guard.

Footsteps could again be heard coming up the stairwell, and another figure appeared.

"Henry?" said McCloskey.

"Fields? What are you …?"

"I know what they want," said Fields. "They told me."

"He's delirious," said Campbell.

The room started to hum. The Guard was standing near the front window. Campbell grabbed the talisman off the table and moved past Fields. He held it out to the Guard. They hesitated. His weapon still drawn, McCloskey took a step back and the Guard took a step forward.

"All right, come and get it," said Campbell. He was remembering what Zahra had said, that the talisman had to be *handed to them by a living soul.*

Fields flinched; McCloskey could see him out of the corner of his eye.

"Henry," he said, "stay there." McCloskey took another step back and the Guard took another step forward.

Vera Maude stood frozen next to the table, her hands over her mouth.

Campbell held the talisman out further. Fields noticed it for the first time and leaned forward.

"Henry!" said McCloskey.

"No, Jack, I have to do this."

Fields then dashed and grabbed the talisman out of Campbell's hand. Continuing to hold it up high, he threw himself at the Guard, which tried to take it from him, but they were all propelled through the window and down onto the street.

Vera Maude screamed. Zahra's eyes opened and she began to bring herself slowly out of her trance.

Campbell led the charge down the stairs and out onto Maiden Lane. Fields was lying dead on the packed snow, a pool of blood forming round his head, glass and window frame everywhere. It was a familiar scene, except for the silhouettes of four figures surrounding Fields, arms and legs askew, melted through the snow straight down to the cobblestone. There was no other trace of the Guard. Before a crowd had a chance to gather, Campbell searched the white drifts, raking them frantically, but the talisman was nowhere to be found.

"It must be here somewhere," he said.

McCloskey looked down at Henry, wondering how he would ever explain this to Clara. Maybe she could have seen it coming, just not exactly like this. He put his hand in his coat pocket and pulled out the charm he had discovered there earlier. He suddenly noticed Vera Maude was standing beside him. He turned her away from the scene and held her close.

A constable came running in from the Avenue.

"Call Laforet," said Campbell.

The officer was having trouble pulling his eyes off the body. "It must take a certain madness," he finally said.

"Make that call, please, Constable."

"Yes, sir."

"A certain madness," repeated Campbell.

Snow was falling again, blanketing Henry Fields as well as the dark silhouettes. People were coming out of their houses, shaking their heads and pointing up at the attic window.

Later the following week, after leaving her to sort herself out once again, Campbell decided he should probably check in on Zahra. He also wanted to tell her that there was nothing he could charge her with in the death of Kaufman. The case would be left open for now, a mystery like so many of the events that had occurred lately on Maiden Lane.

Heading up the Avenue to her apartment, he found himself pausing in front of Grinnell Bros. music house and noticed a placard advertising this month's newest record releases. He scanned the list and, seeing something he thought Zahra might like, he entered the store.

A sales clerk tracked down the recording for him. It was a Rachmaninoff serenade. Campbell hoped she didn't already have it. It wasn't much, but he reminded himself it's the thought that counts. He tucked the parcel under his arm and continued his walk. It was a clear sky for a change, and there was even a hint of spring in the air.

He climbed the few steps up to the front door. It was locked. He gave it a hard rap to make sure she heard him from upstairs. A burly, red-faced man answered.

"Excuse me, I'm looking for Madame Zahra."

"She's gone," said the man.

"She stepped out?"

"I mean I came home to find her apartment empty. She's gone."

Campbell's face fell. "Gone where?"

"How should I know?" The man was squinting sideways at Campbell now. "And who might you be?"

"The name's Campbell. Are you Mr. O'Grady?"

"Yes," said the landlord.

"I'm Detective Campbell of the Windsor Police Department. May we talk?"

O'Grady scratched his head. "Haven't even unpacked yet. And the wife's still asleep. Mind if we go upstairs?"

"I was going to suggest that."

Campbell followed him up to the attic.

Apart from the table and chairs, which presumably belonged to O'Grady, the place was indeed empty. Campbell looked around. The only evidence of Madame Zahra Ostrovskaya having lived here were the stars on the ceiling.

"I'm gonna to have that painted over. Now, what was it you wanted to talk to me about?"

"We should sit down, Mr. O'Grady."

O'Grady looked up again at the stars. "She put on quite a show, didn't she?"

"I'm sorry," said Campbell. "What do you mean?"

SIX MONTHS
LATER

Chapter 41

RETURN TICKET

"How can you see anything?" asked Shorty.

"I got good night vision," said Mud. "Runs in the family. I used to watch my ma practise signatures by candlelight and I helped my dad strip parts off trucks in factory lots after dark. Sometimes he needed a small pair of hands. It beat husking corn, which was what my older brothers were doing."

It was dark now, or near dark. A thin veil of starlight hung from the quarter moon.

"You were a born criminal," said Shorty.

"I was bored," said Mud.

"Pick it up, you two." McCloskey was behind them, marching the boys along.

The trio had just finished putting away the day's leftover chicken and frog legs, usually promised to the dogs that hung around behind the kitchen at the Westwood. With their bellies full, the bootleggers were now making their way down Prospect Avenue toward the river, trying not to kick up too much dust. It had ben a dry summer.

Prospect Avenue might have sounded like a clear path to Yukon gold, but it was really nothing more than a tar and gravel drag servicing the salt mines that drilled deep under the Detroit River. And from the foot of Prospect it was a nothing more than a path worn through the tall grass along the shore. They were here to see off a small boat laden with about a dozen cases of rye.

"Wait — listen. Mud, what's that motor?"

Mud turned his ear. "It isn't cops," he said. "Maybe the competition."

"Shorty, are we on time?"

Shorty checked the glowing green dial of his fancy new wristwatch. "Right on the money."

McCloskey gave a whistle and immediately got a whistle back. Thinking they were a safe distance from the roadhouse now, Mud clicked on his flashlight and aimed the lens slowly up and down the water's edge. When Shorty tsked, Mud shot the light directly in his eye. McCloskey was enjoying seeing his boys taking these pokes at each other. He felt like they were finally back on form.

But they remained vigilant. The Westwood had been raided the other night and one of the licence inspector's new tricks was to raid the same establishment again a few days later after the proprietor had paid his fine and assumed he'd be left alone for a while. But one couldn't be too careful. Mud kept the light aimed down low, catching weeds and driftwood until he netted some well-heeled civilian feet in motion.

"Groesbeck?"

"Drury?"

The figure halted just a few feet away. Mud fixed his flashlight on the polished shoes while Shorty hung back in the shadows, his hand tucked in his coat pocket. The two leaders, the Honourable Premier of Ontario and the Honorable Governor of the State of Michigan, shook hands.

"I thought we should meet," said McCloskey. "Is everything in order?"

The cases had been left hidden under some canvas and mouldy old fishing nets during the day, waiting for the rendezvous that was to take place under the cloak of night. Like any successful campaign, it would come down to timing and execution. You can't force these things to happen; these deals sometimes come with a motion all their own, and all one can do is try and steer them in the right direction.

"Looks good."

"Sounds like there's some traffic out there," said McCloskey.

"Nothing we can't handle." McCloskey noticed someone standing behind Groesbeck.

"Good luck then. You know where to reach us."

"Thanks, Drury. Oh — and the balance is in an envelope behind the front desk, under my name."

"Gotcha."

Once the boat had successfully pushed off, Mud dimmed the flashlight and the three stood and watched the vessel disappear across the black water. As the sound of that motor faded, the sounds of others took over. One that came in howling from downriver got their attention.

"He's going pretty fast," said Mud.

"Police?" said McCloskey.

Mud paused. "No … smaller, faster."

"Travelling light?"

Mud paused again, listening to the impact of the bow on the water, the rhythm of the engine. He looked out over the river to examine its surface in the moonlight.

"She's carrying," said Mud.

The motor was revving even louder now, and sounding as if it might be just a hundred or so yards off shore. There was a loud splash, and then another, and then the boat, clearly sounding as if it had spun around, headed back downriver even faster, having just jettisoned its load.

"What the hell was that?" said Shorty.

It got quiet really quickly, as if the sound of this motor scared off all the others. McCloskey thought it might actually have been a police boat, one of the newer models. But then there could be heard a frantic splashing, like arms and legs flailing in the water, followed by a shouting of unintelligible, maybe drowning words.

The boys looked at each other and then McCloskey moved to the very edge of the shore, almost stumbling into the river.

"Mud — the light!"

Mud came over, flashlight shining. He swept the surface of the water with it, careful not to aim it too high.

"*Gau mehng a! Gau mehng a!*"

McCloskey waded in up to his knees. "Mud — over here!" He was pointing to his left, where he could just barely make out someone struggling to shore. By the time Mud's flashlight had zeroed in on them, the person was standing, or limping rather, through the shallow waters. McCloskey got hold of him before he collapsed.

"America?"

"No," said McCloskey. "Canada."

"*Aah … gweilo.*"